The Wrong Side of Memphis

Claire Applewhite

L & L Dreamspell

Spring, Texas

Cover and Interior Design by L & L Dreamspell

This is a work of fiction, and is produced from the author's imagination. People, places and things mentioned in this novel are used in a fictional manner.

ISBN: 978-1-60318-116-7

Library of Congress Control Number: 2009924353

Visit us on the web at www.lldreamspell.com

Published by L & L Dreamspell
Printed in the United States of America

ACKNOWLEDGMENTS

Throughout history, tragedy has influenced art. A broken heart, a distant dream, and a stubborn obstacle all illustrate the tenacity and resilience of human nature. Indeed, a man is at his finest when he is tested to his limits. Success seems secondary to his struggle.

The Wrong Side of Memphis concerns the Journey after the Destination. One evening in the fall of 1996, I listened to a WWII vet recount his war stories. There was another vet in the room who had received several military decorations for outstanding service in Vietnam. Yet, throughout the evening, he remained silent. Later, he told me how he could not talk about his tour in 'Nam—not at all. He admitted a deep sense of shame and remorse. Yet, he was convinced that, like the WWII veteran, he too had served his country and its citizens. At that moment, I realized I unwittingly held a key to a Pandora's Box. The proverbial elephant lounged in the corner, waiting to be fed. He was not going to go away until somebody noticed him.

The characters in *The Wrong Side of Memphis* voice the challenges faced by Vietnam Vets everywhere, even now. How they cope, how they relate, and how they build a new life together despite a devastating past—this is the story you are about to read.

I would like to express my deep gratitude to those who assisted me in the publication and production of this book. No one does a project like this alone, and I want to acknowledge those who so unselfishly gave of their time and talent:

First, thank you to Veterans everywhere, especially Vietnam Vets. This story is for you.

Detective Jennifer Williams, St. Louis County Police, and Mr. Stephen Otten, former Navy Seal, for procedural and tactical advice. Their time and expertise shaped authentic scenes.

Dr. Ellen Harshman, St. Louis University, John Cook School of Business, for teaching me the business of writing.

Professor John Dalton, University of Missouri, St. Louis, who first encouraged me to write this story.

The excellent faculty at the Washington University Summer Writers Institute.

My dear friends, Barbara Green, M.D. and Carolyn Campbell for their support.

Lois Mans, my talented graphic artist and publicist.

Cindy Davis, Lisa and Linda at L& L Dreamspell for patience, encouragement and confidence in my work.

My Airedales, Gracie and Savannah, who showed me the delights of owning an Airedale Terrier.

My family, who regularly helped with computer glitches and discouragement—thank you for not allowing me to quit.

My father, Donald Krieg, who taught me the value of persistence and hard work.

And finally, my late mother, LaVerna Krieg, to whom I owe a debt of gratitude for a lifetime of love.

DEDICATION

To my husband, Thomas A. Applewhite, M.D.

For the past that carved our memories,
The present that shapes our future,
The future we cannot see,
Thanks with all my love.

The best is yet to be,

Claire

One

St. Louis, Missouri
The Jewel Arms Apartments
Saturday, 5:13 p.m.

"Val! It's Mattie, open up!"

Valerie paused by the front door. His sniffles and coughs made her shiver. *That's what I get for being such a sucker. People always latching onto me. Leave. Please.*

Until today, Mattie Torrez was her kind of guy. She liked the quiet ones, with her wine and roses on the side. She liked his smile and the way he lit her cigarette, things like that. But today, Mattie looked haggard and hard. After two months and some change, she still didn't know him. He stammered and weighed every word. Why, he dropped everything he touched, and the pacing, back and forth...

What was that racket?

Now, Valerie heard muffled voices, a ping, a pounding, and the shuffle of feet. Labored breaths echoed in the hall. She should open the door, but tonight, Mattie's problems would have to wait. She hated to rush. Tomorrow she would deal with Mattie Torrez.

If only his mother didn't live upstairs. For a brief moment, Valerie fantasized that Belle had wandered off and vanished, or even died. Before too long, she came to her senses. Inconvenient situations didn't just become convenient, and Belle wouldn't disappear to make her life easier. Right now, she'd better hustle or she would miss the only job she'd booked all week.

Tonight was Big Otto's Birthday Party. That meant Ladies' Night, and Payday for Valerie. In her wildest dream, Otto invited a guest who appreciated her kind of talent, like a Hollywood agent with a one-way ticket to Tinseltown. The dream owned her.

She hoped Otto's Fine Auto Parts wasn't as hard to find as its "skilled automotive staff," and their sketchy party instructions. About a month ago, Valerie's phone rang, and a raspy voice calling himself "Waldo B," rattled off the birthday requests. "As long as the money is green," Valerie said.

"Now, listen up," the dude said. He coughed into the phone, and sniffled while he mumbled. "Big Otto loves his Mercedes, and fudge cake with lots of fluffy white frosting. We think he would love a Blonde in a Mercedes with a fudge cake. Yous can sing, can't cha?" Without a warning, he hung up on her. The nerve of that nut!

She stomped off to her bedroom and yanked a dress from the crammed closet. Valerie didn't want to be late tonight. She loved a good dress, and she loved parties, especially ones with lots of men. The clutter smelled dusty. With watery, itchy eyes, she rummaged in the heap for her gold stilettos.

Valerie bustled about the cramped bathroom. Bottles of perfume and mysterious tonics crowded every space. The flimsy front door rattled. She thought she heard Mattie's muffled voice. For a brief moment, she even thought he sounded a little frightened. She dismissed the notion. His antics couldn't ruin her evening.

"Not now, Mattie, I'm getting dressed. Tomorrow…I'll see you tomorrow. Now, go get something to eat—or drink."

She teased her platinum hair and lacquered the bouffant bubble with cheap aerosol spray. With a graceful hand, she guided the sheer stocking over her knee, where it ended mid-thigh in a thin edging of red lace. For just a moment, she admired her reflection in the chipped mirror. She loved the way her breasts spilled out of the white polyester halter dress. Beautiful, just beautiful. Sooo Marilyn.

"Valerie, baby, c'mon, open up! Now, c'mon!" The doorknob was clattering now, faintly at first, followed by a crescendo of knocks and rattles.

"I told you Mattie, I've got a party with The Big Otto! I'll see you tomorrow."

She outlined her full mouth with Red Devil lipstick, and glanced at the mirror. *That's her,* she whispered. *That's Marilyn, all right.*

She inched into her spiked heels and tiptoed onto the yellowed linoleum in the narrow hall. Someday, she'd get out of this dump. Marilyn wouldn't want to walk on yellow linoleum. Why should she?

Imaginary fans crammed the hushed living room. Valerie slunk to the tiny "stage" where she prepared to serenade her audience. *Someday, I'll be a big star, just like Marilyn.* "Diamonds are a girl's best friend," she crooned in her sweetest soprano.

Rattle and clatter and the wobbling knob shattered the spell.

"Damn it, Mattie!" Valerie's polished red fingers squeezed the knob and turned. She'd give him a tongue lashing this time, she'd had enough.

The pitted mahogany door banged back against the dull plaster. Mattie collapsed onto Valerie's slender frame and they toppled to the drab carpet.

"Val, help. Help me, Va-al. He-ll-p," Mattie sputtered and spit between labored gasps. His eyelids drooped, even as he struggled to focus his gaze. "I love ya, Va-al." His lips were limp and soft. His breaths grew shallow. A thin line of blood dripped from his neck.

Don't panic. You've been in tight spots. Every roll, you've beaten the odds. Her hands were wet with Mattie's blood. She couldn't breathe. Mattie's shirt was stained, just like his crimson tie, his slashed coat...her scarlet-white dress, oh my... Deep in her throat, a scream waited, and waited.

"Mattie, get up!" She shoved his thick legs away from the

front door and gulped some rancid air. Mattie's frantic pleas repeated like a refrain. *Valerie baby, c'mon open up, Valerie baby...* *STOP!* Mattie's wounded hands clutched at the "Marilyn" face; blood oozed from his neck. Her fingers grazed something cold, and recoiled in horror. The wooden handle of a knife protruded from the curve in his spine. Valerie's hand felt numb. "Why Mattie? Why?"

Mattie gasped. "Will you...you...will you...Val, please..." The hoarse voice faded. His head drooped. The lumpy shoulders slumped.

"Wake up!" Valerie slapped his cheek. "C'mon Mattie, talk to me. You can't die." Sticky, red-brown blood covered "Marilyn" and her pretty white halter dress with the satin lining. As long as she lived, she would recall that sticky, bloody mess.

Still clad in the wobbly golden heels, Valerie propped the limp body in front of the worn recliner. The bitter taste of bile rose in her throat. Determined to cope, she swallowed. Her jaw stiffened. Mattie's brown eyes stared in quiet accusation.

Across the hall, a stereo blared the Motown music of the Supremes. The aroma of fried fish hung in the humid air. Somewhere, a television droned to the creak of a mattress. Gray light from the empty hallway cast a dim shadow onto Mattie's expressionless face. Valerie slammed the door. Wild-eyed, she gripped the telephone receiver. Her trembling finger punched the numbers and waited. She felt like a killer. She should have opened that door when Mattie asked, no...begged. It was all her fault. There was a click on the line.

"It's Valerie. You know, Valerie Gains at the Jewel. You know, the Jewel Arms. Yeah." The authority in her raspy voice shocked her. "Apartment A." She took a deep breath, and avoided Mattie's gaze. "There's a dead guy in my living room... What? Yeah, it's an emergency! How would you like it?" She banged the receiver into its cradle and wept. Mattie stared at Valerie with dark, open eyes.

Stashed at the end of the long hall, the tenant in Apartment C enjoyed a distinct privacy. Natasha Weeks treasured the isolation. To her, the dark mystique of Apartment B was an advantage and distraction from herself and her business, which, mind you, was nobody's but hers.

Sometimes, late in the night, the doors in B opened and shut, opened and shut, opened and shut. Muffled voices called for "Walter Hubble," whoever that was. If anyone asked Tasha, she said she never saw nobody, no way, not lately. She never even bothered to look. Tasha's ears heard their sneaky feet shuffling on the steps. No fooling her, no way. One thing she learned in jail was how to listen real good. A woman doesn't listen good, she might die. That's what Tasha learned. Anyways, her ears were what she had tonight. Her eyes sure weren't good for nothing— one of them, anyways.

The left one throbbed like stink from cataract surgery, and Lord, how those pain pills made her dizzy! No barhopping for her tonight. Still, she missed the crystal tumblers at Izzy's Corner, brimming with bourbon and a little water, lots of ice, and a cherry or two. Three of those drinks, and her pain and memories faded and dulled. That friendly buzz dulled her troubles, and guaranteed a return, but not tonight. Tonight, she had to stay sober.

It was funny, but Natasha never thought a guy like Parrish Leach would ever get out of jail, no way. It would be so good to see him again. She couldn't believe he planned to fry up some of his famous catfish, just because she was under the weather. Best fried stuff on earth, yes Lord, though Natasha was cutting down on fried foods these days, counting cholesterol and fat grams, you know.

About five years ago she and Parrish met, when she'd been in the lockdown for passing a few bad checks. What a stupid rap that had been. They could have nailed her for a lot worse. Anyways, she never knew what Parry was in for, come to think of it. But, it must be pretty bad, because he had a life sentence. Tasha guessed he convinced somebody otherwise, yeah.

Anyways, Parrish, or Parry as he liked to be called, was a cook at the Women's Correctional Center when he came up for parole. He liked to brag that he made at least two things better than anyone else—fried catfish and chili. Tasha thought he just might be right about that, too. So, tonight, at her special request, he was frying up a batch of fish in peanut oil, his top-secret ingredient.

Though the sun had set, the air in the apartment hung heavy and hot. Parry rearranged the browning fillets in the bubbling oil, careful not to crowd the pieces. Despite her limited vision, Tasha struggled to watch *Wheel of Fortune* on her one indulgence, a large color television set.

"Tasha!" Parry burst into the bare living room, and wiped his brow on the sleeve of his work shirt. It was his favorite one, with his name embroidered in thick red thread on the front pocket. "Mind if I open the door to the hall?" He cracked the door and a rush of air filled the tiny room with a funny, metallic scent. Parry crinkled his nose in curiosity. "Had to take off my work shirt. Hot as hell in that kitchen."

Tasha sniffed the greasy air. "Don't know if that's much better, Parry. I need to get me a good fan one of these days. Fish ready yet?"

Parry wasn't listening. His dark eyes, ever alert, scanned the dark hallway. He was sure he had seen someone creeping along the narrow corridor. He pressed his finger to his lips in a gesture of silence, and peered into the dingy vestibule. A faded brick propped the wide entrance door against the cracked green plaster walls. Mild breezes rustled the trees that framed the doorway, casting lurid shadows into the moldy dimness.

Something wasn't right. Along the way, Parry learned to trust his feelings. The first night in the St. Louis City Jail, two guys he didn't trust from *hello* beat him and beat him again. A man *learns*, hear? He wiped his strong hands on the dishtowel knotted at his waist, and crept along the frayed carpet. Then, he slammed the thick front door, and returned to the end of the hall

in utter blackness amid the smells of peanut oil, mildew, and....
He shook his head. Whatever it was, it didn't smell right.

It wasn't until he served dinner in the cramped dinette,
though, that they noticed. Natasha rose to take her seat at the
rickety card table. Parry saw her good eye widen in horror. From
the front door to the kitchen, a fresh trail of bloody footprints
stained the carpet.

Across the hall in Apartment D, a leggy redhead turned up
the stereo. Dimond"Di"Redding loved Motown music, especially songs by the Supremes or Aretha Franklin. She grabbed the
vacuum cleaner and began to dance, but her leg didn't want to
cooperate. Chunks of shrapnel from a mortar attack in 1968 had
caused a permanent limp, but Di had no time for self-pity.

In the distance, a siren wailed. Di squinted into the darkness,
but she didn't see anything or anyone that raised suspicion. That
is, until suspicion exploded at her doorstep.

An ambulance dashed to the curb at the Jewel Arms. Brakes
squealed, and Di heard muffled voices outside her window. Like
fireworks on the Fourth of July, the red and blue lights glared
through the dusty venetian blinds in her living room. Seconds
later, she heard the pounding on the massive front door of the
building. When she rose to answer it, the familiar twinge pulsed
down her left leg. A bare yellow bulb in the foyer illuminated the
problem. Someone had locked the front door.

Di barely opened it and the paramedics rushed straight to
the door of Apartment A. Through a crack in the doorway, Di
observed a woman she didn't know. In fact, Di only moved in
two weeks ago; she didn't know anyone. Surely though, she would
have noticed this blonde. She was probably an actress, looking
like Marilyn Monroe the way she did—except for the stains.
Crimson blood drenched her dress.

Di tried not to stare, but the gore, coupled with morbid curiosity, conquered her courtesy. Soon, other faces appeared to
gawk at the mess. Amid this tenuous commotion, Di encountered

her neighbors. The retired couple from Apartment E, Edith and Edward Mars, poked their heads into the hall, followed by Parry and Tasha from C.

Parry wore a gray shirt with the red embroidery. Some dark stains saturated his damp shoes, and for a moment, Di wondered why they looked as wet as they did. After all, it wasn't raining—yet. The second floor sounded like a tomb.

The fresh stains on the hall carpet drew mixed reactions from the bystanders. When they carried the body out, Di noticed the gritty footsteps leading back to Tasha's apartment. Parry and Tasha noticed them too, and so did a man dressed in a pale gray suit and yellow tie, the same one that now stared at Parry's stained shoes. The elderly couple retreated to Apartment E, like turtles to their shells. A uniformed policeman remained with Valerie.

The man in the gray suit approached Parry, carrying a small black notebook. "Detective Rick Valentino," he said. He extended his hand to Parry, his eyes registering the long scar stretching from Parry's left cheek to his clavicle. Parry focused on the beretta that peeked from Valentino's leather shoulder holster. He nodded in response to the perfunctory introduction. Other than that, he said nothing.

Tasha's silence said way too much, in Valentino's opinion. He noticed the fresh suspicion in her right eye. He had a very weird hunch that she'd had some experience with police detectives—maybe too much. He'd check out a few things on this Tasha Weeks.

There sure was a lot of noise out here. He glanced over his shoulder, and observed the protocol in action. Police officers slapped yellow tape on the area outside Apartment A, while lab technicians swarmed around the scene. Cameras clicked and snapped.

"Why don't we go inside where we can talk?" His steady voice never wavered.

He escorted Parry and Tasha down the narrow hall that led

to Apartment C. His eyes followed the incriminating footsteps. Those crimson stains knew how to talk. Valentino listened.

Di cracked the apartment door, and peered into the lonely hall. The odor of fried catfish lingered in the air—an odd accompaniment to the bloody footprints and the yellow tape. She locked the door and wondered whether such incidents were typical of St. Louis. She'd always thought of the Midwest as uneventful, even boring. So far, she hadn't been bored.

She'd moved here because she wanted some peace. *Peace*—the word made her laugh. Somehow, she sensed she might have come to the wrong place for that.

Di's thoughts were interrupted by the shrieks of protest out in the hall. She put her ear to the door and eavesdropped. "You bastard!" shouted Valerie. "I told you everything you wanted to know and now you're hauling me in! I knew better than to trust a cop!"

"You should have known better than to move a body, lady," said a man's voice.

The front door banged, punctuating her objections. Through one of the narrow living room windows, Di witnessed the theatrics; a woman in a white halter dress, splattered with blood, forced into an idling patrol car. Her platinum hair glimmered through the back window. The car sped into the blackness.

Footsteps stopped outside her door, interrupting her thoughts. The loud knock seemed to be right there in the livingroom. Through the peephole, Di glimpsed the swarthy man in a gray suit, accessorized by a gaudy yellow tie. Wasn't he the same guy who tossed the blonde in the backseat like a bag of cheap laundry? Why would he want to talk to her? She didn't know anything about anyone in the building, period.

"Who is it?" she said through the door.

"Detective Valentino, Homicide. Like to talk to you for a few minutes." His voice was forceful and gruff, yet void of emotion.

Confused, Di again cracked the door. The detective flashed

his badge through the opening. "All right to come in?" In a flash, his black eyes searched the room.

"Sure." Di stepped aside, knocking a dish filled with M&Ms, her favorite candy, onto the yellow shag carpet. The detective watched impatiently while she stooped to retrieve them, one by one.

"I don't have all day, lady. Mind if I ask you a few things?"

"Go ahead," said Di, popping a green M&M into her mouth.

"Mind if I sit down?"

Di gestured to a leather sofa pushed against the far wall. "Be my guest."

A book titled *Talking to Heaven* lay on the coffee table in front of him. He reached to open it, and then stopped himself. Di settled into a worn wing chair in the corner.

"I might as well tell you first off, there was a murder here tonight. Or did you already know that?"

"I heard the commotion in the hall earlier, if that's what you mean. I didn't know what it was about." She didn't like Valentino's interrogation technique. She'd seen a lot better.

Valentino scribbled something in his black book and grabbed a pack of cigarettes from his coat pocket. Di noticed the 9mm Beretta pistol in his shoulder holster. It was more modern than her own gun, Don's sterile CIA Hi-Power, now stashed behind the Minute Rice in the kitchen pantry.

"Mind if I smoke?" he said, while he fumbled for his plastic lighter.

"Yes."

Valentino shook his head and replaced the cigarettes. A corner of his mouth curled. "May I have your name, Ma'am?" He settled back into the sofa.

"Dimond Redding. My friends call me Di."

Valentino frowned. "Diamond? You mean, like the jewelry?"

"It was supposed to be diamond, but they misspelled my

name on the birth certificate. As I said, my friends call me Di, so it doesn't matter." She crossed her long legs, folding her arms across her chest.

"Yeah, well, like I was saying Miss Redding, about the murder."

"It's Mrs. Redding. What about it?" She didn't choose to be a widow, not that it was any of Valentino's business.

"Did you know the victim?"

Di uncrossed her legs and popped a few more M&Ms into her mouth. "Who was the victim?"

Valentino leaned forward and studied Di's face. His knees hit the edge of the chrome and glass coffee table and he winced. "His name was Matthew Torrez. Friends called him Mattie."

Dimond thought for a moment and recrossed her long legs. At 5'10", she would have towered over Valentino. "No, I didn't."

"Didn't what?" Valentino was instantly alert.

"I didn't know him. Look, I just moved in a couple of weeks ago. The fact is, I don't know anybody in this building. I'm not going to have much information for you."

Valentino paused, scrawling in his notebook. He took a deep breath. "Strange. Very strange."

"What?"

"The people in Apartment C say they know you."

"I don't know why they would say that. They don't."

"Okay." Valentino pulled some gum from his pants pocket. "Mind if I chew gum?"

"Nope."

"What about the hooker across the hall from you?"

"Hooker? Did you say hooker? What kind of place is this?"

"Look, Lady Di, it's pushing 11:00. We're all tired." His forehead wrinkled in confusion. "Okay, maybe she's not a hooker, but I've been in this business long enough to know what one looks like. Like they say, if it quacks, it's probably a duck."

Di grabbed a fistful of M&Ms. "Mind if I eat a little candy?"

"Very funny. So, you're telling me you just moved here and don't know anyone. What brought you to St. Louis?"

For the first time that night, Di laughed out loud. "I was looking for peace and quiet, if you want to know the truth."

Valentino waited, his pen poised in mid-air. "Go on."

"Used to have relatives here. Well, I guess I still do, but they're six feet under now. Buried out in Calvary Cemetery, you know, up north." She shrugged. "They liked it here, said it was a good place to retire. Cost of living isn't too bad, got some people who spend their whole lives here. I was afraid it might be a little too quiet for my taste, but it's not shaping up that way, is it?"

"You're a little young to retire, aren't you? I'm nowhere close."

"I was a field nurse in Vietnam. Got hit in the leg by some shrapnel. Then I came back and got a job at the VA Hospital. I could probably retire, but what else would I do?"

"You're kidding," Valentino smirked. He eyed the petulant woman before him. He didn't see a wedding ring.

"Where's your husband?"

"He died."

"I'm sorry."

"It's okay."

"What happened?"

"Don was a Green Beret, if you want to know, Special Forces. Died in the jungle. I've got his medals if you'd like to see them."

Valentino studied a random spot on the rug. Di knew she had embarrassed Valentino, but she thought it was best to tell people the truth about her late husband, especially the nosy ones.

Outside in the cavernous vestibule, a group of party-hoppers stormed the hall. Immediately, they faced the yellow tape that bordered the area outside Apartment A. Amid exclamations and muffled observations, they pounded their way up the creaky stairs.

"Look, it's late." Valentino rose from his seat and yawned.

"I'll be in touch. This case could go on for awhile."

"Why do you say that?" She was sure that Don could have had it under wraps in half the time it was taking this guy.

Valentino ignored her question, glancing at the black rotary phone near the edge of the end table. "Didn't know they still made phones like those. I like it. Mind if I take your phone number?"

Di shrugged and set the candy dish on the end table next to the phone. "Go ahead, but there's not much else I can tell you. I'm sure the other tenants know more about things around here than I do."

Valentino placed his black book in his coat pocket. He seemed to be deep in thought. "I can't say much about all of this. I ought to leave without saying a thing. But, I'm sure our paths will cross again before this murder is solved, with you being right across the hall from the crime scene and all. Frankly, I don't believe you *don't* know anything about this guy. You must have heard something, or seen somebody. Every tenant in the building is a suspect right now. Fact is, that victim owned some weird props."

Di frowned. "What are you getting at, detective?"

"Most corpses don't carry mega diamonds in their pockets, do they?"

"What?"

"This guy, whoever he was, had a diamond rock in the front pocket of his overcoat. It must have been at least four carats. Hooker swears she doesn't know anything about it. I thought it was strange she hadn't lifted it before we got there." He turned and opened the door.

"Maybe she didn't know he had it on him," said Di.

"Yeah, right." Alone and weary, Valentino walked through the door and into the steamy August night. He unlocked his car door and glanced at the bright, full moon. "It's you and me these days, Mr. Moon," he muttered.

I'm always lonely...I'm always alone. You think too much, you know that?

He drove into the darkness for some answers.

Two

Sunday, Late Morning

Parry sat in his jail cell, waiting for someone to tell him there was a misunderstanding, a simple human error—like a case of mistaken identity. Every minute that passed seemed to lessen the possibility. Yet, he had to believe it existed. It was all he had.

He yawned and rubbed the stubble on his chin. He hadn't shaved since Friday morning. Trapped on his cot, and clothed in a wrinkled orange uniform, he'd slipped into despair when he heard footsteps approaching. He glanced up to see a guard unlocking his cell door.

"Leach!"

Parry stared at the guard. He hadn't slept all night.

"What's up, Leach? Look alive, man. You have a visitor. Five minutes and counting."

Parry frowned at the news. Visitor? In here? Shackled, he shuffled down the corridor to the visiting room, where Tasha sat on the other side of a Plexiglas divider. She wore a faded navy blue dress and a hat that fit close to her round skull—her Sunday best. A fresh piece of gauze covered her left eye, secured by two long pieces of adhesive tape. She looked petrified, but not because a jail was unfamiliar to her. Rather, because it was.

The guard pointed to a chrome kitchen chair. It looked like a bite had been taken out of the seat's foam rubber stuffing and the red vinyl cover was brittle and torn. He sat down and the tired seat whooshed in agony. At the sight of Tasha's downcast face, the hopes he had been nurturing vaporized. Nevertheless, he suppressed his thoughts, and gave her a warm smile. "Tasha, girl! Man, is it good to see you!"

Tasha extended her weathered hand towards the glass partition. "Parry, don't you worry, I'm going to get you out of here. I know you didn't do nothing."

He rubbed the back of his neck. "Well, you might be the only one thinks that." He sighed despondently. "What am I going to do? That lawyer they give me don't know straight up, and 'sides that, he's some white guy don't believe a thing I say anyways. I can tell." He took a deep breath. "I'm as good as gone, girl."

"Parry," whispered Tasha, "don't say that, now."

Parry leaned closer to the glass. "You the only one can help me. That detective spent all a last night interrogating the hell out of me." He shrugged his sloping shoulders. "It don't look good. Nope, it don't look good at all."

"But you didn't even know the guy was killed! He was that ho's boyfriend, Parry. Everybody knows that."

Parry stared at his feet. He didn't respond. Tasha gripped his hand tighter.

"You didn't know that guy, did ya?"

Parry raised his chin and gazed at her. He bit his lip before speaking. "Yeah. I knew him. Oh yeah." His dark eyes narrowed with hate. "He turned me down for a job when I first got outta jail. I asked him for any kind of work. You know, I'd do anything he needed doing, girl. But naw, he couldn't give a black man a job at his fancy car dealership, no way. He said it's because I had a record, but you know that wasn't it. He just want to keep good money out of my hands. Keep me hungry, so I go rob somebody again for something to eat. He probably like it if I starved to death." Parry laughed bitterly. "But that ain't my style. You know that." He punched the palm of his hand with his fist, and stared past the glass at the cinder block wall.

Tasha retracted her hand. Her face was lined with worry. "No way," she murmured. "That ain't your style." Her jaw stiffened as she added, "Mine neither."

"Leach!" yelled the guard. "Time's up!"

Sunday Afternoon, around 2:00
The Jewel Arms Apartments

The tinny doorbell chimed, and Di squinted through the peephole. In the dim hallway, she saw a thin, almost sickly woman with chocolate-colored skin. A square of gauze concealed her left eye, and a red bandana handkerchief wrapped tightly concealed most of her grizzled black hair. Her hands balanced a plate covered with aluminum foil. A loud knock sounded on the flimsy door.

"Miss!" said a hoarse voice. "Miss, you got a minute to talk?"

After all that had happened last night, Di wanted to be alone. Most of all, she needed sleep, and time to think. The knocking persisted. "Miss Redding! It's Tasha Weeks from C!"

Weeks. That name sounded familiar, but besides that outrageous woman across the hall, she didn't know any of her neighbors. How did this stranger know her last name?

Di smoothed stray wisps of hair from her face as she cracked the door. She tried to smile at the visitor, but the woman looked so pitiful in her faded housedress and scuffed slippers, an awkward stare was all she could muster.

The woman thrust the plate into Di's hands. "I brought you some brownies." Her full lips broke into a wide grin, and she pointed to the end of the hall. "I live in C, just down there," she said, extending a clammy hand. "Like I said, my name's Tasha Weeks. Pleased to meet you."

Weeks...Weeks, thought Di. She still couldn't place the name.

She gripped the plate tighter, the smell of fudge and powdered sugar wafting to her nose. "What a nice thing to do." Her lips curled in a hesitant smile. Sensing the woman's uneasiness, she gestured inside her apartment. "Won't you come in?"

Tasha leaned closer, so that she could preview the living room. "Just for a minute, if you don't mind." She slid past Di into the stark living room, and stood in front of the leather sofa.

Di gestured with one hand, the other still holding the plate of brownies. "Please, sit down."

Tasha covered the left side of her face with her hand. "I don't usually look like this, but I just had the surgery on my eye."

Di set the plate on the coffee table in front of her visitor. "I hope it's nothing serious."

Tasha threw up her hands. "Lord, if it's not one thing with me, it's another." She gazed at her feet. "I-I don't know how to say this."

Di remained silent, but a perplexed frown crossed her brow. Outside, speeding cars rumbled along the narrow city street. Tasha looked up, her right eye widening in excitement. "You knew my brother Ant, didn't you?" Her voice almost trembled in accusation.

Di remained by the door, arms folded over her chest. She wore a denim workshirt with the sleeves rolled up, and a pair of khaki slacks. "What brother? Who are you talking about?"

Tasha rambled. "I saw your name on the mailbox in the front hall. Ain't too many people with a name like Dimond. I knew you had to be the same person."

Di clasped the doorknob. "I'm afraid I don't know what you're talking about, Miss Weeks." *Weeks.* The name nagged at her memory.

Tasha remained seated on the sofa, her legs spread slightly. "You were a nurse in Vietnam, weren't you?"

Di removed her hand from the doorknob. "A long time ago, yeah."

"Well," laughed Tasha, shaking her head, "you might not remember—I guess you don't, but you wrote letters for him—to me—a couple times when he was too bad off to write. I got those letters, and they got me through some rough times, yes, Lord."

The woman yanked some frayed envelopes from the pocket of her blue flowered housedress. A stray letter dropped to the floor beneath the coffee table. She held the envelopes at a distance, and viewed them with her good eye. "This your handwriting?" She leaned forward and offered the letters to Di.

Di frowned, but accepted them. For the life of her, she couldn't recall having written letters for anyone named Ant. Yet, that certainly looked like her handwriting. On the outside of each envelope she read the address:

Miss Natasha Weeks
St. Louis Municipal Jail
St. Louis, Missouri 63103

They were all postmarked 1968, Saigon. "Why are you showing these to me now?" She was feeling uneasy. *How was she going to get this Miss Weeks to leave?*

"I got more than that at home, Miss Redding. They from his friend, Buck, telling me how good you was taking care of my brother. He say you a real fine woman with a good heart."

Di softened a little at the compliments, yet remained wary. The woman wanted something from her—what? Di fingered the envelopes, turning them over to find the return address of one Antoine Weeks.

In a flash, Di saw him, lying on a cot in the field hospital in Saigon, his upper body swathed in gauze, his face bruised and burned. She stared intently at the forlorn woman sitting before her, and struggled to find a resemblance beneath the bandage that concealed her left eye. She couldn't see anything to corroborate such a claim. Yet, Natasha possessed these old letters.

Di handed the pages to Tasha, and noticed the desperate look on her face. "Your brother must have been a fine soldier, and you have every right to be proud of him, Miss Weeks. But what can I do for you now?" The question blasted a barrier. Now, Tasha chattered so fast it bordered on gibberish. "Parry's in trouble. I don't have no one else to ax. He didn't do it. I know he didn't. But that cop in the suit's trying to set Parry up to make it look like he did. Parry called me this morning and axed me to bail him out of the jail, but I don't have no money, Miss Redding. I'm hardly able to get around by myself right now." A wild spark illuminated her good eye. Her hands flapped like they were on fire.

Di reached for the doorknob. The door opened before she spoke. "Miss Weeks, I'd really like to help you, but…"

Tasha raised her hands in a halting motion. She gulped some air to steady her nerves. "Please, just hear me out. I know I made some mistakes in my life…" She paused and hung her head. "Some mighty bad ones. I don't deserve nothing. But Parry, you know, he's not like me. He's a good man, just like Ant. He already done his time, Miss Redding. He don't deserve this. I can't leave him in there to take the hit."

Tasha jabbed the air with her index finger. "I bet I know who killed him. Was that whore who be living down in A. That Gains woman, you know. She'd do anything to anybody."

"What are you talking about?" said Di. She didn't want to admit that she knew anything about the murder last night.

"'Bout the dead white guy last night, you know. That detective…"

"Valentino?"

"Yeah, that's him. He took Parry downtown with that Gains woman, but Parry say he gonna let her off."

Di approached her visitor cautiously, intending to help her up from her seat. Up and out. She should never have opened the door in the first place. Sitting in the shadows, a sloppily taped bandage over her eye, Tasha gave her the creeps. "Miss Weeks," she said, latching onto her bony elbow, another arm around her stooped shoulder, "I'm going to have to ask you to leave now."

Natasha refused to budge. She dug her terrycloth slippers into the faded carpet. "You got to help me, Miss Redding. Parry's like my brother now. He's all the family I got." She tugged at the dingy envelopes in her pocket. "I know you the kind of person who could help me."

"I don't mean to be rude, but you have to leave now. I'm sorry about your friend, I really am." Di felt a twinge of guilt as she perused the woman's worn clothes. "But, I really can't get involved in all of this. I just moved to St. Louis. I'm barely settled myself." She motioned to the clutter around her.

Solemnly, Tasha hung her head, and folded her hands. When she raised her head, her chin jutted forward with conviction. "I know one thing, Miss Redding. Parry done cooked fish at my apartment last night. He didn't kill nobody."

She struggled to her feet and shuffled toward the door without looking back. "You're already involved, Miss Redding. The killer did business right outside your door—that's right now—while you ate your supper."

She twisted the knob and stepped into the half-light of the corridor. Her voice echoed in the shadows. "Parry locked up all nice and tight, and that detective ain't looking no more, but the killer still out there, Miss Redding. Believe it."

The door slammed. Di stood in the darkened room and took a deep breath. She didn't want to think about Natasha Weeks or her brother, or the woman across the hall. What if Tasha came back? She didn't want to be there. She grabbed her purse and decided to leave the apartment.

Outside, the gray sky had gone from gray to green. A tornado sky, thought Di. The tension in the air seemed to crackle with delight. Maybe it had been Tasha's visit, but the last time she'd felt like this was years ago, in that Saigon hospital. In her memory, she was there, visiting with Ant again, and writing another letter to his sister. That was another lifetime, in a senseless war, fighting a relentless foe.

Though it was years later, Di couldn't help but see the parallel. Time had gone by, but the past remained. She started a new life, and faced the ugly truths that challenged her optimism. Still, her past lived on in the present.

Tasha had been right about one thing. It had puzzled her in 'Nam, and now, the dilemma returned to haunt her. Once again, a man was dead. Senseless violence demanded justice.

Who killed this Mattie Torrez? Somewhere, a murderer wandered free, waiting to kill again.

Believe it.

Three

Memphis, Tennessee
Late Afternoon, Sunday

"Well, Vanna, that just about does it." Elvin slammed the trunk of an old silver Cadillac, parked in the driveway of his small brick bungalow. A FOR SALE sign on the manicured lawn advertised his departure. The Airedale, officially named Savannah, lounged beside him. He smoothed the dog's floppy ears and grinned at her fuzzy face. "Think I ought to check the mailbox before I leave?"

Tires screeched behind him. Vanna leapt to greet the untimely but familiar visitor. The petite blonde hustled from the backseat of a red convertible, and clacked up the driveway in spiked, backless heels. Tousled curls framed her round face. She stomped past Elvin with her pug nose aimed at the heavens and her pink plastic sunglasses slightly awry.

"You could say hello, Cherie."

He stood with his hands in his pockets, and watched Vanna bound playfully around her former mistress. His wife stood with her back to Elvin, and fumbled with the keys to the front door. Vanna snatched the pink purse and dropped it at Elvin's feet. Its contents spilled onto the concrete driveway.

"You're gonna need this stuff, Cherie."

Elvin bent down to gather the various lipsticks, cigarettes and a lone Visa card. He glanced at the card, and slipped it into the purse. The name, "Walter Hubble," was not familiar. He approached his wife, who continued to ignore him. Quietly, he set the purse down on the porch behind her.

"Look, Cherie," he said, "this divorce thing is stupid. I'll do anything to make it work, you know that. Just tell me what you want. That's all you got to do."

The woman faced him. Elvin couldn't tell whether he saw hate or frustration in those green eyes—maybe both, he decided. "Damn it, Elvin. Why are you doing this?"

"I love you, Cherie." His voice quivered. His hand grazed her slender elbow. "I'll do anything…"

She pushed him. Her tiny body stiffened as if it might explode. "It's over, Elvin!" Her voice was filled with fury and scorn. "Don't you get it, or what? I got myself a new man now." She stamped her foot on the concrete. "I don't want to be your wife. Anymore. Got it? I don't know what else to say to your Dixie-fried head!"

A siren wailed in the distance. Two young boys pedaled their bikes down the sunny sidewalk. Vanna chased them, running mightily after something she would never catch. A lump rose in Elvin's throat. He couldn't help feeling that he and Vanna had a whole lot in common.

"Oh hell! Just take it all, why don't you?" Cherie tossed the loose keys into the magnolia bushes that edged the porch. "I've got to get out of here." She stomped down the driveway, and flopped into her car. She turned up the radio, and shook her tiny blonde head. The ignition key turned; the red car sped down the sunny street. Fifteen years sputtered, withered, and died.

For the first time in his life, Elvin Suggs was speechless.

The Jewel Arms, Belle's Apartment

Belle lay in the back bedroom, shivering under layers of faded quilts. A weak, skeletal woman, she was always cold. Chronic bad health and a stroke, aggravated by her bouts with alcohol and prescription painkillers, left her partially paralyzed on the left side.

Despite her protests, her son Mattie had hired Rose Honeycutt, a stocky, middle-aged nurse-aide to care for her.

For all practical purposes, Belle was deaf, particularly when she didn't want to hear anything. As a result, Rose rarely spoke to her, nodding occasionally as Belle prattled on about the past, and sometimes, the present. Any topic sufficed, as long as it involved wrestling.

Rose set a mug of warm milk on her night table, but Belle took no notice. She was preoccupied with her running commentary on the wrestling match on the small black and white television set.

"Did you see that left hook?" the old lady cackled as she kneaded her fists together in delight. "He got him down again... Look at that, they're down for the count!"

Belle ignored the nurse's movements. In the throes of action, the television screen blacked out completely. "I was watching that!" said Belle, as she noticed the remote control in Rose's hand. "Turn it on!"

Rose's mouth curled in a soft smile. She extended her plump hand toward the old woman. In her palm, she held three capsules, which she offered to her with a motherly nod.

"What's this?" As Rose lifted the old woman's head, Belle's tone became childlike. Although she couldn't explain her trepidation, she feared the younger woman. "I didn't think I was supposed to have any more pills today."

Rose tipped the mug toward Belle's cracked lips. "You've been too agitated, Belle. You need something to help you sleep. The other pills will help kill the pain. I don't believe people should have any pain."

Belle stared at her in the dim light of the cluttered bedroom. She felt confused. She felt that way a lot lately. She didn't recall complaining about any pain. Certainly, she had no reason to be agitated. "But I don't feel any pain tonight, Rose."

"Of course you do." Rose's thin mouth curled at one corner. "Now, let's get going. I have a date tonight."

The old lady gulped each pill, followed by a sip of the milk. The bitter taste made her wince. "Take this away, Rose. It tastes bad."

Rose gripped the mug in her meaty hands. Her plump face relaxed. "Good night, Belle," she said with a smile. She turned off the lights and shut the door. "Sleep tight, honey."

Di's Apartment, Later that night

The phone buzzed. Di wanted to ignore the call, but decided to answer. It might be Valentino. "Yeah," she said. "Who is this?" There was a caller waiting. She could hear the breathing. Static crackled on the line. "Come on, who is this?"

She slammed the receiver into the cradle, but seconds later, it rang again. She let it ring three times. "Yeah, who is this?"

"Well, aren't we friendly tonight?" said a familiar voice.

"Elvin! Did you just call me?"

"Yeah. I'm talking at you, ain't I?"

"No, I mean about a minute ago. Somebody called and hung up."

"Why would I do something like that? You know I never give up the chance to talk."

"Yeah, well, what's up?"

"You're gonna die when I tell you." Elvin paused. "Well, girl, I was thinking 'bout coming up to St. Louis for a little while. Thought I might pay you a visit and do a little looking around. Thought I'd drive up tomorrow. Probably be there after supper sometime."

Again, Elvin hesitated. "You in some kind of trouble?" he said, his voice thick with the drawl of his native Memphis.

"Not me, exactly. Don't worry yourself, Elvin." Di's laughter melted into concern. "Say, what's up with you? You sound a little bit tired."

Seconds passed on the end of the line. Finally, Elvin cleared his throat. "Cherie left me last week."

"See you tomorrow, El," Di said. In haste, she replaced the receiver.

No explanations were needed. Di and Elvin owned a certain understanding. Di's late husband, Don, had been Elvin's closest friend, and together, they had served in Vietnam. Elvin Suggs suffered beside Don Redding when he died, shot down in the sweltering jungle. Elvin had personally delivered Don's gun to Di, along with Don's final words to his wife.

Now, Elvin Suggs needed a friend. There was one number that he called; the conversation had been short. Too many words would blur the basic message that defined their friendship. Simply put, the subtext read like this: they were there for each other, no matter what. Period.

It was understood. Period.

Four

Far too alone and dangerously busy, Rick Valentino felt lonely. After he left Di's apartment late Saturday night, he stopped for some White Castle hamburgers, and rushed to his studio apartment on Hampton Avenue. He really craved a cold beer—maybe two or even four—but his friends at the AA meetings warned him there would be times like this. The hamburgers would have to do.

For the most part, he liked his job, but it never failed to puzzle him when someone was murdered. Killing was such a primitive thing for a human being to do. He accepted it, but he couldn't understand it. Murder victims always made him feel so vulnerable, and he didn't like that feeling at all.

He had two suspects. Well, he thought as he popped two Alka Seltzers, there is really just one. So far, the evidence was circumstantial, but he thought he had the goods to prove Parry Leach had struck again. He shook his head and undid his tie. Some guys just never learned. He probably shouldn't have kept the blonde in custody overnight, especially wearing that filthy dress. He chuckled to himself as he brushed his straight, white teeth. It wouldn't hurt to keep her kind locked up on a Saturday night.

He snapped off the lamp on the night table and tumbled, exhausted but restless, into the simple double bed. He had to notify the next of kin tomorrow, just as soon as they firmed things up down at the morgue. He would never get used to that part, either.

The streetlamps cast a dull glow through the bedroom window. Shadows danced on the wall. A hearty wind whistled through the rustling leaves. Valentino stared at the ceiling. Awake and frustrated, he craved a drink—just one little, tiny drink. He tried to relax, but something bothered him about the old couple next to Mrs. Redding. He couldn't forget their interview, though they seemed innocuous, maybe too much so. What was wrong here?

At first, they hadn't wanted to let him in, but his badge convinced them it would be the wise thing to do. Edith huddled behind Edward, a tall but stooped gentleman with thick white hair, dressed in a tan cardigan sweater and rumpled gray slacks. He had a large, beak-like nose. A pair of thick glasses with heavy black frames obscured the expression in his black eyes. Edward peered through the crack in the door at Valentino. At the glint of the badge, he squinted through the glasses.

"May I come in?" Valentino asked. When he got no response, he added, "I'd just like to ask you a few questions. Just a few minutes of your time, sir, and I'll be out of your way."

Still intimidated, the elderly man shuffled aside when Valentino entered Apartment E, next to Di. It reeked of coffee grounds and lilac air freshener. Valentino couldn't decide which odor was stronger.

He'd never seen so many ceramic knickknacks in one place. A box overflowing with coupons and receipts crowded the kitchen table. Beside it lay a large pair of kitchen shears. A stack of recycled aluminum TV dinner trays crowded the countertop next to the refrigerator, along with a collection of empty jars of various sizes. Once he was inside, the couple continued to ogle him in silence while they all stood in the living room. They did not offer him a seat on the afghan-covered sofa. Valentino started talking.

"I'll make this as brief as possible, folks, but I want to make sure I don't miss anything. I'm sure you can understand that." Again, he received no response. The tension in the room crackled. He pulled out his black notebook and clicked his ballpoint pen. "First of all, could I have your names?"

The woman peeked at her husband. She was a bird-like woman, with steel-colored hair and large brown eyes. She wore a lavender housedress covered by a thin gray sweater. She appeared to be cold, even in the heat of the late summer. Her lips trembled, and she clutched her husband's elbow for support.

"We are Mr. and Mrs. Edward Mars," Edward replied in a gravelly voice. He shoved his hands into the front pockets of his worn slacks. Edith continued to grip his arm.

Valentino scribbled in his notebook. "Okay, that's a good start. Now, as you might already know, there was a murder here this evening, we estimate somewhere around 6:00 p.m. Now, naturally, due to the location of your apartment, I'm interested in anything or anyone you might have noticed that might have been, oh, let's say…unusual." Valentino raised his shaggy brows suggestively.

Edith replied. "We didn't notice anything, did we, Eddie?"

There was a short pause as the old man shifted his feet from side to side.

"Mr. Mars?" Valentino asked. "Would you care to comment?"

"N-no."

"Where were you around 6:00 this evening, sir? Were you together?" Valentino's pen was poised for his response.

Edward Mars fumbled with his thick glasses, struggling to straighten them with trembling fingers. "Why, we were right here in the kitchen, eating our chicken pot pies." He coughed, and coughed again, before he retorted, "Of course we were together, Detective. Where else would we be?"

"We always have chicken pot pies on Saturday night," Mrs. Mars said. "We watch *Wheel of Fortune* during dinner."

"Right," Valentino said, noting their remarks in his black book.

"Did you come out into the hall when the ambulance arrived? Did you hear any commotion?"

Neither replied.

"Folks, it's not a hard question," joked the detective.

"No, we didn't," Mrs. Mars said, pulling her gray sweater tighter.

"Didn't what?"

"We didn't notice anything," Edward said.

Valentino noted the close proximity of the kitchen table to the door. "A man was stabbed right outside your door and you didn't hear anything?"

Edward nodded, a deadpan expression etched on his lined face. "That's right, Buddy."

In a cavalier manner, Valentino closed his notebook. He acted like he had just finished a Sunday pot roast, and was about to sample a coconut cream pie.

"Well, I guess that's about it then. Thanks for your time." Valentino turned to leave, placing his hand on the doorknob beneath the assortment of locks and chains. Suddenly, he turned around, a look of enlightenment decorating his face. "I was just wondering about something else. Did either of you know a man named Matthew Torrez?"

The woman's eyes widened. Valentino glimpsed some recognition in them.

"Who?" she asked.

She obviously struggled to contain her emotions. Edward looked nervous.

"Matthew Torrez was the victim's name, ma'am."

Valentino turned to Edward Mars. "What about you? Did you know Matthew Torrez?"

Edward's eyes were cold and defiant as he asserted, "I do not know anyone by that name."

Now, Valentino shifted restlessly among the plain white sheets, struggling to fall asleep. The image of the old man's glasses burned in his brain, along with the declaration that he did not know Matthew Torrez. Because of their age and frail appearance, he didn't believe the Marses were murder suspects, at least, they weren't ex-cons like Parry Leach—he had checked, and yet, he had the feeling they knew more than they were saying. He punched the feather pillow in frustration. Why would they lie? What were they hiding—and why?

Valentino was finally in a deep slumber when the phone call pierced the silence. It rang four times before he could answer it, knocking the phone onto the thin carpet. Clumsily, he picked up the receiver. "Valentino," he mumbled, his voice heavy with sleep.

"Hey, Princess!" It was Reggie down at the station. Reggie was five years away from retirement, a heavy-set black man who had spent his career as a St. Louis City cop. He was unflappable.

"What's up?" Valentino peered through the blinds at the gray dawn. "What time is it?"

"Time to get up, Princess. I'm working and you should be too."

"Yeah, yeah. Did you call just to call me names?"

"Got news, my man. We ran a background check on that stiff your guys brought in last night."

Valentino sat up, all ears. "Go on."

"Name's Matthew Torrez, thirty-five years old, cause of death, exsanguination from a severed right carotid artery, but you already knew that." Valentino heard the rustle of paper as Reggie continued. "Owns a foreign car dealership in Clayton. Ran his Social Security Number. Got yourself a big fish this time, Rick. Probably has his first dime."

"Interesting, I guess."

Reggie gave a sly laugh. "Guess where the lady lives, my friend?"

"Where?"

"The Jewel Arms on Watson. Sound familiar?"

"That's where the guy was murdered."

"Yep."

"What's the connection?"

Reggie chuckled. "With his mama? What you oughtta be wonderin' about is the connection between him and that Gains woman you hauled in. Quite an operator, that one."

"Yeah, well, that can wait a little. I've got a very likely suspect under wraps for now. I think I got lucky on this one."

"Besides, you got to break the news to his mama."

"Can't you guys ever give me a break? You know where she lives as well as I do. It's gonna take me a little while to get cleaned up after last night."

"Then she can just be happy a few minutes longer, can't she?" joked Reggie.

Valentino hung up and sat on the edge of the creaky bed. He would have to think about this for a minute. Did Belle Torrez know Valerie Gains? If she did, how much did she know about her? Did she know Parry Leach? In the same way that Valentino knew that dusk followed dawn, and cats liked tuna, he was certain Mars knew something about Torrez. He wasn't telling him, either. Did that make Mars a liar—or a coward? Edward refused to divulge any knowledge of the victim, even though Valentino suspected he was hiding something, be it ever so small.

He stood and flipped on the overhead light. It hurt his bloodshot eyes. The clock said 6:45 a.m. If he hurried, he could get over to the Jewel Arms in an hour, before this Belle Torrez had a chance to leave.

No time like the present. He stumbled into the kitchenette to make coffee.

Less than an hour later, Valentino stood at the top of the landing and gathered his wits. Through the stained glass windows, the morning sun fought to illuminate the peeling letters on the old apartment doors. Somehow, the building seemed a little nicer in the morning. The cheap paper, embossed in black and gold, complete with ripped and curled edges, remained legible. Still, thought Valentino, a building like the Jewel deserved more attention. He sniffed the putrid air and winced. The rank hall reeked of dust and strong coffee.

A door opened to his left, and a short, stocky man in a white terrycloth bathrobe snatched a newspaper from his doormat.

"Hey!" he said to Valentino. From the cheerful expression in his voice, Valentino surmised that this was the man's version of a greeting.

Valentino reached for his badge. "Detective Rick Valentino. I'm looking for Apartment G."

The man looked puzzled. "It's that way, Mister," he said. He pointed to the other end of the hall. A Texas accent flavored his speech. "You sure you want G? An old lady lives there, you know."

"Yeah, I know. Thanks."

The man shook his head. "You never know about some people, I guess."

Valentino had pulled out his notebook. "Your name, sir, if you don't mind?"

The man's face brightened. "Denton Smith." He extended his free hand. "From Dallas."

"Texas boy, huh?" said Valentino as he scrawled his notes. "How long have you lived in this building, Mr. Smith?"

"Call me Dent, will you? Oh, I'd say close to six months, now."

"Know many of your neighbors?"

"Oh, I see people come and go, you know."

"Uh-uh," said Valentino.

"Like, there's the Silvers down that way—he's in medical school. Then there's the lawyer across the hall from me—black guy named La Mour." He chuckled. "Don't see much of him, especially on the weekends."

"Oh, yeah?"

"Yeah. And the old lady, well, you never see her. But that plump-like gal she's got looking after her is always making a racket around here. Like, she got in a fight the other day with the old lady's son. I think he's the one hired her in the first place."

Now, we're getting somewhere, thought the detective. "Her son, you say?" Valentino tried to conceal his excitement. He was sure too much interest could dry up his source.

Despite Valentino's caution, Dent suddenly clammed up, and shifted from foot to foot. "Oh, it wasn't much, really. I get carried away sometimes. Everybody gets into it once in awhile, don't they?"

Valentino thought for a moment. "Yes, I guess they do." He pointed down the hall. "You say G is this way?"

Dent nodded, and tightened the belt on his bathrobe. "That's right. Oh, and detective?"

Valentino turned to face him.

"I'd appreciate it if you didn't hear any of this from me, you know?"

Valentino winked. "Gotcha."

Five

Annie and Benjamin Silver occupied Apartment J, located directly above Di Redding. They slept late Sunday morning, as they always did, and dressed to go to brunch at Ben's mother's house. This was a ritual they'd observed every Sunday since their honeymoon, a long two years ago.

Annie was a tall, wiry woman, two years younger than her husband, with long tanned legs that were toned and shapely from her daily run. Her blonde hair was highlighted and waist-length, but she usually wore it pinned up in a twist in the back of her head. She had a naturally sunny disposition, and seemed oblivious to Ben's chronic depression. At least, that's the impression she gave those around her.

Annie worked as a medical technologist at University Hospital, and Ben followed his dream. That's what people told him, he liked to tell people. He was not a very enthusiastic medical student.

A tall and muscular young man, Ben wore thick, wire-rimmed glasses. The gray strands that streaked his black hair belied his twenty-five years. The perpetual hangdog expression, in particular, led most people to believe he was much older and very depressed. These days, he tended to communicate in grunts and moans.

The couple had stayed in the night before because Ben wanted to study, whether he needed to or not. Annie wanted to go out for a hamburger, maybe even see a movie. However, her request fell on deaf ears, and after four beers, she passed out in front of the television set. She drank on a regular basis these days, although she wouldn't admit it, even to herself. Ben had isolated himself in the tiny second bedroom immediately after dinner.

When they quietly descended the vinyl treaded steps to the first floor, they were shocked. On a quiet Sunday morning, neither expected to confront a yellow-taped murder scene, smeared thoroughly with dried blood.

"What happened last night?" said Annie, trying to focus her bloodshot eyes. She sniffed at the musky odor in the narrow hall.

"How the hell should I know?"

"You were up studying, weren't you?"

Ben's face flushed with anger. "Unlike you, I concentrate on what I'm doing. You watch too much of that damn TV."

Annie stood in front of Apartment A, her sheer summery dress a stark contrast to the grisly site. "Poor Valerie. All those parties finally caught up with her, I guess. I wonder if she had any family."

"Who cares?" Ben threw up his hands in disgust. "She should have expected it, living such a trashy life. It would be better if her family never found out about any of it. It's certainly nothing to be proud of."

"She was a nice person! And she wasn't a hooker, if that's what you mean. She was one of those celebrity impersonators that entertain at parties. She expected to be an actress someday."

Across the hall, Di lifted her tousled head from the sofa. She had fallen asleep watching television, and now, the argument roused her. She didn't recognize these new voices.

"It's just like you to stick up for that kind of scum," said Ben. "And now that scum is gonna make us late for my mother's." He grabbed Annie's arm and gave her a harsh shove.

"Don't touch me like that!" she said, pushing him away. The

move landed him with a thud against Di's door, and she opened it as Ben jerked Annie's arm with a harsh shove. Even in her disheveled condition, she seemed to intimidate them. At least, that was her gut feeling. "What's the problem here?" Di asked.

"Sorry," said Ben grudgingly. He plunged his hands in the front pockets of his khaki trousers. "I didn't know anyone had moved into D."

"Glad to meet you." Annie extended her hand. "I'm Annie Silver and this is my husband, Ben." She smiled, displaying a row of perfect white teeth. "When did you move in?"

"About two weeks ago." Now, Di noticed Ben's hand in the middle of Annie's back, nudging her toward the front entry door.

"I'm afraid my wife talks too much," Ben said, his voice tense with pent-up anger. "We're going to have to move on now. She's already made us late again, as usual. Mother hates it when she does that."

"But Ben, I was just going to ask our neighbor about Valerie."

Di observed Ben's reaction. She sensed the tension escalating between the couple. She decided to introduce herself, not only to be friendly, but also to find out more about Valerie. It seemed like Annie could be a regular chatterbox.

"My name's Dimond Redding, but no one calls me Dimond," she said, flashing a smile. "So just call me Di, okay? Now, what were you saying about Valerie?"

Ben stamped his foot furiously. "If you two *ladies* would like to shoot the shit, do it on your own time, will you? Mother's waiting!"

Annie glanced at the dark bloodstains outside Apartment A. "Look, I'll be back a little before dinnertime. Maybe we can talk then. I mean, if you want to."

"Sure." Di noticed the way Ben gripped his wife's arm, digging his fingers so tightly into the flesh that the surrounding skin bulged. He shook his head as he propelled her through the front entrance, dragging her down the front walk toward the narrow street.

"Stop it, Ben! That hurts!" Annie, attempted to shake off his hand.

Di watched through the front window as Ben hurled his wife into the passenger seat of a compact car. He slammed the door, barely missing her hand.

"Now I'll have to drive like a maniac!" He struggled to roll down the window. "It's all your fault!"

The tires screeched while he pulled away from the curb. As Di reached to close the door to her apartment, she glimpsed the bloody rug across the hall. She couldn't help herself. Instinctively, her thoughts turned to Annie.

Sunday Afternoon, around 4:15 p.m.

Myles La Mour felt exceptionally good. Maybe a little weary, but still very fine. It had been an outstanding weekend. As he pulled up to the curb in front of the Jewel Arms, he weighed the chances of spending another one just like it.

He stepped out of his black BMW and smoothed his gray Brooks Brothers suit. Then, he grabbed his leather briefcase, which had been in the backseat since he left his law office last Friday night.

Fresh out of law school, Myles was a strikingly handsome man of African American descent, with hazel eyes and a carefully trimmed moustache. His clothes were impeccably coordinated, and custom tailored to fit his tall, athletic build, which he maintained with regular workouts. He had a presence about him that attracted the ladies on a regular basis.

He strolled along the sidewalk whistling, despite the ominous green-gray sky. "Tornado weather," he muttered, opening the door to the entry hall.

The smell of frying bacon permeated the air, and Myles sniffed appreciatively. He collected his mail from the black mailbox labeled *La Mour* and suddenly, he noticed the yellow tape.

Stunned, he stepped in the hallway, just outside of Apartment A. Still gripping mail and briefcase, he surveyed the blood stains. The sound of approaching footsteps echoed from the concrete sidewalk. The screen door whined and Valerie Gains entered the building. Jangling keys broke the silence while she fumbled in her snakeskin purse.

"Well, hel-lo to you." Myles scrutinized the curvaceous blonde, still clad in her blood-stained dress. "You all right?"

"Do you mind?" Valerie pushed her way past him.

"Uh, are you supposed to go in there?" Myles pointed to the area in front of Valerie's apartment, still outlined in yellow tape.

"I live here. Nobody tells me what to do. So buzz off!"

"Don't believe we've met, Miss...?"

Valerie turned her back and she inserted the key into the cheap lock. "I don't know why we would," she said, and shoved the door.

"Would what?"

"Meet." Valerie slammed the door in his face.

The rebuff did not offend Myles. He considered it a temporary setback. The yellow tape and bloodstains were far more unexpected. He lingered a moment, studying the gory scene. You never knew what a weekend would bring, he thought, whistling as he thumbed through bills and catalogs. He climbed halfway up the creaky wooden stairs when he heard it.

"Oh, Mr. La Mour?" asked the lilting voice.

Myles halted, and turned to see Valerie Gains standing in her doorway of Apartment A, clad in a filmy red robe, trimmed in red ostrich feathers. He was confused. Not only by her sudden warmth, but also that she knew his name.

"Yeah, that's me," he said. The musty hallway suddenly seemed too hot. Valerie ran her fingers through her platinum hair.

"You're a lawyer, right?" She smiled, batting thick black eyelashes.

"That's right, Miss…"

"Gains. Valerie Gains. I'm sorry for my behavior before, but I've been so upset lately, and I—well, I wondered if you might be able to help me with a little problem. That is, if you can forgive me, Myles."

Myles. *Now it's Myles.* He observed the outline of her body beneath the folds of the sheer lingerie. His tie felt like a noose.

"A lot depends on what your problem is, Miss, uh, Gains." He loosened the length of red silk and inhaled twice. "Right now is probably not the best time to discuss your personal affairs. Perhaps you could give me a call at my office tomorrow." He descended the creaky stairs, fumbling in his coat pocket with each step he took. "I don't seem to have a business card, oh here's one." He handed her the card.

Rivulets of sweat dribbled from his temples. As he stood in front of her door, he felt queasy. "What happened here?" He pointed to the tape, and craned his neck to scan the disheveled living room in Apartment A. It had been dissected by the police.

Valerie raised a penciled eyebrow. "You don't know?"

"Why would I? I've been away for the weekend."

"I thought everyone knew by now. It's in the morning paper. Why don't you come in for awhile? I'm awfully lonely, and after what I've just been through, I could use a few drinks."

Myles was tempted, he really was. If he hadn't just spent the weekend with a woman like Frieda, he would have relented, even though something told him it wouldn't be smart. Hell, his bones were tired, and he had to be in court early the next morning. He reached for Valerie's smooth palm and squeezed it.

Why did it hurt so bad to be so smart? He could ponder that question for years and never know the reason. He would be smart once again, he told himself. But just once, he would like to know what it felt like to…*forget it, just forget it.*

"I like a drink once in a while myself," he said, "But I'll have to take a raincheck. Be sure and call my office."

Valerie leaned against the doorway, and sucked a drag from

her cigarette. One shoulder of her robe slipped, exposing her
smooth, creamy skin. "Oh, I will," she said, with a knowing grin.
"...Myles."

Valentino stood outside Apartment G and straightened his
tie. He needed to look just right when he spoke to Belle Torrez.
Before he could knock, however, he overheard a shrewish voice
raging from somewhere inside the apartment.

"How do you expect to get better when you won't take all
your medicine? And your nuisance son—he comes around all
the time, checking out every move I make!"

He heard a low mumble in the background that Valentino
couldn't identify, followed by a cracking sound that might have
been a slap. "How the hell do I know where he is?"

It sounded to him like a good time to interrupt the activi-
ties. Valentino tapped on the door. There was a scuffling sound
inside, as if the furniture was being rearranged. He waited, and
knocked again.

"I'm coming, I'm coming," said a woman's husky voice.

The door opened, and Valentino encountered a plumpish
woman in her forties. She was short, and wore the dyed blonde
hair pinned in an elaborate updo, a sharp contrast to her gray
sweatshirt and denim stretch pants. She brushed a stray curl from
her forehead and glared at the detective.

The flash of Valentino's badge quickly replaced her irritation
with shock. When she didn't respond, Valentino persisted, painfully aware of the reason for his visit. "Mrs. Torrez?" He was almost certain that she was not, but he hoped her reaction would
divulge some information.

The woman giggled. "How old do you think I am, Mister?"

Valentino perused her lumpy body, and decided to ignore
the question. "Is there a Belle Torrez here, ma'am?"

"You don't have to get that way with me, Mr. Val-Val—" She
squinted at his identification while she stuttered, and the effort
seemed to fluster her all the more.

"Valentino."

"Whatever. Belle Torrez lives here, yeah. So do I."

"I have some information to discuss with Mrs. Torrez. May I come in?"

The woman planted herself in the narrow doorway. Her flabby body stiffened in resistance to his request. "Nope."

"Is Mrs. Torrez in right now?" He craned his neck to peer into the apartment, hoping to catch a glimpse of whoever had provided the other half of the muffled conversation he had overheard. He saw no one. The only noise was the voice of a television newscaster droning in the background. A stainless steel walker stood in the far corner. The air smelled stuffy in the way that only sick rooms can.

"Listen, Mister, I could have you carted away for harassing us this way. Mrs. Torrez is a very sick woman. She's…she's asleep right now."

The woman placed her stubby fingers on her ample hips, as if to emphasize her authority. Valentino counted five rings of various styles and stones on each hand.

In a flourish, he clicked his ballpoint pen. "I didn't catch your name." He raised one eyebrow, and waited for her response.

"I don't need to tell you my name."

"No, you don't. I can just take it from the mailbox downstairs, Miss Honeycutt. Would you be the housekeeper?" He scribbled in his notebook.

Rose was insulted by the last remark; that was the last straw. "It's *Mrs.* Honeycutt, and I am not a housekeeper. I am a professional nurse. Mrs. Torrez's son hired me to run things around here, and I do it my way."

"I see," said Valentino. The edge of his mouth retracted, almost like a sneer. Just outside the apartment door, his foot stumbled on something soft—like the morning paper. He picked it up and handed it to the woman. "I'll come back later. In the meantime, you might check the obituaries."

He left. He never saw the suspicion in her blue eyes. The sound of jangling keys made him turn and strut down the hall, he observed a well-dressed man clutching a briefcase. Obscured by the shadows, his free hand struggled to unlock his apartment door.

"Need a hand there, pal?" He approached the landing.

Startled, La Mour glanced over his shoulder at the detective. "Oh, don't worry, I'll get it right one of these times," he said, setting his briefcase at his feet. "That's what I get for living in such a cheap apartment, I guess." He laughed pleasantly. "Leaves me money for the finer things in life, though."

"Oh, yeah?"

Myles La Mour frowned and turned his back. *Yeah. Oh yeah.*

Who was this busybody? Myles wrangled with the keys again, fully aware the stranger still stood behind him. Finally, he conquered the lock and the door surrendered, causing him to lose his balance. He tripped over the cumbersome briefcase and fell into the living room, which was furnished in glass and chrome.

"You all right there, pal?" said Valentino.

Myles hardly thought the man's interest sincere. In fact, it offended him that the stranger had stepped inside his apartment, but he controlled his urge to tell him to get the hell out. Instead, he stood up and smiled before gesturing to the open door. "Thank you for your concern. Now, if you'll excuse me…"

Before he finished his sentence, the man flashed a badge in his face and introduced himself as Detective Valentino, which meant nothing to Myles. He felt weary, and wanted nothing more than a shower and a ham sandwich. But this guy, this Valentino, had other plans.

After Valentino helped himself to a seat in the living room, Myles reluctantly positioned himself on the sofa across from him. The obnoxious Valentino asked a lot of questions about how he'd just spent his weekend, all of which Myles considered highly up close and personal. In Myles' opinion, the guy was outrageous, but he answered the questions in hopes that when he finished,

Valentino would be too. Myles was wrong.

"So," said Valentino, "you're telling me you were gone all weekend, is that right, Mr. La Mour, and you didn't know a thing about the murder until a few minutes ago?"

"That's right. Are we through here?"

"Not yet." Impatience overwhelmed him.

"Look, I've told you all I know—which isn't much."

"Tell me about Matthew Torrez. Did you know him?"

"Yeah, you could say that."

"You were friends, enemies...what?"

Myles folded, then unfolded, and refolded his hands, floundering to find the right words. "Is this on the record?"

Valentino sighed. "That is my plan, but plans can change, can't they? Speak freely, my friend. You can trust me."

Myles didn't buy that line for a minute. "I'm an attorney, Detective. This is off the record."

"Gotcha."

"Torrez was the kind of guy that people either loved or hated. You know, people tended to...you know...react to him one way or the other."

"What about you?"

Myles proceeded with caution. He had to watch his facial expression. Ever mindful of his words, he laughed nervously before he began to speak. He hated speaking ill of the dead, but there was just no nice way to say what he had to say. He shifted position on the sofa and leaned forward, elbows resting on knees. "How can I say this, Valentino? The man was a bigot. A dyed-in-the-wool, racist bigot." Myles' eyes blazed with an inner fire.

"I don't need to tell you how hard I've worked to get where I am right now. Okay, I'm fresh out of law school, I'm not established yet or anything, but..." He pointed to the two diplomas on the plaster wall from Saint Louis University. "I am the first in my family to graduate from college, not to mention law school, even though they were all smart enough to do the same. The thing is, they didn't have the *opportunity*."

Valentino opened his mouth to speak, but Myles interrupted, shaking his fist in the detective's face. "No, let me finish. You asked for this." His eyes narrowed with hate. "People like Matthew Torrez, they don't believe in opportunity for people like me. They don't understand that I want the same things they want, and I'm willing to work just as hard for them—maybe harder."

"What makes you so sure of all this, Mr. La Mour?"

Myles escorted Valentino over to the window and pointed at his black BMW parked in front of the building. "See my car out there? I went in to Mr. Torrez's car dealership one day, ready and fully able to pay for that vehicle. Mind you, I had just come from work, and was still dressed in my suit. I wandered around that showroom for thirty...forty minutes. Only attention I got was from a security guard. Guy tailed me like I was getting ready to rob the place. For a minute, I thought he would arrest me. Finally, I asked if there were any salespersons available, and out comes Mr. Matthew Torrez acting all huffy like I was bothering him or something."

"And?"

"And, he asks me if he can help me, informing me he's the owner and all that stuff. I tell him I'm looking to buy a BMW."

"Okay."

"Okay, so he says, 'Sir, are you aware of what a BMW costs? Maybe I could interest you in something more reasonable.'"

"And I say, 'No, I came here because I want a BMW.' Well, now he gets all squirrelly on me and finally says, 'Sir, can you afford such a car?' That was it for me."

Valentino looked confused. "But, Mr. La Mour, you did get the BMW, didn't you? Or didn't you buy it from him?"

Myles relaxed a little, even chuckling a bit at the question. "Buy it from him?" He shook his head. "After I showed him my business card, after I told him what I thought of that question, and especially after I asked him what he thought a judge might think of the question, he practically gave me the car."

"He didn't admit he discriminated against you, did he?"

Myles grew serious. "Discrimination is the most dangerous when nobody says anything, detective. It's the little things that say the most. Of all people, your kind ought to know that."

Myles paused. He was out of breath, but felt a lot better. "You'll have to excuse my temper back there, but I harbor some strong feelings on the subject of Mr. Matthew Torrez. I'm afraid it will take a while to forget what I know I should forgive."

"Yes, I can see that, Mr. La Mour."

Myles rose and smoothed his rumpled suit. "So, is that what you wanted to know? Did you get what you came for?"

Valentino rose and extended his hand to his host. "Yes, I believe I did. Thank you for your candor."

He tiptoed into the hall and paused for just a second, to digest Myles' testimony. How could he be sure of the convenient claim that he was gone all weekend? Yet he didn't get the feeling the lawyer was lying about anything—far from it. This Torrez guy was shaping up very differently than expected. So far, no one seemed to have missed him at all. It was disturbing.

"Excuse me." The voice startled him. Valentino felt a tap on his shoulder. He turned to see Denton Smith, still clad in his terrycloth bathrobe. Valentino couldn't help himself. "Say Mr. Smith, don't you ever get dressed?"

Dent looked surprised at the question. "Why should I?" He shrugged. "I don't go out much."

"Really? Don't you work?"

"Work?"

"Yeah, you know, like in a job?"

Dent laughed. "Oh, that. I work from my apartment."

Valentino stared at Dent's bare feet. "Just what is it you do?"

Dent scanned the hallway and the darkened stairs. "Listen, would you like to come in for awhile? I don't like to talk out here where everyone can hear."

"But, there's no one here."

"You never know who's listening. Trust me."

Valentino felt confused, but had planned to ask Dent a few

questions later anyway. Now, he planned to ask a lot of them. "Uh, sure there, Mr. Smith. Lead the way."

Before long, he sat on Dent's brocade loveseat, drinking tea. A tempting plate of muffins garnished the coffee table. Dent flopped in a velvet wing chair, facing him. This time, Valentino felt uneasy; he didn't enjoy the feeling. He took a sip of tea and replaced the cup on the saucer. "Mind if I smoke?"

Dent looked nervous. "Smoke?"

"Yeah, you know, smoke. Like, in cigarettes? If it's a big deal, why..."

"No, no, not at all. I want you to be as comfortable as possible," Dent said. He glanced skittishly around the room. "It's just that I'm a little worried about the ammo..."

"Ammo? What ammo?"

Dent glanced over his shoulder. "That's what I wanted to talk to you about."

"I'm all ears." Valentino pulled his black book from his suitcoat.

Dent gestured wildly at the book. "Oh no, I'm afraid that won't do. This is just between the two of us."

"You have to understand that I have a job to do here. I'm sure by now you're aware that there was a murder here Saturday night, and that the victim's name was Matthew Torrez. It was in the weekend paper." His face brightened. "Say, have you ever heard of a guy named Parrish Leach?"

At the mention of Leach's name, Dent grew hysterical. "Please, I didn't know he had a record!"

"Record? What record? Mr. Smith, don't tell me that you sold Parry Leach a gun of any kind."

"I never would have if he'd been straight with me about that."

"Slow down, Mr. Smith. You've just lost me. You say you sold Parry Leach a gun?"

Dent took a deep breath. Valentino thought the man was going to cry.

"Please, have a fresh muffin, won't you?" He offered the plate to Valentino. "They're lemon-poppy seed—my favorite."

"No thanks, I'm not much of a muffin person, Mr. Smith. Back to the gun, please."

Disappointed, Dent set the plate on the coffee table. "I'm a legitimate, registered gun dealer, Detective. I know it's frowned upon these days, but I have an appreciation for them—as works of art, you see. I don't know if you can understand that or not. It's not a popular viewpoint, I know."

Valentino nodded, even though Dent's confession shocked him. The man in the bathrobe didn't impress him as a gun dealer, no way, no how. But then, maybe that wasn't a fair conclusion on his part. What did a gun dealer look like, after all? "Go on."

"Parry Leach approached me about two months ago and asked to buy a gun for self-defense. I didn't find that unusual. He seemed very concerned about his personal safety, though."

"Mr. Smith, did you know at the time that Leach had just been released from jail? Possession of a firearm violated the terms of his parole, you know."

"Of course I didn't know. I never would have sold him the gun if I had."

Valentino sighed and focused on the small crystal chandelier suspended from the ceiling. He weighed every word. "Excuse me, but as a firearms dealer, aren't you required to do a background check?"

"Well, yes, of course, but you know, I work on a highly selective basis."

Valentino shook his head. "You have to do better than that."

"I work by referrals only. That protects me from, shall we say, questionable customers."

"Okay, so as I see it, here's the million dollar question: who referred Parry Leach to you?"

Dent shifted in the chair, tucking his bare feet beneath his compact body. "Do I have to answer that question?"

"You do if you want me to overlook your colossal, king-size, careless mistake."

Dent paused for a moment. "The person who referred Parry Leach to me was Matthew Torrez."

"I see." Valentino swallowed the last gulp of tea. Dent Smith was full of surprises today. "Say, do you mind if I have one of those muffins now?"

Di watched Valentino slouch down the creaky steps. He looked a bit haggard.

"Mrs. Redding!"

"You just missed the fireworks, Detective. Ben Silver is the guy you should be talking to, I'm afraid."

Valentino pulled out his black book. "How do you spell that?"

"C'mon Valentino. S-I-L-V-E-R. Give me a break."

"So, what's the problem with Mr. Silver?"

"You're the detective, remember? Okay, I'll give you a hint. He's one of those guys that gives you the feeling they'd just love to kill somebody, just to see what it feels like."

"It's that obvious? What does this guy do? For a living, I mean?"

Di feigned a half smile and stared at the spot where the Silvers' car had been parked. "He's going to be a doctor."

Valentino slammed his book shut. "Great."

"Isn't it?"

"When did they say they'd be back?"

"Not until late this afternoon."

"Okay. Anything new with you? Like, any new items you'd like to suddenly recall about last night?"

"I just gave you my one and only hot tip for today."

"That's it?"

"That's it."

"Well, I think I've done enough damage for one day. If anything comes up, give me a call."

"Remember what I told you. The Silvers live upstairs—in Apartment J, I think."

Valentino waved and ventured into the muggy afternoon heat. His mouth still tasted of Dent's lemon-poppy seed muffins. They would never replace a cold beer. Just the thought of one caused him to stop and think. He shook his head and sauntered toward the curb. *Forget the beer, Val, forget the beer. I said, forget the beer, Val.*

Time to check out Parry Leach's new gun. *Val! I said, forget the beer.*

Six

Weary and confused, Di guided the shopping cart to the truck in the nearly deserted parking lot. She usually didn't buy this much food, and certainly not this much beer. The checker had given a funny look as she scanned the cases of Busch. With Elvin on his way into town, though, Di needed a good supply. The dog food was quite another story. There were so many brands to choose from, and they all looked the same. In an attempt to make an educated choice, she bought the one with the best-looking dog on the package.

As she loaded all the groceries into the back of the old Suburban, she suddenly realized she didn't know if pets were allowed in her apartment. Well, with a murder investigation going on, she didn't think anyone would worry about a little bitty dog. Di started the engine and wound her way through the narrow city streets, lined with cars on either side. They weren't meant for a truck.

She felt like a jerk for turning her back on Ant's sister the way she did, but really, she didn't even know her—or this Parry guy, for that matter. What Tasha needed was a good lawyer, or at least somebody with impressive connections, not a newcomer like her.

She docked the Suburban at the corner in front of the building, and glanced up at the murky sky. The air felt clammy and it smelled like a storm was on the way. She hurried to unload the food.

As she stepped to the rear of the vehicle, the squeal of brakes stunned her. The car stopped so close to her back that she could have sat on its hood. Annie Silver leapt out of the passenger's seat. "Ben, you almost hit her!" she shrieked, running over to check the damage. "Are you all right, Mrs. Redding?"

For a moment, Ben fumed in the front seat, his face flushed with anger. Annie looked frightened, and took a step backwards. Finally, he emerged from the driver's seat. "Didn't you see me coming?" he demanded of Di.

"I was getting ready to unload my truck," said Di. "I didn't expect anyone to pull in that close."

Ben smirked. "Well, it was almost your funeral, Lady. Better be more careful. Come on, Annie, let's go. I've got to study."

"But Ben, I was going to spend some time with Mrs. Redding, remember?"

He grasped Annie by the shoulders, and glared at Di. "Stop bothering my wife," he threatened, as he pushed Annie into the building.

Di had gotten two bags into the apartment when the storm exploded. Rain pelted the roof of the truck as she watched from the front window. The heavy clouds were dark. The potent thunder crashed. White lightning crackled across the sky. She decided it would be better to move away from the window and get the rest of the groceries after the storm ended and Ben Silver disappeared for the evening.

As she started to put the food into the empty refrigerator, a long white envelope slid under the door.

Oblivious to the mysterious message, Di turned on the radio. "And a 50% chance of showers later on tonight," said the disk jockey on the oldie's station. "And now, let's hear from the Queen of Soul."

"R-E-S-P-E-C-T," declared the voice of Aretha Franklin.

The phone rang. Di crossed the room to answer. "Yeah," she

said casually. There was a caller waiting on the other end, she could sense that, even as static crackled on the line. "Who is this?" Frustrated, she hung up. Seconds later, it rang again. She let it ring three times before picking it up again. "Yeah!"

"Hey again," said a familiar voice.

"Elvin! Did you just call me?"

"Di, is this a game? I call you all the time."

"No, I mean about a minute ago. Somebody just called and hung up again. This is the second time for this, Elvin."

"Why would I call you to hang up? Cherie said I was dumb, but I'm not stupid."

"Yeah, well, what's up?"

"I'm callin' you from, let's see, down on Chouteau and Grand. Awful hard to see through this rain. How do I get to your place?"

"Oh, you're not far. Just go south on Grand up to 44 West and take it to the Hampton exit. I'm in a place called the Jewel Arms. Big old brick building with stained glass windows, flat roof, you can't miss it."

"Me and Vanna are pretty hungry 'bout now. There's White Castle across the street. We might stop for a few burgers on the way."

Di listened, but didn't reply. Her eye had drifted over to the area in front of the door, and was now fixed on the envelope.

"El?"

"Yeah?"

"Hurry up, okay?" She cut the line and dialed the number on Valentino's card, studying the name that was neatly typed on the front.

He picked up on the first ring. "Valentino."

"Detective? It's Di Redding. Someone just left an envelope under my door."

"I should care or what?"

"It's addressed to you."

"What?"

"You want me to open it?"

"No, don't open it." He paused. "Jeez, it's pouring outside. Listen, I'll be over early in the morning anyway—I'll get it from you then. Are you all right?"

Di barely heard. She was watching the apartment door. It was weird, but she thought she felt a presence on the other side.

"Mrs. Redding, are you there?"

She listened as the door to the main entrance creaked and the storm door banged shut. Yet, as she peered into the sheeting rain, twisting the phone cord this way and that, no one seemed to be outside the building. Her voice quivered with uncertainty as she said, "See you tomorrow, Detective."

Elvin and Vanna arrived around 11:00 p.m. Di had just about given up on them when she heard the gas-guzzling engine of the Cadillac rumble up to the curb. The dog's bark was a dead give-away. She ran out to the front sidewalk to meet them, just as Vanna relieved herself on the lawn under the glow of a street lamp.

Elvin looked exhausted, but was as talkative as ever. "Di! Don't you look great!"

"Is that your dog?" asked Di, gawking at the thick-bodied Airedale.

"Shore is," said Elvin. "She's a beaut, ain't she?"

"She's so…large," said Di, searching for the right word. "Elvin, I don't know if I can keep a dog that big in the building without people noticing." She opened the main front door and stood in the foyer. Elvin ogled the yellow tape.

"Oh, we ain't gonna stay here. I noticed a Holiday Inn right off the highway on the way in. Which one is yours?"

Di twisted the knob to her apartment door and pushed. "This is the place. Make yourself at home, buddy. The thing is, I don't think they're going to let you have a pet in the room, especially of any size. I've got an extra bedroom, you know. It'll work for tonight, anyway. But the dog, El…"

Elvin gazed at Vanna with tenderness in his eyes. "Well, Vanna's got to have a place to stay. If I could just leave her with you for one night, Di, I could go to a motel for the night."

Di cringed at the thought. She had very limited experience with dogs—or cats, or birds, or fish for that matter. Vanna sniffed the candy dish with her large black nose.

The enormous terrier reminded her of a wire-haired pony. She shook her head. "Elvin," she insisted, "I don't care what anyone says. If Vanna stays, you do too."

At 7.55 Monday morning, Valentino pulled up to the Jewel Arms, and parked behind a silver Cadillac with Tennessee plates. He'd had a hard time finding a place to park, unusual for a weekday. He glanced in the rear view mirror, and wiped dry toothpaste from his mouth. The big Caddy intrigued him, and he recorded the number in his notebook.

It hadn't gotten hot yet, but he could tell the day would be another scorcher. As he strolled up the sidewalk toward the Jewel Arms, his heartburn flared. He hated to be the bearer of bad news, but he had to notify Mrs. Torrez of her son's murder.

The main entrance was locked. Forcefully, he knocked and waited for a response. There was none, nobody, *nada*. Again, he pounded the wooden door. This time, however, Valentino heard a bark. Sounded like it belonged to a large dog, but in his experience, you could never tell the size of a dog by the amount of noise it made. Funny, he hadn't noticed any pets Saturday night. Perhaps they had been frightened, like everyone else at the Jewel Arms.

As he waited, the barking grew louder and closer. Bees grazed in the lilac bushes bordering the sidewalk. The door opened, and a tall, freshly shaven man greeted him. By his side stood an Airedale Terrier very much like her owner—tall, muscular and fit. The man wore blue jeans and a gray T-shirt with the letters POW across the chest. He held a steaming mug of coffee.

"Morning," said the man. "What can I do for ya?"

The surprise welcome unnerved Valentino. Still, he flashed his badge and delivered his standard introduction: "Detective Rick Valentino, Homicide."

The man grinned broadly. "Elvin Suggs, Memphis. Come on in!" The dog lounged on the step, and refused to budge. "'Scuse me, could you hold this, just a second, sir?" Elvin handed the mug to the detective. "When Vanna gets comfortable, she just don't want to get up, you know? I'm kind of like that, too."

Without a sound, Elvin hoisted the dog into the foyer and wiped his hands on his blue jeans. The muscles in his forearms resembled tennis balls. "There!" He held out his hand. "I'll take my coffee back now, thank you."

"Right," Valentino said. He eyed the rows of mailboxes in the front hall, and searched for the name of Torrez. There it was, on the same mailbox with another piece of red labeling tape, bearing the name Honeycutt in raised white letters. "Say, do you live here?" Valentino reached for his notebook.

"Me? No. I got in from Memphis late last night, matter of fact. Just visiting a friend."

"Oh yeah? And who might that be?"

Elvin gestured to the door of Apartment A. "Old friend of mine, Di Redding."

Valentino raised his eyebrows. His antennas sprang up. "Really? And how long do you plan to stay, Mr.…uh…"

"Suggs, sir. Elvin Suggs. That's S-U-G-G-S for your little book there. As for how long I'm gonna be here, well, I don't have any particular plan right now. All this mess," he said, as he gestured to the taped-off area in front of Valerie's apartment, "does kind of put me off, to be straight with you. Might stay awhile, might not. I'm self-employed, see."

"I see," muttered Valentino. This was one strange guy. Funny he would show up right after the murder. He decided to keep an eye on him—and Mrs. Redding. He stood. "Well, I need to be moving on."

"Have a good day," said Elvin, grabbing Vanna's collar.

"You too." As he made his way up the rickety steps, he considered Mrs. Redding's new visitor and shook his head in disbelief. He would never have guessed a guy like Elvin Suggs was her type.

Seven

Elvin hummed and hustled while frying up some bacon and eggs. Vanna wrinkled her nose at the aromas. He arranged a plate for himself and placed a fried egg on top of Vanna's food, now piled in a used aluminum pie plate. Di was still sleeping.

After talking with Valentino, Elvin remained curious. As soon as Di woke up, he would ask her about this Saturday night murder. He looked up to see Vanna nosing around under the coffee table. She seemed to be stuck.

"Come here, darlin'." Coaxing, pleading, he liberated the dog from beneath the table legs. The sound of rustling paper caused him to check her jaws. Sure enough, she was chewing again, but this time, an envelope.

"Vanna, darlin', give me that delicious envelope, now." Elvin bartered a bacon strip for the letter. He blotted the paper against his blue jeans. The dog's saliva caused the ink to smear slightly, but Elvin made out the name, and a Saigon postmark with a return address for Antoine Weeks discreetly placed in the upper left-hand corner.

Like an electric shock, memories flooded his senses like they were fresh—though they were more than thirty years old. He envisioned Ant with him in the jungle, searching for Don. They had found him minutes before he died. Ant had been like a brother to him. No, he *was* a brother.

This was a letter to his sister, Tasha, the one he constantly yacked about. Still, he wondered what it was doing on the floor in Di's apartment. Did Di know Ant's sister? Elvin yearned to read it, if only to rekindle a piece of a cherished friendship, but he restrained himself. He didn't do things like that.

"El? You in here?" Di emerged from the back bedroom clad in black jeans and a white blouse. Her red hair was tousled and she wore no cosmetics. Still, she had a magnetic charisma, despite the dark circles beneath her blue eyes.

"In the living room," he answered. Vanna ran to Di, her tail wagging as she tried to jump up to lick her face.

"Hello, Vanna," Di said in a strained voice. Liking the fuzzy dog was such an enormous adjustment.

Elvin remained unusually quiet. Finally, he spoke. "Di? You remember Don talkin' about a guy called Ant?"

"What?" Di yawned, and combed her hands through her hair.

"You ever hear of a guy named Antoine Weeks?"

Di hesitated a moment. "Yeah, I think so. It's been so long since all that happened, El."

Elvin held up the tattered letter. "I found this on the floor. Well, no, Vanna found it, and I took it away."

Di stood next to Elvin. The minute she glimpsed the handwriting, Elvin noticed the recognition in her eyes. "This yours?"

Di shook her head. "Nope." She took a deep breath. "I had a visitor yesterday. She brought some letters with her to prove her identity. She must have dropped one by accident, I don't know—maybe not. Actually, she lives in this building, down the hall. Her name's Natasha Weeks."

"You're kidding! Ant's sister lives here? That's great!" He reached for the doorknob. "I think I'll go on down and do a little reminiscing!"

Di grabbed his elbow. "No, wait a minute. It's not so great. She's pretty down on her luck right now."

"So what? I am, too. We can have a few beers, you know, share some memories."

"Elvin, Tasha Weeks came here yesterday because she wanted

me to help her get her friend—whom I have never met—out of jail."

"Jail?"

"Well, it's a long story, but there was a murder here Saturday night, right across the hall."

Elvin lumbered back to the Formica kitchen table, and resumed eating his cold breakfast. After one bite, he threw down his fork and dumped the food into Vanna's dish. He poured a cup of black coffee into a mug stamped POW.

"I was fixing to ask you about that," he said.

"I guess you noticed the stains on the carpet."

"Sure, I did. But there was a guy poking around here early this morning, too. Called himself Valentine."

"That's Valentino. He's a real pest. He arrested Tasha's friend—whoever he is—and now she says he's the prime suspect."

"Valentine thinks he did it?"

Di ignored Elvin's error. "Oh, yeah. But she's just as sure he didn't. She claims he was with her all Saturday night."

Elvin sipped his coffee. "I still don't see why I can't pay her a visit. It's Ant's sister! Me and Ant and Don—we were like that!" He held up three fingers pressed tightly together. "At least we ought to return the letter. Don would want us to. And besides, it's the right thing to do."

At the mention of her late husband's name, Di relented. "You're right. I'm just not sure what to say to her."

"Oh, don't worry 'bout that." Elvin swiped at the air. "I'll do all the talking. We'll go visiting tomorrow afternoon, shore 'nuf.

Elvin slammed the refrigerator door. It was mid-morning and he was thinking hard about Ant and the sister; he wanted a Coke, or a beer. Anything cold would do.

"Di!" he yelled to the back bedroom. "I'm going out to get some more beer! You need anything?"

The door opened and Di appeared in her bathrobe. An aqua tinted cream frosted her face. "Oh my gosh, Elvin, I forgot the stuff I left in the car last night!"

"Huh?"

"I bought beer yesterday, but the storm broke before I got the chance to unload it. My keys are over there by the candy dish. You mind getting the rest of the stuff out of the car?"

"No, ma'am." As he opened the door, Elvin grabbed the keys, and Vanna bolted into the hall. Before he could stop her, she scratched wildly at the door of Apartment B across the hall. Her sharp nails marred the cheap wood; the force of her strength weakened the simple lock. Elvin yanked at her collar, and cautioned her, while the muscles in his arm bulged with strain.

"Quiet, little lady! They're going to throw us out in the street! Now, come on!"

The terrier refused to budge. Like wrought iron in wet concrete, her wire-haired legs sunk into the thick carpet.

"Mr. Suggs!" said Valentino. He clomped down the steps with amusement in his eyes. "Having a little trouble with your dog?"

Elvin grinned in embarrassment. He struggled to move the ninety-pound Airedale, but as usual, Vanna was just as determined as her owner. Her resistance intrigued Valentino. "Your dog seems interested in something inside Apartment B there, Mr. Suggs. Do you know why that would be?"

Elvin shrugged. "No, sir, I don't."

Valentino circled Vanna, who had entrenched herself on the welcome mat. He rapped on the door. There was no answer, yet he noticed that the door seemed to rattle when he knocked. The latch was not fastened securely. Again, he knocked, and the flimsy door surrendered.

There was no escape. A smeared trail of crusty blood wound from the living room into the narrow kitchenette. The dog didn't need a search warrant. Free to explore, Vanna put her large nose to the floor and trailed the distinctive scent.

Valentino poked his head into the spartan living room. He turned to Elvin, who was eager to restrain his dog. "Shh," he said, putting a finger to his lips. "Let her go."

"She ain't coming back, Valentine. I'm going in."

Valentino reached for his gun. "Watch your step. There's blood on the floor," he whispered. "I'm right behind you."

Except for a few folding chairs and a card table, the living room was empty. There were no pictures on the walls. The kitchenette had a Formica table with two chrome chairs with cheap plastic seats. Except for one surprise, Elvin and the detective would have abandoned the scene. Vanna made them look a little longer, and try a little harder.

Edward Mars was propped against the oven door, clad in his pajamas. The original hue of the fabric was a mystery. The thick black-framed glasses had been carefully arranged on his beak-like nose. His face was puffy and gray. Vanna was sniffing the corpse, unsure of what brand of human she had discovered. Edward's head lolled on his sagging chest.

"Grab your dog, Suggs!" shouted Valentino, even as he strained to mute his frantic voice. As Elvin coaxed Vanna out of the apartment, Valentino was overwhelmed with a rare sense of guilt. How could he have suspected Ed Mars of murder? His hand shook as he grabbed his cell phone. "Reggie! Valentino. Get the guys back over to The Jewel Arms." He turned his back to avoid the splattered red puddles that lacquered the faded linoleum. "We got another murder."

There was patent pause before his hoarse voice coughed a response to the inevitable question. "No, Reggie. I'm not kidding."

11:00 a.m., Valerie's Apartment

Valerie lounged in her waterbed, propped up on a pile of pillows. She normally slept until noon, but not today. When a lady had a few bills, she booked a lot of dates. She scrounged in her purse for the little black client book, and tried to quiet her nagging conscience.

These "dates" were strictly a temporary thing, she assured herself. The second her agent called she'd quit forever—and that was a promise. She sucked a drag from the cigarette and stubbed it out in a plastic ashtray she'd lifted from some motel. One glance at her red lingerie jogged her memory. *It was time to call that slick-looking lawyer man.*

She sat near the edge of the bed, and rummaged through the night-table drawer. Where was that business card he gave her yesterday? Maybe she would get a few of those for herself. A little publicity never hurt anybody. There it was, stuck between the pages of the TV Guide. *Myles La Mour, Attorney at Law.* She fluffed her platinum curls. In her professional opinion, that little white card didn't do him justice. He was one fine looking man. Why, from the way he dressed, he must be loaded. She crossed her firm legs and punched his phone number in short, staccato strokes.

"Mr. La Mour's office," said a perky young woman.

Valerie sat a little straighter and raked her matted hair with her tapered fingers. She wasn't sure how she should approach this fine-looking lawyer man. Her voice cracked with sleep. "Say—is Mr. La Mour, um, *available?*"

An uncertain pause linger. "May I tell him who is calling?"

"Tell him it's Valerie Gains, from his building. I'm sure he'll remember me." She fumbled in the drawer for a cigarette, and cradled the receiver against her shoulder.

"Hold, please," said the secretary.

Valerie lit the cigarette with a BIC lighter, and waited. She had nearly finished it by the time she heard Myles' smooth voice on the other end. "May I help you?"

"Myles? Is that you? I hope I didn't get you at a bad time."

"Not at all, Miss Gains. In fact, I'm glad you called."

Valerie loved the sound of his smooth voice. "Well, Myles, as I said yesterday, I need a little help with a small, a very small problem, and I wondered when we could get together to discuss my situation."

"Let me put you through to my secretary. She schedules all my appointments."

Valerie hesitated. This wasn't going well at all. She uncrossed her legs. Slightly lowering her voice, she persisted. "If you don't mind, I really don't feel—I don't know—I don't feel relaxed in an office atmosphere—if you know what I mean."

Myles did not respond. Valerie thought she heard another person breathing in the background, but she ignored her instincts. As long as she got what she wanted, she didn't really care what anyone else said or heard. It didn't matter.

"I was thinking that we might meet tonight for a few drinks at the Sunset Hotel." She giggled. "Since you couldn't make it yesterday."

"Miss Gains—"

"Please, Myles. Call me Valerie."

"*Miss* Gains, if we were to meet somewhere other than my office, I feel I should bring someone along to assist me. My secretary, for example."

Valerie repositioned herself on the Jello-like mattress. Her body sunk. Her tolerance was fading. Was this guy stupid or what? Okay, forget it—she could deal with his attitude. She would take a fresh approach. "I'm going to be at the Sunset Hotel at 9:00 tonight. I'm going there to be with you."

"The one out on Route 66?"

"That's the one, honey. I can't wait to see you."

A few seconds passed. Finally, Myles said, "Goodbye, Valerie."

Again, Valerie giggled. "Bye, bye, Myles."

Di's Apartment, Same Day

When Elvin and Vanna barged into the living room, Di dropped the newspaper, stunned. For a moment, Elvin posed in the doorway, pale-faced and tongue-tied. Vanna collapsed on the carpet.

"You look like you just saw a ghost, Elvin. Did you get any beer while you were out?"

"You're going to have to move out of here."

Di threw the crumpled newspaper on the floor and sighed. "What's gotten into you?"

"How long you been here?" Sweat trickled down his temples.

"Two weeks, maybe a little more. Besides what happened Saturday night, what's the problem?"

Before he could explain, the sound of a siren interrupted the conversation. A police car slid to the curb in front of The Jewel Arms. Di rushed to the door in time to see Valentino usher two police officers into Apartment B. In the distance, a siren whined.

Elvin grabbed Di's arm in time to stop her. "Don't go in there, Di. That guy's already gone."

Di resisted his restraint. He looked surprised at her physical strength. "Maybe I could help them, Elvin. I am a nurse, remember?"

"Please, just leave it alone."

Di couldn't hear him. Now in the mysterious Apartment B, she made her way back to the kitchenette. Without usual restraints of her own, Vanna became comfortable on Di's sofa. Unable to stop his friend, Elvin stood in the dim hallway and waited. Within minutes, a speechless Di returned.

"I asked you not to go in there. You can't live in a place like this. Something bad's going on here."

"But I signed a year's lease, Elvin. I can't just move like that." She snapped her long fingers. "I'll tell you something else. The rents in this town aren't exactly cheap—at least not as low as I'd like. I can afford this place. Besides," she repeated, "I just got here."

They stopped talking and listened. Valentino was rapping on the door of Apartment E.

"Oh no," whispered Di. "I'll bet he's getting ready to tell Mrs. Mars about Edward."

Elvin poked his head into the hall and grinned. "Shore 'nuf," he said. "He's right where you put him, Di."

Valentino waited for someone to answer the door at Apartment E, idly tapping his foot on the shabby carpet.

"Anyone home, Valentine?" said Elvin, his voice drifting through the half-open door. Elvin didn't know how to whisper. His words were always louder than normal.

"No, there doesn't appear to be," remarked Valentino, making his way over to Di's apartment. "Under the circumstances, I find that strange, don't you?" He nudged the door ever so slightly. It creaked, and cracked a little wider.

"I believe you have some sort of envelope for me, don't you Mrs. Redding? Mind if I come in for just a second?"

Elvin waved him inside the room. "Come on." Di simply glared at him before snatching the note from the overstuffed mail rack.

Vanna sat up on the sofa when he entered, and the detective pointedly ignored her. Di delivered the long white envelope. He opened it with his thumbnail, while his dark eyes perused the room.

"Thank you, Mrs. Redding. I don't mean to spoil your little visit, but I suppose Mr. Mars' demise has already had that effect."

Di felt ridiculed. What right did he have to question her guests? "Elvin's an old friend of my husband's, detective. They were in Vietnam together. Not that I owe you any explanation."

"Hey, you don't have to explain anyone to me."

Elvin interrupted their sparring. "This ain't what it looks like, Valentine. In fact, I'm still a married man, I think."

"Intriguing," said Valentino. His brow furrowed while he read the note. "But frankly, I'm not that interested in your personal lives—except for one thing."

"I'm waiting," said Di.

Valentino gestured to the dog. "Does she mind if I sit down?" Vanna didn't move, nor did Elvin command her to relocate. "Okay then, I'll make this quick. Up until just a few minutes ago,

I thought I had the person who killed Matthew Torrez in custody. And, I still might—but now, I'm not sure of anything."

"Would someone like to tell me what's going on here? Elvin thinks I should move. Is that what you want to me do, too?"

The remark alerted Valentino. He scratched his ear, carefully formulating his response. "How do I put this? No, I do not want you to move, because I need to keep track of your whereabouts for awhile. At least until I figure out who killed poor old Mr. Mars in there."

"What? Kill Mr. Mars! You don't think I would do such a thing, do you?"

"What I think you would do doesn't matter, Mrs. Redding. What matters are the facts." He turned to Elvin. "Mr. Suggs, the fact that Mr. Mars was murdered right after your arrival does not look good. In fact, I think you'd better come down to the station with me. I have a few friends I'd like for you to meet."

"Sir, I was, and I am, a United States military veteran, and proud of it. Anything you have to say to me, I believe you can say right here. I have nothing to hide."

Valentino contemplated his refusal for just a second, all the while conscious of the Airedale's presence. "What do you do for a living, Mr. Suggs?"

"I do a little of a lot of things. Right now, I'm between jobs, you might say. I'm between houses and marriages, too."

Valentino cocked his head. "Really? Where are you from?"

"Memphis, Tennessee, sir."

"Ever been arrested?"

"No sir."

"Mr. Suggs, did you know Edward Mars?"

"How could I?"

"Answer the question, Mr. Suggs."

"No sir, I did not."

Valentino scribbled in his notebook. He paused, and weighed his words before he spoke. "I have no grounds to arrest either of you, but I have to inform you that until I figure out what went on in there," he said, gesturing to Apartment F, "you're both as guilty as anyone else. You could leave, that's true, but if you decide to bolt, it won't look good. How long do you suppose you'll be around?"

Elvin shrugged his meaty shoulders. "I can stay for awhile, as long as my money holds out. Things at home are kind of up in the air right now, anyway."

"One suggestion." Valentino raised his index finger. "And it's only a suggestion. For the sake of appearances, you might consider staying in another apartment, perhaps even in this building. You never know what some people might conclude from this, uh, arrangement."

"Why would anyone care, Valentine?"

"I don't even know if there are any empty places in this building," said Di. "Anyway, what business is it of anyone's who stays in my apartment?"

At that moment, she turned around to see Vanna, shredding the newspaper on the living room carpet. Particles of M&M shells clung to her tan beard; chocolate-laced drool dripped onto the carpet.

"Elvin," she said, "it might not be a bad idea, if we can work it out."

"Mrs. Redding, you should know the note you just gave me was a notice from the management of The Jewel Arms, advertising three empty units in this building. They thought perhaps I would be interested in one of them for surveillance purposes. Of course F is now out of the question, although it would have been optimal, being on the first floor. Apartments K and H are upstairs, each in the center of the hall. Do you think one of those work for you, Suggs?"

"Suppose so, but I don't know any of the particulars. And, Vanna here has to have a place to stay."

Valentino placed the notebook in the pocket of his black suitcoat. Then, he scribbled something on a scrap of paper and ripped it from his black book.

"There's a phone number in this note to contact regarding the empty units." He handed the scrap to Elvin.

"Why didn't your friend arrange for these to be delivered to you in person?" Di asked. "Why did she arrange for this to be it shoved under my door?"

Elvin waited for a second before he spoke. "This is a little co-incidental, Valentine. Do you trust this situation?"

"I'm sure there's an explanation," replied Valentino. "In the meantime, do yourselves and me a favor and stick close to home." He winked at them as he opened the door. "I'm going to get some lunch."

The pair watched him as he got into his metallic blue Mercury sedan. Di turned to Elvin. "What's his problem? Why would he care if you stayed in my apartment or not?"

Elvin was busy recording Valentino's license plate number. "I'm gonna run a check on him myself. Something's not right here."

"What's wrong now?"

"A lot a things wrong, girl, but something he just said rang my bell. Maybe it means something and maybe it don't, but I'm gonna check it out just the same."

"You lost me, El."

"You ever met your landlord?"

"Come to think of it, no. I pay the rent to a company called 'Jewel Management.' I don't know why they slid that note under the door the other night. The whole thing doesn't add up."

"I don't trust names without faces," said Elvin. "Trust me, I got my reasons."

Eight

Monday, around noon

Valentino sat in the Night and Day Lounge, and ordered a cheeseburger platter with onions. He chugged some ice water while he waited, and watched the cars through the plate glass window. The sky was darkening again, turning that weird shade of green. "Brenda!" he shouted.

"Shut up, Val!" yelled the waitress.

"Hurry it up, already! I work for a living!"

The skinny brunette barely turned around as she seared him with her razor sharp tongue. "We're short today, but I guess you can't see that, blind man. If it wasn't for me, you wouldn't even have a table, so get off my ass!"

Valentino's mood had plummeted. All he could think about was how wrong he'd been about Edward Mars. Overnight, Edith became a widow. The thought jolted him with another realization. He still hadn't told Belle Torrez that her son was dead. As soon as he ate, he'd hustle back to the Jewel Arms to do some more dirty work. Days like this, it was hard to keep going.

He pulled out his notebook and checked the note he had saved from The Jewel Management. It had been carefully sandwiched between the frayed pages. "Apartments F, H and K vacant and available for occupancy—weekly rates." Who, he wondered, was The Jewel Management?

Without a word, Brenda slid the platter in front of him. She stuffed the check between the greasy salt and peppershakers. He poured too much salt over the sizzling fries and bit into the loaded cheeseburger, pondering the situation as he chewed.

Did he have one murderer, or two?

Rose waddled down the hallway, and clomped down the wooden steps in her extra wide Keds. It was so good to get away for a while. The old lady drove her crazy. She didn't know how she would tell her about Mattie, but it had to be done soon. Arrangements had to be made. Why, just yesterday afternoon, she'd had to slip away to identify his body down at the morgue. She worried about the way she kept Belle so drugged up all the time. It was downright dangerous. One of these days, it might catch up with her, and then what? Nobody would understand how goddamned annoying that woman could be.

She pounded her way down the steps and into the musty foyer. Immediately, her throat burned from the stench. Somebody ought to clean up this mess. It was a good thing Belle couldn't see—or hear, or walk, or...what the hell, thought Rose. What did it matter what Belle could do?

Now, this was odd. Rose squinted at the yellow tape across the threshold of Apartment B. She had never seen anyone come or go from that place, except...well, she wouldn't count her own comings or goings from anywhere, for that matter. She crept closer, and found herself staring at the dark stains in front of Apartment A. Wouldn't do any good to ask that whore about anything. What the hell, she had a few minutes. Maybe she'd ask that black gal in Apartment C. Seemed like she was always home. Guess she didn't have to work for a living like she did. Lucky, that's what she was.

She trudged down to the end of the hall and leaned on the doorbell. God, what an irritating noise it made. No wonder people were crabby when they answered the door. She stood in the hall, and wondered why it always seemed so dark, no matter what time the of the day. Come on! Fuming, she punched the buzzer again. Her free time was running out.

Someone pushed on the other side of the door. A lot of shuffling and mumbling before finally, the barrier cracked. A flustered Rose faced Tasha. At first, she avoided staring at the scarred eye, and looked elsewhere when she spoke. Her obvious discomfort embarrassed Tasha, and she shielded the eye with her hand. Tasha's demeanor became intimidating, for reasons Rose did not completely understand.

"Didn't mean to startle you," she stammered, "but I wondered if you could tell me what happened next door."

Tasha shook her head in confusion. "What?"

Rose pointed to the yellow tape. "See that? I just wondered what happened in there. I never knew anybody lived there."

"Who are you, lady?" Tasha demanded.

Rose shifted from foot to foot, her white Keds threatening to split at the sides. She gestured upstairs. "I live upstairs, in G. Name's Rose—Rose Honeycutt. Look, I'm sorry to bother you, but I thought—"

Tasha interrupted. "I don't know what you want, Miss Honeycutt, but I ain't got any, hear? I mind's my own business, and I'd advise you to do the same." With that, she slammed the door.

Rose raised her beefy shoulders and sighed, lumbering toward the wide screen door. She stepped out into the humid air. The sky was darkening; she wondered if she should keep her appointment at the salon. She shouldn't have worn a sweatshirt today, but hadn't had time to do any of her own laundry, what with cleaning all those soiled sheets. Well, she'd go get her hair bleached now, and then she'd feel a lot better. That is, at least until she got back.

Tasha waited until the screen door slammed before she opened the door and peeked into the hall. She ventured into the dimness to inspect the doorway of Apartment B. That white lady was right about the tape. She wondered who had put it there—and why.

Just then, a fuzzy dog lunged at her slippered feet, knocking her to the ground. It stood over her, licking her face with a big, rough tongue.

"Vanna, girl, let the lady up!" said a man's deep voice, laced with a Southern drawl.

Tasha glanced up and saw a tall, muscular man in a gray T-shirt and blue jeans, jerking at the dog's collar with his hands. She shielded her left eye from the overzealous dog.

"Vanna, sit!" yelled the man. Tasha felt herself being lifted from the floor. The man carried her down the hall to Apartment A.

"Di, open up! It's Elvin!"

"Elvin, what in the…" exclaimed Di. She opened the door and stared. She could not believe who Elvin carried in his arms.

Despite her protest, Elvin settled Tasha on the sofa. Back in Di's apartment, Tasha felt awkward, especially after her rejection. The big one was a complete stranger, though he seemed nice and very strong. She knew how Di felt about helping her or Parry—guess her brother hadn't meant that much to that nurse after all. A rattling sound clattered while Vanna scrounged in the candy dish, rearranging the M&Ms.

"Elvin, now you've just got to do something about that dog," insisted Di.

Tasha smiled weakly and rubbed her face. "It's okay, Miss Redding. She didn't hurt me."

Elvin looked at the two women in surprise. "You two know each other?"

"This is Tasha Weeks," said Di in an embarrassed tone.

"Well, spank my britches, it's good to see ya! Lord almighty, can you believe it? This is almost as good as having Ant here himself."

Tasha's face lit up at the mention of her brother. "You knew Ant?"

"Shore did." Elvin extended his hand. "Here, let me help you up. I'm Elvin Suggs. Ant and me was in Vietnam together." He squinted and looked at Di. "Wasn't you telling me about some problem the other day?"

Tasha sensed Di's discomfort and answered him. "I didn't have the right to come in here beggin' like I did, Miss Redding. But I didn't know what else to do. Still don't."

Elvin hooked his thumbs in the pockets of his jeans. "You need money, Miss Weeks? Is that it? Because if Ant's sister needs anything, I…"

Tasha put up her hand and she shook her head. "Naw, it's nothing like that. Don't get me wrong, I ain't rich or nothin', but I don't need much to get by anyways."

"Then what do you need?" asked Elvin. Vanna plopped down in front of his feet. Di looked at the canine accusingly, but held her tongue.

Tasha hesitated, her request having been rejected once already. She smiled nervously at Di before answering the question. "I got a good friend named Parry Leach. He helped me so much in the past, I don't know what I'm gonna do without him. 'Cept now, I'm gonna have to."

"I don't get ya."

"That detective been snooping around here lately, what's his name?"

"Valentine," Elvin said.

Tasha shook her head, wrapped in a red bandana. "Somethin' like that. Anyways, he's charging him with that white guy's murder across the hall."

"Mr. Mars?" exclaimed Di.

"Naw. Some guy named Mattie Torrez, some silly name like that." She stomped her foot, clad in a terry cloth slipper. "He didn't kill no one Saturday night. He was in my apartment, cooking us some dinner, on account of my operation, you know." She touched her left eye in reference. "Just 'cause he got a past, they sure he did it. They don't need no more than that." Tasha watched Elvin ponder the situation.

"I don't know your friend, Miss Weeks…"

"Tasha."

"Tasha. But I know what it's like to have one of your best friends taken away. I can't make you any promises now, but I can look into things for you," said Elvin.

"You a cop or somethin'?"

"Kind of. Back home, I'm a private investigator."

"But I can't pay you, Mr. Suggs."

"You're a friend of a friend; it don't matter to me. I don't know what I'm gonna find anyway. Your Mr. Leach may be guilty. Might not take much time to find that out, either. By the way, call me Elvin, won't you? You're makin' me feel old with that Mr. Suggs stuff."

Tasha shook her head and reached into the worn pocket of her housedress. She offered a five-dollar bill to Elvin.

"I won't take your charity. Ant wouldn't have it. Neither would Parry."

At the mention of Ant's name, Elvin softened. Antoine Weeks had been as proud and independent as a man could be. He took the money. "I'll look into things for you. But remember, no promises."

Tasha nodded. She didn't know if she could trust this weird white guy, but he had been a friend of her brother's. Besides, he could deal with that white detective better than she could.

"Thanks, Elvin," she said, shaking his hand.

She turned to Di. "And I didn't mean to disturb you the other day, Miss Redding. Today either, for that matter." She glanced at Vanna, lounging at Elvin's feet. "Bet you feel safe with her around, don't you?"

Di surveyed the mountain of dog and a spark of recognition crossed her face. "I guess security's getting to be a problem around here, isn't it?"

Tasha turned to leave. "Yes, Lord."

After the door closed, Di faced Elvin, still clutching the five-dollar bill. "Elvin, what are you thinking?" she scolded. "We can't get involved in these murders. For all you know, Parry Leach is as guilty as sin. Heck, Tasha could be in on it, too."

"If there's one thing I've learned in my life, it's that things aren't always what they seem. In fact, they're usually not." He walked over to the window and looked at the overcast sky. "Heck, I might not be alive today if I'd believed everything they told me in the military. If there's one thing I got real good at, it's reading between the lines. I learned to pay just as much attention to the things they didn't say, as I did to the things they said. Maybe more, because I'm telling you, that's where the answers are hiding."

"So what are you saying?"

"I'm saying I will look for myself, no matter what Valentine says. I have to get a feel for what doesn't feel right. And you're going to help me."

"Wait just a minute…"

"You're a suspect too, girl. Don't forget it. But you know you didn't do it, though, don't you? Well, so do I. And even if Mr. Leach did kill the first guy, he couldn't have killed old man Mars. Whoever did is still out there." For a rare moment, Elvin was quiet. "It'd be better if I did take an apartment upstairs for awhile. We could both keep a better eye on things that way. Think I'll move into K, right above the Mars' apartment. You still got Don's gun around?"

Di nodded.

"Good. Think Vanna could stay here? She's a great watchdog, and it would be easier for her to get outside that way."

Di glowered at him. "You know what the answer to that is."

Elvin laughed and the tears streamed down his ruddy cheeks. "I know, I know. If I go, Vanna goes with me."

Nine

The red convertible screeched to a stop in front of the white-pillared mansion. Cherie Suggs bounced from the driver's seat. It was 92 degrees and humid in Memphis, Tennessee, and the air smelled of honeysuckle and magnolias. She surveyed the pile of suitcases and shoeboxes in the backseat, and sighed. Maybe Walter and his worthless brother would help carry her stuff.

At the thought of fat Arnold Hubble, Cherie's temperature surged. Why didn't Walter see him for what he was and kick him out? Then, everything would be perfect. She managed a weak smile. Maybe that's the next thing she'd work on—after she divorced Elvin, shore 'nuf.

She clacked up the wide steps and dug her key from the depths of her pink clutch purse. The knob turned, and Cherie stood on the marble floor of the foyer, soaking up opulence and air-conditioning. This is what she deserved, and by God, now she had it. That silly Elvin could never have given her such a house. She deserved better. Walter Hubble was better. Well, he was! He was richer, anyway. All this thinking made her head hurt. She would stop it right now, this very minute.

"Have a snack with me, cutie?" The reverie shattered. Arnold Hubble waddled into the foyer with a platter of bologna, cheese, and potato chip sandwiches, slathered with mayonnaise. At 5'6, he weighed 262 pounds on a light day. At one time, he had been handsome, but now his face was bloated, and his cheeks so puffed his eyes were mere slits. His head seemed to melt into his neck, and his flabby belly hung over his belt like melting rubber.

Cherie brushed him aside, almost pushing him. "Where's Walter? I got my stuff from the house out in the car."

"What?" Arnold said. Bits of potato chips sprayed onto the marble tiles, and mayonnaise dripped down his chin.

"Put that plate down and help me carry my stuff!" she screeched.

"What's wrong, sugah doll?" drawled a resonant voice from the second floor. Walter Hubble stood on the landing, staring at the feuding couple below. A three tiered crystal chandelier extended into the foyer, secured by a single brass chain, which he flipped on to see them better among the shadows. Cherie's surly demeanor vanished, and she transformed herself into the child woman of Walter's dreams. "Walter, darlin', give me a hug!"

She ran up the wide steps and threw herself into his arms. He embraced her, but with less enthusiasm than usual.

"I didn't hear y'all squabblin' down here, did I, sugah?"

Cherie's lower lip extended in a pout. "Well," she whined, "I drove all the way here in this vile heat with my stuff, and now Arnold won't help me carry it in!"

Arnold looked up from his plate, gulping his last bite. "I was just finishing my snack here." Mayonnaise dripped from his crumb-encrusted chin. "Cherie knows I'll do it shore 'nuf."

Walter smiled and nodded, displaying his perfectly capped white teeth. "See thah, sugah. No need to get yourself all riled up. Why don't we go upstahs for while?"

Cherie batted her spiky eyelashes, coated with layers and bits of mascara. She managed a sly smile.

"There's my little lady. Be a good girl, now." Walter guided her into an upstairs bedroom. "Arnold, baby brothah, you'll bring in the little lady's things, won't you?" He winked at Arnold. "Wouldn't want the sugah to melt." He slipped into the bedroom, slamming the door behind him.

Arnold looked up the stairs before he headed out to the car, baking in the Memphis sun. "Not yet, anyway," he muttered.

With his windows rolled down despite the heat, Ben Silver waited in traffic. The air conditioning was broken and he didn't have the money to fix it. At only 2:00 in the afternoon, he'd finished his work for the day, and decided to unwind before a night of studying. He relished having the apartment to himself for a few hours before Annie returned from work.

He pulled up to the Jewel Arms and scouted for his usual parking space. "What the f…!" he shouted into the steamy air. A silver Cadillac occupied his usual space and half of another one.

"Shit!" He punched the dashboard and pounded the accelerator, the compact car squealing the length of the narrow city block. A young mother started to cross the street with a toddler, while pushing another baby in a stroller, when suddenly the bumper of the car was upon them. She grabbed the hand of the curly headed blonde, and swerved the stroller. Ben stomped on the brakes. They fled, looking over their shoulders at the human monster. The terrified looks on their faces fueled his anger. He didn't realize how red his face was, or how his fury stretched his lips back from his teeth so that he resembled a rabid dog.

"Wimps!" he yelled, and turned to circle the block. He decided he would never become a pediatrician. He couldn't stand seeing slobbering kids all day with dumb mothers like that one. Snagging an empty spot on a side street near the alley, he wondered exactly what kind of patient he could stand to see all day. He drew a blank. Well, he'd have to think about that one much, much later. No rush, after all, right?

He began to relax when he pulled up to the grimy curb. He slammed the car door, not bothering to roll up the window or push the lock. Take it, he thought, and grabbed his white coat from the backseat. It was a crummy car anyway. One of these days, he'd get himself something really nice. Like a BMW Z-3 convertible. Yeah. A real chick magnet. He wouldn't be able to keep the women away—he just needed a better car, that's all.

He strolled up the uneven sidewalk, clumps of grass sprouting from between the cracks. He glanced at the silver Cadillac once more before opening the door to his building. It had Tennessee plates. That pissed him off. Nobody from Tennessee deserved his parking space.

Oh no, here comes that dumpy broad that lived right across the hall. Always asking how to take care of that old lady. He shook his head as he dug the mail from its cubbyhole. You really had to be stupid to take a job like that.

"Hello there, Mr. Silver," said Rose. She paused to retrieve her mail. "Or are you a real doctor, yet?"

Ben looked at her freshly coiffed hair, dyed an ashen shade of platinum. It was pulled back from her wide face so tightly that it stretched the skin. Ben thought her face looked like a bowling ball. Why did fat gals always do that?

"Yeah, hi," he muttered under his breath, ignoring her question. He turned his back as he took a step up the stairway.

"Say, what do you think about all of this?" She waved her frosted white nails at the yellow tape outside Apartments A and B.

He glanced over his shoulder. "People bring their problems on themselves, don't they?" He climbed the steps, slammed the door, tossed the bills and whatever on the second-hand coffee table, and flipped on the porn channel. Finally, some peace.

Maybe he'd give that hot nurse from Oncology a quick call before Annie got home. Then, her silly prattle would start and he'd have to answer questions about his day. Who cared about his day? He didn't. He wished Annie would mind her own business. Nosy people bugged him.

Reluctantly, Valentino pulled up to the curb outside the Jewel Arms. He had to break the news to the old lady this afternoon, and he needed to see Mrs. Mars. He strode toward the old brick building; his cheeseburger lunch made him belch. He popped an antacid lozenge. The heartburn sizzled in his chest.

With his hand on the knob of the screen door, he chose to approach Belle Torrez first, on the premise that hers was the older news. That criteria didn't make it any easier, though, when he passed the Mars' apartment on the way upstairs.

The dense air reeked of stale grease. He wondered why apartment hallways were always so dark. While he padded his way to Belle's apartment, he felt like someone watched him. That couldn't possibly happen here. The old building didn't lend itself to stealthy surveillance. Still, he turned around and peered into the shadows. And saw no one.

He pressed the buzzer and stood in the hallway, mentally rehearsing his words. Close to a minute passed, and again, he punched it. He scanned the hallway. It looked empty, and yet, he sensed an unfamiliar presence.

"Who's there?" A husky voice yelled through the thin door.

Charming. "It's Detective Valentino, Miss Honeycutt. I'd like to talk to Mrs. Torrez."

"Why?"

"Open up. Or, if you prefer, I can come back with some assistance. It's up to you."

Seconds passed before he heard a rustling sound on the other side of the door. Slowly, cautiously, the barrier between them disappeared, and Valentino faced the stocky blonde, still clad in her sweatshirt and stretch pants.

"May I come in?"

Rose waved him inside the apartment. "Guess you're gonna anyway, right?"

He nodded and entered the cluttered living room, furnished with Victorian style antiques. At one time, Valentino speculated that it had been elegant. Now shabby, its upholstery was worn and faded, the carved mahogany legs pitted and scratched. The overgrown sofa and wing chairs overpowered the living area, and the Tiffany lamps cast a surreal glow. The close, sick room smell permeated the air. Valentino noticed the walker was absent from its usual corner. He coughed, struggling to ignore the heartburn.

Rose stood in a rigid stance, her hands posed on her well-padded hips. Before he could speak, Rose lashed out at him. "You think you're so smart, don't you? You want to talk to Belle? Even after she saw the obits this morning? You're a fool, detective. What do you think she can tell you, huh? What do you think she's gonna say about her son's murder? What would any mother say?"

Valentino stifled a burp, patting his inflamed chest. "Is Mrs. Torrez in?" He glanced over the nurse's burly shoulder as if waiting for Belle to appear, balanced precariously on her walker.

"Of course she's in. She's probably asleep," said Rose grudgingly. "She was beside herself when she saw the notice in the paper, but I felt I had to be the one to tell her. It just wouldn't do for her to hear about Mattie from a total stranger." She paused, weighing her words. "He was all the family she had, you know."

"No, I didn't know that," said Valentino. "I still need to talk to her—in person."

"I can see if she's awake, but, I doubt it. The news exhausted her strength, what she had. I'm really the only one who can communicate with her. Even I'm not sure what she's able to understand sometimes."

"I need to talk to her—today. I'm not leaving until I do," insisted Valentino.

"Okay, okay." Rose made her way to the back bedroom. Valentino attempted to follow, but she pushed him back into the living room. "Look, she's not even dressed. Just set yourself down over there, and I'll try to get her up."

Valentino hesitated, but decided to make his way to the rose velveteen sofa against the far wall. The sick room odor made him nauseous. Rose's noncompliance had more than aroused his suspicion, but he was curious to see her performance. He checked his watch. It was 2:30 p.m. After five minutes, he became restless, and wandered around looking at the pictures on the wall—Mattie by himself, Matt and his mother. In the kitchen, a key rack sported a veritable collection of old keys. One key was marked "Mars."

Fifteen minutes passed before Rose reappeared—alone. "I'm

sorry, detective. I just can't seem to rouse her. I warned you, this is usually her nap time."

Valentino stood up and faced her. "Okay, lady, I've been patient—more than I should have been. I'm going back now."

He strode past her into the back bedroom, the pungent odor growing stronger with each step. Rose didn't try to stop him. She stood with her arms folded and watched, her face expressionless.

He was disappointed. Indeed, Belle was asleep; snoring with abandon, mouth open, head tilted back. By the bed, he noticed the walker. On the floor, he saw the morning paper. It was turned to the obituaries. The smell of soiled sheets and lavender caused him to gag, and the taste of raw onions and ketchup once again rose in his throat.

"Okay, Mrs. Honeycutt, I'll come back again," he said on his way into the living room. "I suppose I need an appointment next time." His voice was wry with sarcasm.

"Why do you need to talk to her? I've made all the arrangements for Matthew's burial. There's nothing Belle can tell you that I can't." She sneered at him. "I'll probably be her legal guardian before long, anyhow."

Valentino studied the plump nurse and bit his tongue.

"I'll be back, Mrs. Honeycutt." His hand on the door, he had a sudden thought.

"Would you know if Belle knew Edith Mars?"

Rose's face brightened at the change in subject.

"They were friends at one time, yeah. Before Belle got so sick. Why?"

"No reason. Have a good day."

He eased the door shut and descended to the first floor to question Edith Mars.

Ten

A pleasant breeze heralded the approaching autumn. With all of the windows rolled down, Elvin and Di cruised down Hampton Avenue. The music of the Supremes, Elvin's favorite, blared from the CD player. Vanna occupied much of the back seat. She savored her ride as much as the human passengers, her stand-up ears flopping in the afternoon sunlight.

Elvin pulled into a drive-through lane at McDonald's, and leaned over to the speaker to place his order. His T-shirt flattered his muscled physique. Elvin's looks did not go unnoticed by the young female cashiers.

"Hey there, ladies!" he shouted. "Yeah, would you give us a grilled chicken sandwich, hold the mayo, a couple of big Macs, one large fry, and two cheeseburgers, hold the buns."

There was a pause while the cashier reviewed the order. "Sir," she countered, "Did you say to hold the buns on the cheeseburgers?"

"Yes ma'am, I did. Vanna only likes the burger part. Could you add a large Dr. Pepper and a diet Coke? Oh, and a large water for Vanna."

The young cashier repeated the order in a confused voice. "Is that right?"

"Yes ma'am. Thank you kindly. Oh, and could we get the burgers in a separate bag? We'll need a lot of napkins too, if you don't mind."

The cashier ogled the fuzzy-haired terrier, lounging in the

back seat, her ears standing at attention. "No problem, sir."

Di slunk down in the front seat, covering her face with her hands. "Elvin, this is so humiliating. I got her dog food, you know."

Elvin smiled his famous grin. "She'll eat that too, don't worry about that."

"I don't mean that. It's just that you don't treat her like a dog."

Elvin grew serious. "Di, she's more than my dog. She's my partner. I count on her to do things I can't do."

"Like what?"

"Like protect me. Like track down missing stuff. Like guard my house when I'm not there." He laughed. "'Course now we're both not there. Wanna go to a park?"

Di glanced back. The ninety-pound Airedale stared back with alert eyes. She sniffed the air and yawned.

"This is so unsanitary," Di said, stashing the bags of food on the floor in front of her.

Elvin ignored her. "Okay, so where to?"

"There's Wilmore Park over that way. They've got some picnic tables, I think. There's even a lily pond."

"Show the way, girl."

Vanna poked her head from the rear window and the warm breeze smoothed the wiry hair on her broad face. Fifteen minutes later, they had a picnic beneath a large oak tree.

"Isn't this grand?" said Elvin. "Like it, really do."

"Hi, guys," said a familiar voice. Vanna looked up from her cheeseburgers, and barked in protest. Di turned around and her patience snapped.

"What do *you* want?"

Valentino chuckled. "You're always so cordial, Mrs. Redding. I didn't mean to barge in where I'm not wanted, but actually, you are just the folks I'm looking for."

"Oh yeah?" Elvin popped a French fry into his mouth.

"Why is that?" asked Di.

Valentino shoved his hands deep into his pockets and looked up at the late afternoon sky, fading above the rustling trees. "I haven't been able to find your neighbor, Mrs. Mars." He frowned and pursed his lips. "Have you?"

"Don't know the lady, Valentine. Is that really her name?"

"Well, Suggs, I'm very sure you recall the scene in Apartment B. You know, the body in the bloody pajamas?"

"Yeah?"

"Edith Mars was his wife, El," said Di, "and as far as I know, that's her real name. It's nothing to joke about, detective. I haven't seen her around, if you want to know, but then, I hardly knew her. The Mars kept to themselves most of the time. The few times I saw them, I was getting my mail, and they acted like they were afraid of me. I felt like I made them nervous when I talked to them, so I left them alone. Where could she have gone?"

Valentino observed the dog, smacking her lips appreciatively, with bits of melted cheese clinging to her beard. "That's what I need to find out, Mrs. Redding."

"I hope she's alright," said Di.

"What are y'all gettin' at?" Elvin's expression indicated he already had a good idea.

"I might as well say it. I just hope Mr. Mars was the only victim this time. It is imperative I locate Mrs. Mars as soon as possible."

"What are you going to do?" asked Di.

Valentino took a deep breath. "I was hoping you could help me get a key to the Mars' apartment."

Di frowned at the suggestion. "How?"

"I noticed one with the Mars' name on it hanging on a rack in Belle Torrez's apartment today. I have a feeling they wouldn't let me borrow it, but I'll bet they'll loan it to you, Mrs. Redding."

Di pondered the idea for a moment. She wondered if she should trust Valentino. "What do you think, El?" she asked her companion.

"If we borrow the key, we go in too," he said.

Di could see Valentino did not want that much assistance.

"I think that's fair, detective. That way, it will be the truth when I say I need the key to check on Mrs. Mars," Di said.

"That's not the way I like to work, guys."

Di crossed her arms. "Fine, get the key yourself."

Valentino sighed. "Okay, you win. This time. Let's go."

Eleven

Myles shoved some papers into his briefcase and locked his desk. He always locked his desk at the end of the day. He firmly believed a man could never be too careful.

It had been a good day, and now, he was looking forward to an intriguing evening at the Sunset Hotel. While he put on his suit coat, he reflected that perhaps his judgment of Valerie Gains had been too hasty. Just because she looked like a hooker didn't mean she was one, after all. Maybe he just needed to get to know her; then he could talk to her about changing her image. He believed in judging a person by their inner qualities. He had every intention of getting to know Miss Gains. He grabbed his briefcase and began to whistle. This could be fun, he decided.

When he opened the door, however, he encountered an unexpected visitor. With her hand extended in mid-air, the woman looked sheepish, and oddly familiar. She was dressed in a baggy print housedress, with scuffed black loafers on her flat feet. Her most memorable characteristic, however, was her scarred left eye, which remained half-closed. Through her good eye, she ogled him.

"May I help you?"

"Mr. La Mour?" asked the woman.

"Yes."

"I know it's kind of late in the day and all, but, I only need a few minutes of your time."

"Did you have an appointment?" Myles peered over her

stooped shoulder for his secretary, Olive.

She waved her hand in response. "No, no. I'm coming here for a friend."

Myles glanced at his Rolex watch. "Miss, I'm afraid I already have an engagement this evening."

"I know it's quitting time and all, but could you spare just a few minutes?"

Myles studied the weary soul that stood before him, and decided to grant her request. He secretly kicked himself for his generosity. "I only have a few minutes," he said ushering her into his paneled office. He gestured to the red leather sofa on the near wall. "Please, sit down." He squinted at her face, struggling to place her in his memory. "I don't believe I caught your name."

"Natasha Weeks. Just call me Tasha."

"Sure," said Myles, sitting in the chair across from her. He leaned forward, his elbows on his knees. "Now, what can't wait till tomorrow morning?"

"I got this friend, see, down at the jail. He needs a lawyer bad, but it cain't be any kind of lawyer. He got one they give him, but he some white guy Parry don't trust."

Myles put up his hands as if shielding his face from the heat of a forest fire. "Wait just a minute there. This sounds complicated. I think you're going to need quite a bit of time to explain your problem." Again, he glanced at his watch. It was 6:15 p.m. "And time is something I just don't have right now." He pulled out a business card from his wallet and handed it to her. "Here, take this. Why don't you give my secretary a call tomorrow morning, and we'll see what we can arrange?"

Tasha took the card, shifting it from hand to hand. "You a brotha, ain't ya? Ain't got time for anothah brothah, that it?"

Myles got up and gestured toward the door, wondering how this woman found him. "No miss, you've got me all wrong," he insisted. "It's simply that I have got an appointment with a client. By the way, where did you hear about me?"

Tasha's right eyebrow went up in surprise at the question.

She chuckled softly. "Lady named Valerie Gains told me all about you, Mr. La Mour."

"Miss Gains?" Myles whispered under his breath. A million questions ran through his mind at that moment, but Myles decided it might prove more fruitful to ask Valerie for answers. The simple woman who hunched before him seemed a little slow-witted for his taste.

They stood on the front steps of the office building in the orange sunset. Myles glanced toward the highway and tried to gauge the rush hour traffic. He put a hand on Tasha's rounded shoulder. "I don't want to appear rude, but I really have to leave. Please call Olive tomorrow and schedule a time when we can talk about all of this. I do need to be on my way now."

"I understand." Discouraged, Tasha descended the pitted concrete steps.

Myles' BMW sped off before she reached the street.

A red chiffon dress had never looked better. Valerie strutted into the Sunset Hotel Bar, and searched the darkened lounge for Myles. She didn't see him, but at a little past 6:30, she wouldn't, and not for a while. Unable to find a seat, she walked out into the lobby, and scrounged in her satin even bag. If she had to wait until seven o'clock, she needed a damn cigarette.

Well, she wouldn't sit by herself. She'd go back and wait in the lounge, if she could get a seat. Must be a salesman's convention in town—all these bored, lonely men crowding up the bar like this. A lighter suddenly appeared in front of her face.

"May I?" asked a man's voice.

Valerie turned to see an olive skinned man in a black suit. Her confidence sank like a bricks in lake. "No thanks, detective," she said, stuffing the cigarette back into her bag. Her heavily lined eyes hardened. "I didn't do anything."

"Offering to light your cigarette doesn't mean I think you did anything, Miss Gains," Valentino said.

"Just wanted to get that part straight."

He smiled. "Sure. So, can I buy you a drink?"

Valerie kept an eye out for Myles while she spoke. "No, not tonight, anyway, but thanks." She sensed that her refusal had somehow alerted Valentino. *To what?*

"Why not, Miss Gains?" His dark eyes were piercing, and one side of his mouth curled.

"I don't owe you any explanations. This is my time, so bug off." Valerie turned and stomped off to the ladies' room. He couldn't follow her in there. What did he want with her, anyway?

Amused, Valentino slipped into the bar. He had avoided them ever since getting out of rehab five years ago. He'd been sober for five whole years. He could afford to relax a little bit now. For once, he didn't have an agenda. One beer wouldn't hurt, he decided. Anyway, he deserved it. He wasn't looking for trouble. Just a bone-tired, off-duty cop, looking to unwind.

He ordered a beer from the bartender and collapsed in a far corner booth. While he stared through the plate glass window into the lobby and watched the people, his mind wandered to the events of the afternoon. Mrs. Redding and her visitor had been useful, though he still didn't know how much he trusted either of them. They got on his nerves, but still, they'd managed to get the key to Edith Mars' apartment. This whole case got more bizarre by the minute. He closed his eyes and gulped his beer, replaying the afternoon in his head.

He and Suggs waited downstairs while Mrs. Redding went upstairs to ask for the key. It amazed him how easily she had managed to get Mrs. Honeycutt to give it to her. She even convinced the nurse to call the Mars' apartment, but there was no answer. Then, according to Mrs. Redding, the nurse had shaken her head, remarking how she always dreaded the day when she might have to use that key, and how glad she was now that she had one. You just never knew, she told her, when your time might come.

Valentino sensed a weighty stare, and glanced up and around, yet he didn't see anyone familiar. He gobbled a handful of peanuts from an amber ashtray, and smiled to himself. It made him recall the nervous feeling Suggs' dog incited in him, the way it sniffed around the Mars' apartment. He washed the peanuts down with another gulp of beer. He wasn't used to being nervous and in control at the same time. When he had searched the apartment he had felt that way, and once again, the feeling had returned.

When he first entered the stuffy apartment, followed by his entourage, he hadn't noticed anything unusual. In fact, he was inclined to turn around and leave, convinced he had made a terrible mistake in entering the place without a warrant. Even under the circumstances, he probably had, but it wasn't the first time he hadn't waited for paperwork to do what he had to do. Life didn't wait. At least, his didn't.

That damn Suggs poked around the place faster than he did. At least, the fool hadn't touched anything. Even when his monster dog began eating the leftovers on the kitchen table, Suggs managed to pull her away without leaving any fingerprints. He finished the last swallow of beer. That's the part that nagged him. Mrs. Mars didn't seem like the type to leave with leftovers still on the table. Suddenly, he realized the problem. There had been only one plate on the table. Edith ate her lunch alone that day. Valentino leaned back in the booth. It looked like she had left in a hurry. What did all of it mean?

While he sat pondering the puzzle, he stared through the plate glass at the happy hour crowd, anxious to numb their worries. He studied the empty glass. Well, it worked for him. He got up to leave, and his eye caught a glimpse of a platinum head in red chiffon. She waved and smiled, and for a split second, he thought his luck was looking up. His hopes were quickly dashed when he saw that the greeting was not meant for him. A morbid curiosity overcame him. Who had earned an evening with a girl like Valerie Gains?

The well-dressed man who approached her looked vaguely familiar, but Valentino's foggy memory could not place him. Even after a full day's work, Myles looked dapper and charming.

He had a million-dollar smile on his face, even though his leather briefcase lent the appearance of a business dinner. Valentino fought the urge to trail them. After all, he was off-duty, and for once, Valerie didn't appear guilty of anything—yet. Still, his instincts were aroused. When he watched the unlikely couple turn the corner, he itched to follow them.

The itch won.

Twelve

Early Wednesday morning, Elvin discovered the key to his new apartment in his mailbox, and mounted the creaky stairs to explore his new digs. He had nearly reached Apartment K, when Vanna let out a series of barks punctuated by low growls. Elvin turned to face his new neighbors, the Silvers, emerging from their unit next door. Vanna continued to snarl and lunge at Ben.

"You can't have that piece of rug in here," he challenged Elvin. "We had to get rid of my wife's cat when we moved in."

Elvin responded cheerfully, sizing him up in his mind all the while. "Don't get yourself riled so early in the mornin', there. Vanna's a friendly gal, ain't ya, baby?"

Despite Elvin's encouragement, Vanna sat on her haunches, growling between her teeth. Ben reached for his pocketknife.

"Whoa, whoa, whoa, there pardner." Elvin took a step towards Ben. "I wouldn't do that if I were you." He grabbed Vanna's stout leather collar, pulling her towards himself. "I'll take care of her. Why don't y'all just get where you're going?"

Ben's dark eyes narrowed. "You big hick! You're the one with the Tennessee plates, aren't you? Now, you're moving in with that beast! Get out of my space, Jethro!"

He shoved Annie's back, a gesture that was not lost on Elvin. "Come on, Annie, move it!"

At the end of the hall in Apartment L, a man opened the door, clad only in his bathrobe, and bent down to grab his newspaper. "Howdy!"

Without a word, the Silvers rushed down the hall. Annie hustled forward, propelled by her husband. She looked back over her shoulder before she started down the steps. A look of fear and misery haunted her blue eyes.

"Say buddy," the man said to Elvin, the newspaper still in his hand, "You moving in or what?"

Elvin gazed at the bare legged tenant. His white terrycloth robe was embroidered with the letters *DS* on the front in golden thread. The short man padded toward him on the thin carpet. His broad smile dominated his overly tanned face, and his light brown hair grayed at the temples. He thrust his free hand toward Elvin in a bold handshake.

"Denton Smith, sir. I'm very pleased to meet you." His wide smile displayed his extra white teeth.

"Hey! Elvin Suggs." Vanna bounded into the hall. "This here's my dog, Savannah."

"Gorgeous. Absolutely gorgeous. Airedale, right?"

Elvin beamed. "Yep. You really like her?"

"You won't believe this, but I used to have a dog like that when I lived out West. Did a little bit of everything, but she was a born hunter. Great watchdog, too." He stopped, suddenly growing serious. "You might need her, living up here."

Elvin frowned. "What do ya mean there?"

Dent glanced toward the door of Elvin's new apartment. "Mind if we talk in private? 'Scuse me, what did you say your name is?"

"Elvin—Elvin Suggs."

"Well Elvin, I'm feeling a little funny standing out here in the hall like this. Mind if we step inside your place for a minute?"

Normally, Elvin wouldn't have thought twice about such a suggestion, but this man, this Denton Smith—well, he was friendly, shore 'nuf, and he did like Airedales...Elvin had to wonder about a man as eager to talk as himself, that's all. Never met one before Dent Smith here.

"Mind if we use your place, Mr. Smith? My apartment's not

fit to live in yet, I'm afraid."

Dent shook his head. "No, not at all. Glad you thought of it. Call me Dent, will you? Everyone else does."

Soon, Elvin relaxed on an ivory brocade loveseat with a glass of lemonade and a plate of homemade banana nut muffins. A copy of *Guys 'n Gunz* magazine rested on the coffee table in front of him. White French Provincial furniture graced the apartment; it might have been 1960's vintage. Dent sat across from him on a matching loveseat, wearing his bathrobe. Vanna lay by the door.

Now behind closed doors, Dent began to whisper. "Listen, Elvin—that's right, isn't it? I thought so. Well Elvin, I think that medical student slaps his wife around. I can't say for certain now, but there's been times she's come out of there with bruises on her legs."

"On her legs?"

"She's a runner, you know. Goes out in shorts, little T-shirts, things like that. Couple nights ago, I went over to borrow some sugar, and he wouldn't let her come to the door."

Dent leaned closer, and Elvin was sure he noticed blue eye shadow on his eyelids, perhaps a little pink lipstick on his lips. He began to fidget. "Listen," he said while he rose from his seat, "I promise I'll keep my eyes open."

Dent raised his arched eyebrows at the suggestion. "You going somewhere? I have so much more to tell you. I write an advice column for *Guys n Gunz*, you know. And you haven't touched my muffins."

Elvin downed the glass of lemonade in one swallow. "Yeah, well, the day's a wastin'. I'll be around, Dent."

Vanna rose when Elvin reached the door. "Let me show you out," said Dent. "Really, you must try my muffins sometime."

Elvin hustled out to the hall, breathing hard. "No muffins for me, thanks." He headed back to his apartment, and slammed his door—quickly.

Valentino shadowed Valerie and Myles until they boarded the elevator. At one point, he hid behind an overgrown potted plant. He was dying for a cigarette, and the truth was, another beer, or a beer and a shot of bourbon. Yeah, a beer and a shot would really hit the spot.

After they got on the elevator, he lost them. What was he doing anyway, he asked himself. He approached the elevator and examined his motives. What did he hope to see? Whatever they were doing could be perfectly legitimate. Right—and he was Elizabeth Taylor. He glimpsed the red glow of an exit sign off to his left and decided to take the stairs up a few flights. Maybe roam the corridors a little. He sniffed the air. It was filled with the scents of steak and potatoes, but there was something else—what was that smell?

Again, he smelled it. Now, he recognized it. It was White Diamonds, Valerie's perfume. Oddly, that wasn't the scent that bothered him the most. Tonight, Valentino smelled a rat.

Valerie stepped onto the fifth floor with Myles behind her, walking as if in a trance. She chattered on about her hair and her makeup, and how they'd stopped making Red Devil lipstick. Whatever and why was it that they stopped making such a good seller, she asked. Myles nodded his head in agreement. He didn't notice that Valerie knew her destination. He never flinched, not even when she pulled the room key from her purse. If he thought it was unusual, it didn't alert him in any way. At least, he didn't stop her, in spite of the sweat that was dripping from his temples.

Valerie inserted the key and the door jammed. She struggled and pulled, first on the door, then the key. Oddly, the fuss shattered Myles' reverie. The seediness of the situation alarmed him. Anxiety heightened his senses.

"Damn it!" cursed Valerie. "Myles, could you give me a hand?"

Next to Valerie, snug and firm in her tight red dress, Myles felt like he was choking. He struggled to compose himself, but he had to admit, as much as he knew he should leave, he knew he would not—not yet. Valerie stepped aside, and Myles jiggled the lock. It suddenly unhinged, and he tumbled onto the rose-colored carpet of the hotel room. Everything in that rose-hued room reeked of stale cigarette smoke.

In a heartbeat, Valerie slammed the ponderous metal door. They were alone.

Valentino dawdled in the hallway of the third floor, still dying for a cigarette and a drink—especially a drink. That lone beer had reminded him how badly he'd missed it, and besides, he wasn't supposed to be working tonight. This was his time. He deserved a little reward for all the extra hours he'd worked in the last week. He leaned against the fire extinguisher at the end of the hallway. He wanted another beer, but for some reason, he wanted to know the whereabouts of Valerie and the guy with the briefcase. He really wanted to know why that guy needed his briefcase. Dinging elevator bells interrupted his thoughts.

A man that looked like a waiter emerged from the elevator, pushing a cart that rattled with the sound of dishes. Valentino watched him from his position three doors down, straining to see his gold-embossed nametag. He seemed certain which room he wanted, and stopped outside a door in the middle of the dim hall. Staring at the room number, he tapped three times on the metal door. He waited, but there was no answer. Valentino was in plain view, but the waiter pointedly ignored him. Again, he knocked on the door, this time more firmly.

"Mrs. Torrez! Room service!"

At the mention of the familiar name piqued Valentino's interest. He focused on the waiter. To Valentino, he seemed irritated. Suddenly, he glanced at the room number once again, and moaned in dismay.

"Something wrong?"

The waiter turned to look at him and shook his head. "I can't believe I made such a stupid mistake."

"What is it?"

The waiter shook his head. "It happens when I'm tired. I got off the elevator too soon. You know how it gets at the end of the day."

Valentino snatched the opportunity. "Oh yeah, I know how that is. Say, I couldn't help but overhearing a minute ago. Were you looking for a Mrs. Torrez?"

"Yeah."

The waiter stiffened his jaw and turned his back, pushing the elevator button. When the door opened, and the waiter rolled the cart inside, Valentino followed.

"What floor you want?" snapped the waiter.

Valentino noticed the five button was already lit. "Five will do it for me, too, thanks," he said.

They rode together in silence, and Valentino made a mental note of the place settings on the cart—exactly two. The bell dinged and the waiter rushed off without a word. Valentino stepped out into the wide hall and walked to the end of the corridor.

A maid pushed a cart of soap and towels toward him. "Can I help you?"

"Just looking for the ice machine," he said, watching the waiter out of the corner of his eye.

"It's through that door." She pointed towards an alcove.

Valentino didn't hear her. His ear was tuned to the raspy whisper of a woman's voice, floating from an open door in the middle of the corridor.

"I just love champagne, Myles, don't you?"

Annie Silver trudged up the sidewalk towards the Jewel Arms with a bag of groceries in each arm, her purse dangling from her shoulder. When she reached the main door, she was forced to set them down on the step. She could hardly open it. Finally, she trudged into the stuffy foyer, and turned to dig her mail from the cubbyhole. A scuffling sound startled her.

"Whoa, whoa, whoa, there girl," drawled a man's voice. Annie turned around and Vanna stood up to greet her, knocking a bag of the groceries on its side. A jar of spaghetti sauce splattered onto the floor. Glass splintered into the air.

Annie's round eyes filled with tears and her shoulders slumped with fatigue.

"Don't cry there, ma'am, I'll clean it up right quick."

She felt a pair of strong hands on her shoulders.

"It's just a broken jar, hon."

Annie looked up at the muscular stranger, threads of gray running through his thick black hair. He smiled.

"I know you. You live across the hall from me. Come on, I'll help you carry the rest of this stuff upstairs."

"But the mess…"

"Vanna and me will clean it up."

Elvin knocked on Di's door. Di poked her head outside and gasped at the mess. In seconds, she focused on Vanna. "Don't tell me—"

"Got some paper towels or somethin', Di?"

"Gonna take more than that, El." She disappeared into her apartment, emerging with a bucket and sponge mop. Elvin mopped while Vanna watched, and Di caught up with Annie, who looked more forlorn by the minute.

"You know, I'm sorry your groceries spilled, but it's good to talk to you again. Why don't you come in for awhile while Elvin cleans this up?"

Di winked at Elvin. Without a word, he continued to sponge tomato sauce and glass chips from the floor.

"I-I guess I could do that," Annie stuttered. "You mind if I put a few things in your refrigerator while we talk?"

Soon they sat in Di's small living room; Annie drank a beer while Di munched some M&M's. Annie sniffed the air. "You really keep a clean house," she remarked. "What is that smell?"

Di laughed. "Pine-Sol. I just finished having house guests." She became more serious. "You know, we didn't get a chance to talk the other day."

Annie chugged some beer from a half-empty bottle. She leaned back in the sofa, and closed her eyes.

"Annie? You okay?"

She nodded, but her eyes remained closed. "Yeah." She finished the beer.

Impressed, Di asked, "You want another one?"

"That'd be great." Annie paused. "Can I ask you something personal?"

Di turned around at the refrigerator door. "Sure."

"If you had a friend, and they told you about something you knew was wrong—say, something you were afraid was going to hurt them someday, what would you tell them to do?"

Di handed her the second beer. She was amazed at the speed with which she drank the first one. "What are we talking about here?" Sat down across from the troubled woman.

Annie appeared more relaxed. The beer relaxed her. "Let's say, this person told you she had a friend who she was afraid might..."

"Might?"

The door burst open, and Elvin entered the small room. "Don't worry Di, Vanna's upstairs." He pointed to the empty bottle of beer. "That's good stuff. Think I'll have one myself."

Suddenly, Annie squinted through the living room window at the curb, and she struggled to her feet. "I've got to go now." She picked up her bags of groceries.

"Why?" asked Di.

"Dinner's not ready." Her eyes filled with tears. "He'll be so mad at me."

"Why?" asked Elvin. Outside, the car door slammed, and Ben Silver's short footsteps clipped the sidewalk towards the front door. "That your husband?"

Annie nodded.

"You shouldn't be afraid of your husband."

"I don't want to go upstairs alone." Her chin quivered.

"No problem. I'm going your way." Elvin grabbed the bags of groceries.

"Oh, Di," he said, while Annie twisted the doorknob. "We need to talk. I've got some news. Don't go away—I'll be back after my visit."

Di sat alone on the sofa in the stillness, thinking about Annie and Elvin's remarks. What was Annie trying to tell her? It seemed so hard to talk to Annie about anything. What was Elvin's news?

The sound of a television shattered the silence. Music blared through the plaster wall like the orchestra played right next to her. Startled, Di sat up and listened. The noise came from the Mars' apartment.

Thirteen

Wild horses couldn't have pulled Valentino from his place behind the potted plant. Another beer, maybe, but nothing else in the world could tempt his resolve, no-sirr-ee. He waited until the waiter boarded the elevator before he ventured down the hall. He risked a big mistake. What if the hooker opened the door? Again, he told himself, he wasn't really working.

The quiet hall bothered Valentino like a festive graveyard. Nothing visibly wrong, and yet, he was tense. No one saw him approach Room 512, but even with his ear to the door, he couldn't hear anything. What had he hoped to see anyway? He decided to keep walking, and glanced at his watch. Nine thirty—time for a beer.

He headed back toward the elevator, just in time to see Myles emerge from Room 512. Disheveled, minus a coat or tie, but still toting his briefcase, he rushed towards the waiting elevator. In his haste, Valentino knew he hadn't noticed him. He could have followed him right then and there, but an even crazier notion entered his mind.

He approached Room 512 and knocked. No one answered. Glancing over his shoulder, he knocked again and waited—and waited. To hell with it. A hard-working man had a right to get drunk, just tonight, just this once. To the bar!

Next to the potted plant once again, Valentino punched the elevator button. Despair filled his heart. The Torrez case had a suspect, but Leach didn't seem like the right guy. He was losing his edge. It had been a week, and now, he had another murder on his hands. The elevator doors opened; he felt the weight of a stare. He turned his head for a second, and they closed again—without him.

It was her, alright, and she looked damned good, until she opened her mouth to speak.

"You followin' me, detective? I'm not afraid of you." She stepped into the hall, wearing the red chiffon halter dress. Her mascara was slightly smeared. "You afraid of me, detective?"

A couple stepped off of the elevator and walked past Valerie, hiding their embarrassment. Valentino approached her. He felt crazy tonight. "Not at all. Should I be?"

Under the dim lights, Valerie's face took on a softness that Valentino had never noticed.

"Feel like a drink, Valentino?" She stood by the half-open doorway. "Or is Ricky working tonight?"

Valentino knew it was wrong. Not smart, either. Not for a minute did he feel manipulated. He wanted a drink, but he could get that in the bar downstairs. At that moment, he realized how Desperate and Lonely had become his new name. His humanity surfaced. "Not tonight, I'm not."

"Good." Valerie eased inside the hotel room, and kicked off a satin shoe. "Let's party."

Di stepped into the dim hall and caught her breath. It smelled rank and rotten. Wheel of Fortune blared from Apartment E. When she knocked, the sounds of crumpled newspapers and short, fast footsteps resounded. The door opened wide; at first, Edith Mars stared at Di with a blank confusion in her eyes. Without warning, the old woman's face melted into a grin. "What a nice surprise!"

Speechless, Di hesitated, uncertain of her next words.

"Is something wrong, honey?" asked Edith.

Di hadn't wanted to be the one to break the news of her husband's death. Where had she been for the last week?

"Well, I heard the television…" Di began.

"Oh honey, I'll turn it down!"

"No, no, Mrs. Mars, that's not what I mean. It's just that the police have been trying to contact you for the past few days. No one's been able to find you."

Edith smiled. "Oh, that! You know, that detective came by with that good looking young man. You know, the one with the big muscles." Her eyes grew wide at the memory. She grew somber. "What a shame it was, the way Eddie died, wasn't it?"

Di blinked, and blinked again. Edith already knew.

"What is it, honey? You don't look so well."

"It's just that…I didn't know that you knew about your husband. I feel so sorry for you. You're all alone now."

"Oh, don't worry about me, honey. I'll get over it. Now, I need to get back to my show before I miss the end. I love to see who wins, don't you? And don't worry," she giggled before she shut the door, "I'll keep the noise down this time."

Later that night, Di lay in bed, replaying Edith's words in her head. She didn't want to think about it, but somehow the moment she learned of Don's death crept into her memory. Alone in the darkness, tears dribbled from her eyes. Don had been one of a kind.

She didn't understand Edith Mars' reaction. She grabbed a tissue from the nightstand and dabbed her tears. Edith shouldn't have been so cheerful.

It just wasn't right.

Valentino awoke sometime after midnight. Beneath the window, a horn blared in the street. He tried to recall the details that found him in this room, but his brain buzzed and blurred. He turned and studied Valerie while she slept. There in the shadows, she almost looked beautiful—almost. Still, the sound of her raspy voice grated on his memory. She had used him, though just hours earlier, she had divulged some very useful information.

He shouldn't have let her seduce him. He'd made a tactical

mistake; he knew that then, and to some degree, he regretted it. But now, he knew things about Matthew Torrez that he might not have learned from anyone else but Valerie. Ditto the guy with the briefcase.

He swung his legs over the mattress and slumped on the edge of the bed. The glow of the streetlight filtered through the sheer curtains. The room stank of stale smoke; suddenly, he craved a cigarette. The table from room service was still over by the window, littered with half empty bottles and glasses of wine and champagne.

Valerie shifted on the bed. His gaze fell on her purse, resting on the nightstand next to her. He wanted that purse, but he wanted to leave, too. He didn't want Valerie to stop him.

Worse, he had draped his clothes over a chair across the room. He didn't remember putting them there. Had he been that drunk? It didn't matter. A clean escape mattered now.

Moments later, he stood before the bathroom mirror, holding his clothes and Valerie's red satin purse. Valerie was snoring. The contents of the purse were unremarkable, except for a business card that would have been equally unremarkable, except for one thing. It stated the name of an attorney by the name of Myles La Mour, which sounded strangely familiar. That didn't bother him. The home address on the card disturbed him. When he pulled on his pants and pondered the fate of the last man who had been involved with Valerie Gains, an even more disturbing thought provoked him.

Matthew Torrez had apparently had some determined enemies. He had also been a lonely man—and an unlucky one. Valentino fingered the card and studied the name, staring at his pale, drawn reflection in the hazy mirror. Myles La Mour had escaped Valerie's wiles. The man in the mirror had not.

"Sugah doll!" Walter was in the house. Yippee, thought Cherie. She couldn't see him, but could hear him. She stood in the kitchen, grimacing as she poured her morning coffee. Dressed in her white baby doll nightgown, fluffs of curls all over her head, she resembled a toy poodle. She heard Walter's slow, heavy footsteps descending the wide steps, and sighed in resignation.

"Baby, where'd you run off to?"

Cherie's stomach did a flip-flop. She didn't think she could tolerate Walter one more day. She didn't understand her feelings. For one thing, Walter doted on her; and he was so filthy, stinking rich. She took a sip of her saccharin-laced coffee. Did she miss Elvin? Maybe a little bit, yeah. Something else bothered her to distraction—maybe that fat, stupid Arnold?

"There you are!" Walter exclaimed. "Give daddy a big ole kiss!"

Cherie clacked across the tile in her white satin heels, adorned with white feather pom-poms. She had just settled on Walter's lap when Arnold waddled into the room, carrying a box of Dunkin' Donuts.

"Brought y'all some breakfast!"

He set the box down and grabbed a jelly donut in each hand. "Don't y'all like donuts, or what? Plenty for everybody!" Globs of red jelly dripped from his flabby chin. He took another bite, and a dab landed on Cherie's white feather pom-pom.

"Oh! Oh! Wa-alter!" She leapt from his lap and grabbed the stained shoe. "My new slippers! Now they're ruined! All because of that fat slob brother of yours!"

"There, there, sugah doll. Daddy will buy a new pair."

Arnold swallowed the last bite of the culprit donut, and reached for another. Oblivious to the hysteria, he asked, "Do I smell coffee?"

"Brothah, why don't you go on and eat those somewhere else?"

"But Wally, we was goin' to talk business this mornin', wasn't we?"

Arnold's eyes hardened, though they flitted across Cherie's skimpy nightgown. Walter noticed his sudden interest.

"Yeah, suppose we were. Sugah doll, why don't you go change, and we can go shopping for some new slippers. Besides, I heard Cartier's is opening a new store downtown." He winked. "But, you wouldn't like shopping for new jewelry, now, would you?"

At the second suggestion, Cherie's pixie face brightened, like a daisy to morning sunshine. She jumped up, and clacked across the tile into the foyer, slamming the French doors behind her. "Bye, bye!" she shouted.

Once on the spiral staircase, however, she waited silently, listening. The idea of Arnold talking business with Walter intrigued her. The brothers' voices buzzed low at first, and all she could make out was the sound of their alternating drones. She wanted to creep closer, but she didn't dare. It was too risky. Besides, her suspicions were probably silly. She started up the stairs when she heard the clatter of a fist pounding the glass table. She descended again, until she reached the bottom step.

"Damn it, brothah, how did Elvin Suggs end up in our buildin'?"

Elvin? Cherie felt confused. What building did Walter mean? She heard Arnold's whining voice, but she couldn't understand the words.

"Ain't this a fine mess?" Walter said. "Now we gonna have to go up there."

Where were they going? Could she go, too? Cherie heard footsteps on the tile, now approaching the French doors. Startled, she tiptoed up the steps to the marble-tiled bathroom. While she ran her bath water, and poured in her strawberry bubble bath, her thoughts turned to Elvin. Where had he gone? She glanced toward the cavernous walk-in closet and flipped on a miniature chandelier. The racks of clothes eased her anxious feelings. She had to decide what to wear today, no matter what Elvin did. Like Walter always said, first things first.

Di sat across the Formica table from Elvin, sipping coffee. Sunday mornings made them feel lazy. Even Vanna slept in the worn sofa in Di's living room. "So, El, you settled in up there yet?"

Elvin scratched his forehead and leaned back in his chair. "Problem is, I don't know how settled I should get."

"What do you mean?"

He shrugged his beefy shoulders. "I mean, I don't know what's goin' on with Cherie and my house in Memphis. I guess I got to make some plans, but you know, so far all the plans I ever made blew up in smoke anyway. So, I'm wondering if I should even bother. Guess I'll stay here another week, anyway. I don't like bein' there when that agent shows my house to strangers, you know?"

Di leaned forward and put her elbows on the table. "While we're on the subject of Cherie, I might as well tell you—I never liked her."

"What? Why you telling me this?"

"I don't want you to feel like you're losing anything because she left, that's all. Because you're too good for her—always were."

Di stopped talking. She noticed Elvin reach for his handkerchief. He wiped his eyes. "Don't talk about Cherie that way, Di. You didn't know her the way I did." He pointed a finger in the air and stabbed it. "Fact is, you're probably right, but you know, we had good times. Don't know why they had to stop, 'cause you know, I was happy."

Vanna looked back at her master, her ears alert and ready. "It's okay, girl," he sniffled, and stuffed his handkerchief into the back pocket of his jeans.

"I'm sorry. I just thought you might want to talk about it. Did you say you had something to tell me?"

Elvin sat up straight, instantly composed. "That's not what I wanted to talk to you about. Let's see, where do I start? I'll start with Valentine." He narrowed his eyes. "Turns out Valentine has a few problems of his own, Di. Not that it makes me happy; it's just interesting."

"How interesting?"

"For starters, he was in rehab five years ago."

The revelation didn't faze her. "Drugs?"

"Not as far as I can tell, but I'm not ruling it out. I'm guessing alcohol."

"Okay, so?"

"So, it looks like he was suspended from the police force for awhile back then. Behavior under the influence, or something like that. Seems he had a thing for prostitutes, too." Elvin shook his head. "From the looks of things, he was a damn good cop before then, judging by what folks said about him."

Di tapped her mug with her index finger. "How did he get where he is now?"

"Your guess is as good as mine. I'd have to ask around to find that out, I think."

"I still don't think he knows straight up. I mean, it doesn't look like he's getting anywhere on this case, and it's been over three weeks. He's got a suspect for the first murder, but nothing on Edward Mars. Something tells me that Parry Leach didn't do the first one. You and Don could have had this thing wrapped up along time ago."

"Got a little more coffee? I don't know about all that—maybe. This one's not so easy."

"What makes it different?"

"The diamond ring, for one thing. Does it mean anything? I mean, the old man Mars didn't have a diamond on him when he died. Why did this Mattie Torrez?"

Di perked up. "El, I forgot to tell you, Edith Mars is back. I talked to her last night."

"Yeah, I was with Valentine when he went to tell her about her husband."

"Didn't you think her reaction was a little lackadaisical, to say the least?"

"Far from it. She was hysterical, screaming and crying. 'Bout what you'd expect. No, I wouldn't say she didn't care at all."

Di didn't say anything at first. This wasn't adding up. "Where did you get all that info on Valentino?"

Elvin grinned. "You know I still got friends out there, girl.

Friends that don't forget a kindness."

"Did you offer to help Valentino?"

"Yeah. Said he didn't need my help. Maybe he doesn't. But Tasha Weeks' friend shore does. I'm just biding my time anyway. Might as well make myself useful. I can work here just as well as I can in Memphis." His musing was interrupted by screams coming from upstairs.

"That sounds like Annie Silver," said Di.

Elvin waited—and listened. "Tell you what, Di. Wouldn't be surprised if that husband of hers was a stone cold killer."

The screams grew longer and louder. "I'm going up there. You want Vanna to stay here with you?" At the sound of Vanna's name, Di's friendly demeanor withered.

"Not that scared yet, are you? Come on, Vanna. Let's get him!"

Arnold sat belted into the driver's seat of Walter's silver Cadillac. Walter lounged in the passenger seat, savoring a gin and tonic. Though it was late September, the Memphis humidity was oppressive. The weather at their intended destination didn't improve his foul mood. They had heard about St. Louis's damp humidity and Indian summers.

"This is a bad move, Wally, if you don't me mind saying so. I don't think your girlfriend ought to be with us."

Walter waved him away with indifference. "This is all too complicated for the little lady, brothah. She won't be any trouble. You'll see."

"How can you say that? We gonna be right under Elvin Suggs' nose, and we walkin' into the middle of a mighty nasty divorce."

Walter poked Arnold in his flabby belly. "That's right, brothah. What I'm going to do here? Wait till he figures out what's goin' on in my building? And don't let's forget, it is my building." He looked out the window at his pillared mansion. "Shit. That apartment's been good to us, brothah. You wanna see the gravy train end? Be a lot simpler to run Elvin Suggs out of town."

Arnold stared at Cherie, clacking down the front steps in her red patent leather heels. He shook his head. "I don't know 'bout that, Wally. Don't know 'bout that at all."

"What do you mean by that?"

"I mean Suggs is nobody's fool. You know he's a professional snoop, and he's strong as a bear. Does he know 'bout you and Cherie? That could get mighty messy."

Walter put his hand in his pocket and drew his .45 revolver. The glint of his gaudy diamond ring in the afternoon sun made Arnold blink. He looked at Arnold before he replaced it, seconds before Cherie slid across the backseat.

"A little ole mess never bothered me before now, did it, brothah?"

Arnold gulped and turned on the engine.

"We on our way."

Fourteen

Tasha had to see Myles La Mour. A strong-willed, determined woman, she felt disheartened after her afternoon visit with Parry. In her opinion, he needed a lawyer like Mr. La Mour, but her frantic calls to his office weren't returned. No one answered his apartment door. What could she do? She just had to find a way to ask him about Parry's case. Well, she just would. Parry's future depended on her.

All afternoon, Tasha patrolled the musty hallway. Around four o'clock, she pruned the scrappy weeds by the chipped front door. Sometime, she reasoned, Myles La Mour would return. When he did, she would convince him that he could be the right man for Parry's case. In her heart, Tasha believed Myles would achieve justice, and the cops would leave Parry alone once and for all.

When the silver Cadillac screeched to the curb, Tasha surrendered her last shred of hope. Who were these people? They were definitely not Myles La Mour. By the light of street lamp, Tasha saw two white-haired, light-skinned men in the front seat. There might be another in the backseat—had more like yellow hair, that one did.

Had Tennessee plates, that Caddy did. Looked just like that white guy's from Tennessee—the one says he's Ant's friend. Didn't look like him though, no way. Didn't get out of the car, neither. What were they staring at? They gawked like they were at a zoo or the circus. Sideshow? Is that what they were thinking? Well, that meant it was quitting time—time for dinner.

Somewhere, a horn blared. A car pulled up beside the Cadillac, and idled in the center of the street. Tasha watched while Ben Silver got out of his car, still clad in a white lab coat, and kicked the passenger door of Walter's Cadillac.

"You big hicks," he said from between clenched teeth, his face glowing with rage. "I warned you, Tennessee. Now, stay out of my way."

"Who do you think you are, homey?" Arnold's beady eyes hardened. He lowered the driver's window. Walter pulled his .45 from his waistband, but said nothing.

"Walter," gasped Cherie, "put that away!"

Walter ignored her. His .45 aimed at Ben's skull, the right moment could be any moment, until another silver Cadillac pulled up behind them. Arnold glimpsed the headlights from the corner of his eye.

"Let him go, Wally. We're getting too famous."

"What do you mean, brothah? Let me get off a few shots here."

"Wally, better let him go. I don't like it neither, but there's a nigger behind you, watching every move you making. Let me take care of this one, Wally." The prospect of another conflict delighted Arnold, but he knew Tasha heard every word he said.

"Y'all gonna need a new space, homey. Stay out of my way."

Ben managed to get back in his own car. His eyes glowered with a fresh vengeance, but he started his car and drove slowly down the narrow street, hunting for another parking space. "I live here, Tennessee," he muttered. "Damn right, I'm a homey." Still, he did not look back.

Cruising home in his black BMW, Myles' curiosity overwhelmed him. He had to take a gander at that tricked-out Caddy.

Arnold sneered when he passed. "Look at that, Wally. Nigger shouldn't have a car like that."

Tasha craned her neck to see where Myles had parked. She

wished she still had two good eyes. It was so hard to see, especially at night. She wanted to run inside, but didn't want to miss her chance to plead Parry's case. Determined to succeed, she remained under the porch light. Myles sauntered up the walk in the chilly breeze, wearing a red polo shirt and khaki pants, briefcase in hand.

"Look at that, Wally, there's two niggers living in your buildin'."

Walter's anger flared. "Their money spends the same, don't it, brothah? Why would I care who lives there? Fact is, long as those rent checks keep coming in, I don't care 'bout this building or the folks in it. So shush."

When Myles approached his mailbox in the foyer of the building, Tasha made her move. She could barely see him when she spoke, and it took all the nerve she could muster to approach a man with charisma to burn; but, Tasha kept thinking of Parry, sitting in that cell. She couldn't tell Parry she'd failed. She couldn't accept defeat. Now was the moment. "Mr. La Mour, remember me?"

"No I'm afraid I don't." He kept walking.

"Please Mr. La Mour, it's Tasha Weeks and Parry is still in jail. You've got to help." She hurried after him. "Parry needs a brother to help him, not some white kid just out of law school."

He stopped and shook his head. "Alright, alright Miss Weeks. Come by tomorrow before my first case, around eight, and I'll hear you out. I can't promise a thing, though. Now, please—have a good evening."

So, she got Parry an appointment with Myles La Mour. Wait until Parry heard her good news!

That night, Tasha shut the door of her apartment, and considered the blonde in the backseat. What she must have to put up with, Tasha could not imagine! One thing Tasha knew, without a doubt. Even with one good eye, and though she still met with the occasional bigot, and though she was, she guessed, considered poor by some, she wouldn't have traded places with that blonde—not ever, no way.

Sometime past midnight she awoke, startled by voices in Apartment B. Voices didn't usually come from that direction. It had been awhile since she'd noticed anything suspicious. She dismissed it, and tried to go back to sleep. She had an important meeting with Mr. La Mour tomorrow morning. She needed sleep to work for Parry.

She had almost dozed off when she heard a tapping at her door. She raised up in bed and listened. Tap-tap-tap. If not for the strange noises next door, she probably would have ignored it, but Tasha convinced herself it might be a mistake not to answer the door; it could be an emergency. She grabbed her worn terrycloth bathrobe and stumbled to the door. She opened it.

Di Redding stood in the hall in her bathrobe. Even in slippers, she towered over Tasha. "Sorry to bother you, Miss Weeks, but..." She glanced toward Apartment B. "Could I come in?"

"Shore, shore. 'Scuse the mess, though. With my surgery and all, I haven't had the energy I usually do, and with Parry in jail, why—"

Di pointed next door. "I didn't think anyone lived there. Shhh. Hear that?"

There was the sound of something being dragged across the floor. "Do we have to talk about this now?" asked Tasha, scratching her head.

"Why don't you come stay at my place tonight?" asked Di. "With all that's been going on, we'd probably both be safer."

"Miss Redding, no offense and all, but—"

Suddenly, they heard the door to Apartment B open, and then, slam shut. The sound of low voices buzzed in the hall. Di reached for the doorknob and Tasha grabbed her arm.

"No, Miss Redding, no..."

The main door slammed shut, and Di rushed to the end of the hall, hoping to catch a glimpse of the intruders. As she stared into the misty night, the only thing she saw was the red glow of taillights. A silver Caddy sped into the chilly blackness.

Fifteen

"Where's my diamond, Rose?" Belle studied the ceiling. It almost seemed as if she thought that she might find it there.

"I'm sure it's around, sweetheart." Rose hustled around the stuffy room, piling the stray glasses and plates onto a brown plastic tray.

"No, no," the old lady insisted. "I wore it on this finger for fifty two years, and now, it's not there anymore." She inspected the ring finger on her shriveled hand, and stared with a blank look in her watery eyes. Rose slouched on the edge of the sagging mattress.

"Honey, I'll look for it when I get back."

Belle frowned. "Where are you going, Rose?"

"You know I go out every Tuesday to get my hair done, Belle. You've had all of your medicine. Now try to get some sleep while I'm gone."

"All I do is sleep, Rose. I want to watch my wrestling." Rose flipped on the television. Belle was instantly absorbed. "Turn it up."

"There you go." Rose adjusted the volume.

"No, louder." Before Belle could make additional requests, Rose had slipped into the upstairs hall. The volume seeped through the door of the apartment. Well, no one up here's home during the day anyway, she thought.

The humidity had evaporated and a crisp, smoky scent wafted

through the autumn breeze. Rose climbed into her old car, and celebrated her freedom. It was the only time of the week that she felt this way, and now that Matt was dead, she wondered how much longer she could stand to take care of Belle. She lowered the driver's window and sped along the narrow street, blissfully unaware of the eyes that followed her.

Valentino had watched her leave every Tuesday for the past three weeks. This time, he would talk to Belle. He felt certain she was alone in the apartment. But, he had a dilemma. How to get in? While he sat in his car, staring at the long apartment building, he had a brainstorm. He hustled up the front steps, and rang the bell of Apartment D.

Di answered the door, even though she had already identified the visitor through the peephole. Reluctantly, she opened the door. "What?" she asked, her arms folded across her midriff.

"I came to ask a favor." Di waited in silence. "I said, Mrs. Redding, I came to ask a favor."

"I'm not deaf."

"You don't like me, do you?"

"What do you want?"

Valentino scanned the gloomy hall before he spoke. "Can I come in?"

"No."

"Okay." He whispered his request. "I need to get a key to Mrs. Torrez's apartment."

"Why are you asking me? I gave you my key. Don't tell me you returned it to that Honeycutt woman. Detective? "

Valentino continued to whisper. "Of course I returned it. Look, you don't have to ask that nurse for anything. Maybe Mrs. Mars has one."

Di rolled her eyes. "And you want me to ask her for it."

"Yeah, and I don't have much time to use it."

"If it would get rid of you for now, then, okay. I'll do anything."

Unfazed, Valentino replied, "Good."

Minutes later, Di stood facing Valentino, the key to Apartment G in hand.

"I'm sick of lying for you."

"What did you say?"

"I told her Rose asked me to check on Belle while she was out. Now, I want to go in with you."

"No way." Valentino extended his hand, waiting for the key.

"Why should I give it to you?"

"Don't forget, Mrs. Redding. In my book, you're still a suspect."

"That's ridiculous. I didn't even know the victims."

"So you say. The key, please."

Di clenched it in her hand. "What are you going to do in there?"

"Depends on what I find." He extended his outstretched palm.

Di surrendered the key and ducked inside her apartment. Valentino couldn't stop her from making a phone call.

The detective hustled up the steps, and crept to the end of the hall. As vacant as it looked, he always felt like someone was watching. He scanned the empty corridor. As he inserted the key, a door at the opposite end cracked—it was Denton Smith—in his bathrobe, out to snatch his newspaper.

"Good morning," Dent shouted.

Valentino nodded and waited, but only for a second. Then, he pushed his way into Apartment G. There it was—that awful smell again. Layers upon layers of odors, like peeling an onion. Menthol and Pine-Sol, coffee and lavender. "Mrs. Torrez!" he half-whispered, his voice hoarse from the strain. "Are you asleep?"

He knew it before he reached her bedroom, though he was somewhat unsettled by the sounds of a wrestling match.

"Rose?" Belle said, languishing in the darkness.

"No ma'am." Valentino approached the sick bed.

"Who are you?" She attempted to sit up, but fell back on the rumpled sheets.

Even in the shadows, Valentino saw the confusion on her lined face. He pulled his badge from the pocket of his suit coat. "Detective Rick Valentino. Are you Mrs. Torrez?"

"I haven't done anything, Mister." Belle kneaded her fists together as she stopped to focus on the wrestling match. "Got him!" she cried.

Suddenly, she stopped talking, and stared at him through hollow eyes. "Did Rose let you in?"

Valentino smiled. "I let myself in. I wanted to talk to you."

With the innocence of a child, Rose simply said, "Oh," before she was again focused on the match. "Did you say you were a detective or something?"

"That's right. Now, if I—"

"Well, I need a good detective."

"You do?"

"I can't find my diamond ring."

Valentino took a deep breath. "Mrs. Torrez, when was the last time you saw your son?"

"My what?"

"Your son, Matthew."

"You must be kiddin'."

"I don't like to discuss these things, Mrs. Torrez, but your son is dead."

"I don't know what you've been smokin', mister, but you're making me laugh."

"What?"

"I don't have a son. Never did."

Valentino stood motionless in the stuffy room, and surveyed the clusters of pill bottles on the night table and dresser top. The old lady cackled with delight while she watched the television screen, completely unfazed by his presence. He wondered if she was a bit demented.

"Ma'am..."

"Just a second, mister." With that, Valentino bent over the bed and switched off the television set. "Hey! That's my show. Where's Rose?" At the mention of Rose, Valentino glanced over his shoulder.

"That's something I want to discuss, Mrs. Torrez. You are Belle Torrez, aren't you?"

"Sure am. Turn on my show."

He was unsure how to proceed, uncertain of the old lady's mental status. "Just one thing, Mrs. Torrez, and I'll be happy to help you find your diamond ring."

Belle's face brightened. "Okay."

"It's about your son, Matthew."

Belle grew agitated and commenced thrashing about the sheets. "I don't have a son, mister, I told you."

"Mrs. Torrez, your son is dead now, but I need to find out what you know about the day he was murdered."

Belle's black eyes grew wide with fright. She began to scream— a long, shrill scream, so loud that Valentino put his hands over his ears.

"Rose! Rose! I need my pills, now. Tony's gone!"

Tony?

Valentino took out his black book and scribbled the name. He was getting nowhere with Belle Torrez, and now, it appeared he had made matters even worse. Maybe it was time to talk to Edith Mars. "Mrs. Torrez, I'm going to leave now, but I'll be back when you're feeling better. How would that be?"

Belle sobbed. "Tony! My Tony!"

Valentino snapped on the television set. Instantly, it pacified Belle, now completely engrossed in the wrestling match on the small screen. Valentino inched his way back through the door. He didn't say goodbye, for fear of distressing Belle again. His hope was that she would forget he had been there. Once he had safely reached the second floor landing, he took a deep breath and prepared to face Edith Mars. It had to be better than his first interview, if he could call it one.

He stood in the hall and waited for Edith to answer the door. She hadn't responded so far, and he had things to do, so…

Suddenly, the front door opened. He stood face to face with Valerie Gains.

"I'll bet he's up there right now." Di sat in Apartment C with Tasha and Elvin, wondering how to proceed.

"Think I ought to go up?" Di shrugged at Elvin's suggestion. "Frankly, I think I'm finding out more on my own. I'm more focused, for example. I am, Di! He's always chasing somebody with a new face."

Tasha leaned forward to speak, and Di noticed a glimmer of hope in her soulful dark eyes. Her left one had healed nicely. All that remained was a bit of swelling at the corner. "Think you can help Parry, Mr. Suggs?" Her voice was soft and fearful.

"Nothin's for sure yet, Tasha, but I'll tell you what I know. Call me Elvin, will you?"

Tasha nodded. She wore a plain white blouse over a pair of black pants. Her clothes were shabby, but they were clean and pressed. Even her pair of white Keds were bleached white, white, white. Tasha dressed to work at the Night and Day Lounge, where she was a cook, a housekeeper, and a, "Whatever else Alfie didn't get done because he was talking on the job." Anyway, she wasn't going to complain, no way, no how. Alfie gave her a job when she needed one. Alfie was okay and alright.

Elvin leaned forward and whispered. "I checked out your friend's record." He shook his head. "Parry's been a mighty busy guy. You know, judging from his past…" Elvin hesitated, "uh, experience, he could be guilty."

Tasha jumped up from her seat and shook her fist. "But he didn't do it! No way."

Elvin held up his hand. "Okay, okay. For now, let's say he didn't do it. I went to see him the other day, see what kind of vibes I got. Personally, I think he's innocent, but my feelings aren't enough to get him off." He paused. "He knew Matthew Torrez, you know."

Tasha hung her head. "Yeah." She stared into Elvin's eyes. "But that don't mean he did it."

Elvin decided not to argue with her. "I've talked to everybody around here now, all except for one."

"Who's that?" asked Di.

"That lawyer named La Mour says I need to check out that lady who lives in Apartment A, but she's never home when I come by."

Tasha's stooped body stiffened and she gripped the sides of the chair. "She's a 'ho. Was her that kilt that white guy?"

"I'll see what I think when I meet her," said Elvin. "There's one other thing."

"What?" asked Di.

"That lawyer said the Torrez woman had him change a will for her a few months ago."

"So?"

"So, it might be important. And there's something else that keeps bugging me. I'm not sure it even matters, but it still bothers me."

"What's that, Elvin?" Tasha's soft voice had melted into a whisper.

"Annie Silver knocked on my door the other night. You know, the medical student's wife?"

"Yeah?"

"Well, she'd had a few beers, for sure." Di frowned in opposition. "Trust me, girl, I know what drunk looks like. Anyway, she said she was lonely and would I like some company? I didn't know what to make of the whole thing, mainly cause of her little outfit." Again, Di frowned.

"What do you mean by that?"

"I mean, she was dressed in a little ole tank top and shorts that—well, they were short."

"I don't see where you're going with this," said Di.

"Anyway, she seemed like the shy type to me."

"I'm with her on that."

"I'm not finished, ladies. Well, there she is, all mellowed out, and I have to say, she was looking mighty good, and who walks up behind her but that worm of a husband of hers, all huffin' and puffin' like some kind of maniac. Now, I wasn't about to ask her in anyway, but this guy pulls some kind of blade out of his back pocket and sticks the point in her back, right out there in the hall where everybody can see him. Even as drunk as Annie was, she knew not to mess with this guy. Something told me he didn't want to mess with me either, and I didn't want to throw any gas on the fire. He said, 'What did I tell you, woman? I'm sick of your running around on me.'"

"What did she do?" asked Di. "She didn't stick around, did she?"

"She started this crying jag, saying she wasn't doing anything wrong, she was just talking to the neighbor. Well, I could tell he didn't believe her, and then, he starts screaming at her. He's pulling her across the hall by her hair, and yelling, 'Remember what happened to the last guy I caught you with?'"

"Who was that?" asked Tasha.

"That's what I'm trying to find out."

Sixteen

"I tell you, Wally," Arnold said, his mouth crammed full of potato chip and mayonnaise bread, "I think it's time we pulled outta this town."

Walter sat on the twin bed at the Sunset Hotel, filing his nails. The scorching autumn sun beamed onto the bedspread.

"Shore 'nough hot up here, ain't it, brothah? Expecting to find me a little cool shade in St. Louis, but I believe it's hotter here than Memphis."

"More ways than one, Wally. More ways than one."

Before they could further their discussion, the door jiggled. Cherie pranced into the room, laden with overstuffed shopping bags, blonde curls frizzed from the humidity, and her pink sunglasses were plunked high on her turned up nose.

"Oh Waallter! I can't wait to show you what all I bought today."

Arnold counted the fancy bags Cherie tossed onto the plush... *What could the woman possibly need or want that Wally hadn't already bought for her?* He didn't want to hear another word about his beer, or his donuts or his Chinese food, shore 'nuf. He crammed a Hostess cupcake into his wide mouth, and chewed, and chewed. Chocolate crumbs and cream filling spewed from his lips, right before the mess dribbled onto the pristine rug.

Still wearing sunglasses, Cherie turned her back to him and slid onto Walter's lap. She planted a full kiss on his mouth. "Could we be alone for a little while, Walter?" she simpered. "You know how I get when it's hot outside." She giggled like a seven-year-old girl. "And it surely is hot today." Walter did not warm to her suggestion. Instead, he coaxed her off of his lap, and onto the king-sized bed beneath him.

"Not now, sugah doll. Daddy has some business to tend to." The woman child slid the sunglasses to the end of her pug nose, and peeked at the white-haired man with the leathery tan. With her lower lip in a pout, she stomped off to the bathroom. The door slammed. Arnold watched her, surrounded by a circle of crumbled potato chips and bits of chocolate cake.

"That's something else I think we ought to leave behind, brothah. I believe in traveling light. And that little gal been weighing us down."

Walter thought for a moment, and then he whispered, "Cain't."

"Can't what?"

"Cain't let her go anywhere on her own now." Arnold frowned, and his swollen face bunched into a mass of wrinkles.

"Why not?"

"You know why not. Cherie knows too much. Sugah got a big mouth. We got connections in this town gonna kill us if we cut 'em off."

"Shore enough, Wally. Shore enough, but they can always find new connections." Walter laughed. It was a low, evil grunt.

"But we the best, brothah. We the best." Arnold grinned, shaking his fist. "Yeah, that's true enough. But ain't we 'bout got enough to retire? I mean, we been hustling this candy for 'bout two, three years now. Where's it all going?" Walter shrugged, as one corner of his mouth turned up in a wry smile.

"You like driving a nice car, do you? Wearing them fine clothes? And don't let us forget, eating good?"

Arnold was silent for a moment. He sat motionless, lost in a trance. Then, he lifted his swollen face, and his eyes were bright with excitement. "So, you saying, if Cherie couldn't tell anyone what she knows about us, we could blow out of here tonight?" Walter shook his head.

"Ain't no point in bringing all that up again, brothah, 'cause she knows everything, and there ain't no takin' it back now. Hell, you done told me that damn husband of hers is up here snooping around in my building. No, there ain't no way we can leave Cherie behind, brothah."

From the bathroom came the sound of Cherie's tinny voice, singing, "Raindrops Keep Fallin' on My Head."

Arnold crumpled a potato chip bag into a ball and threw it into a wicker wastebasket. "You right, Wally, the woman's a talker, alright." He scratched his squarish skull. "And that shorely is a problem."

"Ain't nothin' we can do 'bout that. Right, brothah?"

Arnold got up and waddled over to the window, his back to Walter. Walter shifted on the bed, confused by his brother's aloof demeanor.

"I said, ain't that right?"

Arnold turned to face Walter. His hands were shoved deep in the pockets of his voluminous pants. "They always something can be done," said Arnold. "You remember who told me that, don't you?"

Walter hung his head. "Yeah." His mouth smiled, but his hard eyes did not, even as he caught his reflection in the mirror over the dresser. "Yes, I believe I do recall who said that to you."

"Back for more, are you?" Valerie twirled a lock of platinum hair around a red lacquered nail. Already, beads of sweat were forming on Valentino's brow. Plastered against the door, he wondered how he had been lured into Valerie's apartment. The lonely man perused the voluptuous woman before him, and reminded himself that he knew better. He also knew what it was to be alone with Valerie Gains. He had a problem.

Valerie disappeared into the tiny kitchen, emerging with two bottles of Busch beer. She winked at him as she offered him one.

"I love a drink this time of day, don't you, Rick?"

He shook his head in response. "No, honey, not now. I'm working."

Valerie's mouth curled into a subtle sneer. "So am I, Ricky."

She took a step closer, and yet another, until she was so close he could smell the cigarette smoke on her breath.

His face afire and his body ablaze, he struggled to resist the two things for which he had an undeniable weakness. His hand was on the doorknob. He should leave. He wanted to open the door, and yet...Valerie's expression mocked him.

"You want to leave, do you? Go on." She gestured toward the door, the beer bottle still in her hand. The building was as silent as a chapel, and the late afternoon sun cast shadows through the yellowed Venetian blinds. Valentino felt like a fool. What kind of guy turns down a beer and a woman like Valerie? Edith Mars was probably taking a nap anyway. Besides, the last encounter had been highly disappointing. A trickle of condensation dripped from the icy bottle as Valerie licked her lips. It was all too much for him.

"The offer still good?" he asked. Valerie smiled, and raised a bottle to his parched lips.

"You know what you need?"

Valentino gulped his beer. "What?"

She exploded in giggles. "That's what I thought you'd say." The short red negligee under her robe was an odd contrast to the black stiletto heels. Before this very moment, Valentino hadn't noticed the snake tattooed on her left thigh. He hesitated at the sight of it.

"What's wrong, Ricky?"

"Maybe we should go somewhere else. My car's out front where everyone can see it."

After a quick glance out to the curb, Valerie slid over to the stereo and put on some music by Carlos Santana. She turned up the volume to a low roar, as the sensuous beat filled the apartment. "Better?" she whispered, as she took a step toward him.

"No one will be able to hear a thing." She removed his jacket; untied his tie.

He looked as if he was choking. "You don't like it in the living room, do you?" she whispered in her raspy voice, nuzzling his neck. But the object of her affection wasn't paying attention to her.

He was gazing at the trail of bloodstains between the recliner and the coffee table. The sight of them fueled his resolve. He might be able to get some information after all. He turned the deadbolt. Valerie put her arm around his waist, still holding her beer in the other manicured hand.

"Come on," she coaxed. "I'll show you my waterbed."

Moving to the driving beat of the music, she sauntered toward the bedroom. The hem of the red nightie barely grazed her hips. She never wondered if Valentino was behind her. She didn't doubt it for a minute. Yet, even as he stepped around the bloodstains, he patted his gun. Though he planned to savor this tryst, he expected to emerge from it a wiser man.

At this point, Valerie was still a prime suspect. Yet, while she pulled him down into the folds of the swaying mattress, he didn't want to believe her capable of murder. She kissed him, and her hands slid down his tired body. He forgot about asking her for anything but what she wanted to give him. Besides, his facts were meticulously recorded in his black book; the same black book that had fallen behind the recliner in Valerie's living room.

Elvin pulled his Cadillac up to the curb and sighed. He had just returned from a visit with Parry Leach, and it did nothing to convince him of Parry's innocence. Parry had been suspicious of his motives and close-mouthed, despite Tasha's prior encouragement. He shook his head as he got out of the car. As he walked up the sidewalk toward the Jewel Arms, he noticed Valentino's car.

It was already getting dark outside, though it was only the beginning of October. His watch told him it was five o'clock in the evening. *That Valentine*, he mumbled as he inserted his key into the heavy outer door. *Didn't seem like he ever went home. The poor guy needed to get some friends, party a little, loosen up.* As Elvin stepped into the foyer, he was instantly greeted by the Latino beat resounding from Apartment A, reminding Elvin that he still needed to talk to the tenant that lived there. *Man, that music was loud. Didn't it bother Di?* He sniffed the air in the hall and encountered the scent of a spicy perfume. It almost smelled like cinnamon. He wondered if the detective was still upstairs. Well, he'd go check—right after he got the mail, that is.

He turned his back to retrieve the catalogs and bills. The screen door opened and a young black man dressed in cargo pants and a gray hooded sweatshirt, brushed past him. From the corner of his eye, Elvin watched him rap on the door of Apartment B. It opened immediately, and he disappeared inside, like a bat into a cave. So, someone did live in B, he observed. He guessed he needed to talk to them, too. He wondered if anybody else had met them. In fact, maybe he'd do that right now.

He didn't get the chance. The door to Apartment A opened and he found himself face to face with a very drunk, very jolly homicide detective.

"Suggs! Is that you, Suggs?" Valentino sloshed, struggling to focus his eyes. He was dressed, but just barely, his shirt only halfway buttoned. He had forgotten to zip his pants.

To avoid gawking, Elvin peeked over his shoulder into the living room. It reeked of the cinnamon perfume. His eyes were immediately drawn to the trail of bloodstains on the faded beige carpet.

"You okay, Valentine?" Elvin grabbed his elbow in an attempt to steady him.

"I'm fine! Help me out to my car, will you?"

"You ain't talkin' 'bout drivin' anywhere now, are you?"

"Going to get me some dinner now." His eyelids drooped and he collapsed in the hall.

Elvin smirked at the unconscious detective, snoring loudly

at his feet. He went over to the door of Apartment A, which had remained cracked, and knocked boldly.

"Hey!" he shouted into the apartment. He went over to the stereo and turned off the music. The smell of that perfume was beginning to give him a headache.

"Anybody home?"

It was a tiny apartment, just a one bedroom efficiency, and it wasn't long before Elvin found himself gazing at a voluptuous blonde, sleeping soundly beneath a black satin comforter, embroidered with scarlet roses. The woman lay on her stomach with the covering pulled up around her face. The ashtray on the nightstand was full of lipstick stained cigarette butts; a suspicious white powder dusted its surface. Though he didn't satisfy his curiosity, he suspected she was nude. *All the more reason to leave.* He sure had been wrong about that Valentine. Shuddering, he remembered the drunken man lying out in the foyer.

When he hustled out of the apartment, Elvin was startled. The foyer was now empty. He watched while Valentino swerved down Watson Road, straddling two lanes, and ran a red light. *Too late to stop him now.* He closed the door to Apartment A and crept upstairs to let Vanna out.

It was much later than he thought.

Seventeen

October 25th—it would have been their twenty-fifth wedding anniversary. She shouldn't have done it, but nevertheless, Di allowed herself to linger over "the drawer," as she thought of it, the place where she hoarded the remnants of Don's life. Even worse, she had put The Supremes on the stereo again, if only to drown out the noise from across the hall. She'd cried herself to sleep that night; something after Don died, she promised herself never to do again. Twenty-five years, the things they could have done, the places they could have gone, if only he'd made it too.

Trapped in a fitful sleep, she was lost in a jungle. It didn't look familiar, and yet, somehow it did. Ant was there, and so was Elvin, which was odd, because she hardly remembered Ant, and the four of them had never gone anywhere together. As they moved through the branches and underbrush, a thick fog surrounded them. Some kind of melting jelly dripped from the canopy of overhead branches. The swirling fog grew denser, the goo singed her skin. "Where are we?" she shrieked. "I'm on fire!" But no one answered. She was alone. At least until Elvin and Ant returned to find her sleeping on a pile of dirty uniforms.

"Where were you?" said Elvin. "You should have been there. You could have saved him. It's all your fault!"

"Where's Don?" Even in her dream, her voice sounded clear and rational. "We promised we would take care of each other."

"He kept asking for you. And you were sleeping! Look at you. You were sleeping while they killed him."

Ant pulled out his gun and aimed at her skull. "You deserve to die! It's all your fault! It's all your fault! It's all your fault..." The chant echoed relentlessly. Her head felt like it was going to split.

Di sat up in bed, sweating, trying to catch her breath as she looked around the starkly furnished bedroom. The clock on the nightstand said 2:00 a.m. She must have fallen asleep after dinner sometime, she thought, her mind still hazy. Her stereo still played in the living room. At least that noise in the hall had stopped.

She was in the kitchen, getting a glass of juice, when she heard arguing out in the hall. The voices were angry, even threatening. She pressed her ear to the thin door and listened to the sounds of crackling paper and shuffling feet, and witnessed the magic of money.

🐕

"Wally don't deal with no thief now, Redman," said Arnold. Tired and disheveled, his face was greasy and swollen. Dark wells underscored his beady eyes.

"It's all there, I tole you." Redman stashed a bulging envelope into Arnold's hungry hands. Redman's thin lips curled in a sneer. "I ain't never cheated you before." He took a step closer to Arnold's lumpy body. A thirty-two year old black man, Redman's wiry build belied his strength, but the determination in his eyes did not. "What's your problem, brother?"

Arnold shoved him in the chest. "Only person call me brothah is my brothah, hear? This is a strictly business relationship. If you're smart, which you ain't, you'll keep it that way. Got it?"

Redman reached into his pocket and his fingers grasped at a long folding knife. His jaw clenched so that a vein swelled in his forehead, and the muscles in his neck tensed. He leaned in toward Arnold until their noses almost touched. "Don't you never lay another hand on me," he hissed through his teeth, "or I'll cut your fucking heart out."

Arnold began to laugh, all the while clutching the manila envelope. "You'd be a dead man, Redman."

Redman spit in Arnold's flushed face. He nudged his way past the mound of blubber blocking his path, and blasted through the front door of the building. One breath of the fresh night air revived him. His strength restored, he turned to face Hubble. "I'll be talkin' to Walter 'bout this. Believe it, fat boy."

Arnold stood in the middle of the hallway and guffawed, so hard that his gelatinous belly quivered. "Y'all just do that, Redman. And I'll see to it that it's the very last thing you say with those big ole lips." He spat on the stained carpet in the hallway and laughed like a crazy hyena. "Shore 'nuf."

Di stood behind the door, fighting the urge to open it. Who were Arnold and Redman? Who was Walter? More importantly, what had they been fighting about in the hallway of the Jewel Arms at 2:00 a.m.? She almost called Valentino, but decided against it.

It was probably nothing. One thing for sure, this Arnold was one of the nastiest people she had ever heard. *Shore 'nuf.*

Reggie Combs put his feet upon the desk and dialed Valentino's home number. He hadn't heard from Rick in a week, and he was worried. Worried and tired of covering for him. It wasn't like the detective he knew; at least, the one he had been since he'd gotten out of rehab five years ago. He'd promised Reggie he was a changed man. Reggie decided that had been true, until lately. Valentino's phone was still ringing when Reggie hung up. He glanced at the large black and white clock in the center of the office wall. 7:30 a.m. Where the hell was he?

"Pearl!"

"What!" said the slim, young black woman sitting two desks away.

"I got to run out for a little while. Can you cover the phone?"

"Why me?" She still typed on her computer.

"Look, I'll have to owe you." Reggie jammed his arm into the sleeve of his black jacket.

"You already owe me."

Reggie shoved his pistol into his holster. The gesture was not lost on Pearl. "Where do you want to go for lunch?"

Pearl grinned. "Maggie O'Brien's."

"You got it."

"This must be important."

Reggie hustled toward the door without turning around. "Don't know yet, honey. Between me and thee, I don't know what I'm going to find."

The sky was dark; thunder crackled behind the clouds. Elvin read his mail, accumulated from the week before, as he and Vanna ate oatmeal and watched the Today Show. He groaned as he heard the forecast—90 percent chance of showers. The weather was only a minor disappointment, however, in comparison to the thick manila envelope he found beneath the pile of catalogs and coupons. As he identified the sender, even before opening it, he felt its power over him. He checked the address label. It had originally been sent to his Memphis residence and forwarded to his St. Louis address. Well, he thought, as he cut the thick paper open with his pocketknife, bad news sure knew how to follow directions.

Vanna's ears stood up. She watched her master and sidled closer as his pain became palpable. He paged through the document, and felt his face and his fingers grow numb. His lower lip quivered, and he stifled his tears, somehow managing a weak smile for Vanna. Finally, he closed his eyes. The dog licked his hand. The reason for Elvin's dismay was inconsequential.

Bleary-eyed, he glanced at the television, as a chef showed Katie Couric how to make a soufflé. She laughed as he displayed a perfect example—light, airy and high. "It looks so easy," she giggled.

"With a little practice, anyone can do it."

"Right," Katie said.

"Right." Elvin threw the envelope across the table in disgust.

"Anyone can do it. Just takes a little practice, that's all."

He heard the splash of puddles against tires and looked outside, frowning. He hadn't remembered leaving the windows in his car rolled down. Yet, there was his silver Cadillac, torrents of rain drenching the leather interior.

"So far, so good," he grumbled and grabbed an umbrella from the closet. "What a lousy, stinkin' day."

As he opened the door, Vanna attempted to follow. "No girl, you stay in here." As he ran out to the car, he looked up to see her watching him from the window, ears perked up in anticipation. A quick glance showed him the reason.

"What the..." he said, standing in the downpour. From the window, he hadn't noticed that two silver Cadillacs were parked in front of the Jewel Arms, with Di's old gray Suburban between them. He ran to the car with the open windows and knew it could not have been his, even though it also had Tennessee license plates. The backseat was full of shopping bags and—wait a minute—he knew those sunglasses, he recognized those red shoes. It couldn't be right, and yet, if those weren't Cherie's glasses and shoes, he'd eat his shirt, shore 'nuf.

He crept up the sidewalk to his own Cadillac, which thankfully, was the way he'd left it. He paced back down to the other car once more, oblivious to the pelting rain, and the deepening puddles. Elvin glanced back at the Jewel Arms, now standing beneath a few rays of sunshine, struggling to break through the clouds. Was Cherie in there? Suddenly, his outlook brightened. Maybe she'd changed her mind. Yeah, that was it. She wanted him back. This was all too good to be true.

Elvin was right. It was.

Myles chugged the rest of his orange juice while he checked his watch. Dang, he thought. Seven thirty. Where did the time go? He grabbed his suit coat and briefcase, leaving the burned toast in the toaster. Even if he hurried now, he would be late for his 8:00 appointment, with traffic and all.

He had barely stepped into the hall when he collided with Ben Silver. Ben's glasses came unhinged, and the hate in the man's eyes alarmed Myles.

"I'm a doctor, you shithead! Get out of my way."

Even though Myles was running late, his back was up. "I'm an attorney, sir, but I believe in common courtesy."

Though Ben was feeling hassled, he stopped and turned around to face his neighbor. "Don't fuck with me, Sambo. I'm in a lousy mood."

"Yeah, I noticed."

Myles stayed on the landing, grinning down at him triumphantly. He was not about to lose his temper. His broad smile was like a red flag to a raging bull.

Ben clenched his fists at his sides, his face flushed with anger. "I'm gonna check you out, and you better be a damn good lawyer. That's the only thing keeping me from…"

He froze as the front door opened, and Elvin stepped inside, his face glowing with eager anticipation. "Hey!" he said to the feuding pair.

Ben Silver fumed, and pushed past Elvin into the brisk morning air.

"Thanks buddy." Myles descended the staircase. "Some folks are just not morning people, I guess. You know, I've never seen him smile."

Elvin shook his head. "Just an unhappy guy. Must be hard to live with. "

Myles considered the observation. "Yeah. Look, I'd like to visit, but…"

"Hey, don't let me keep you. Just looked like you needed a little help there."

"Don't give it a second thought." Myles pushed the door open. "Have a good day, now."

"Listen," Elvin said, "have you seen a little lady 'round here? Blonde, real cute, wears a lot of sweet dresses?"

Myles frowned. "I know a blonde lady that lives in there." He pointed to Valerie's door. "But I'm not sure we're talking about the same woman."

"How long she been livin' here, you suppose?"

"Well," said Myles, recalling his rendezvous at the Sunset Hotel, "at least a couple of weeks. She actually consulted me about a legal problem she was having; seemed to be in a hurry to get some resolution."

"You a lawyer?"

"Yes, I am."

Elvin rubbed the back of his neck. "Well, don't that just figure?"

"Excuse me?"

"Nothin' there, Myles, nothin' at all. Hey, maybe we could get together for a beer. I might need a lawyer myself."

"Yeah, sure."

Myles stepped out into the damp air, leaving Elvin to ponder his remarks. His mind returned to the night before, when he had crept into Apartment A. It had never occurred to him that the slumbering woman could have been Cherie. But if it was, what was Valentine doing in there with her—alone and intoxicated? Though he felt a little soggy around the soles, his curiosity overcame him. He had to know.

He closed his dripping umbrella, and placed it in the corner of the foyer before checking the name on the mailbox of Apartment A. Valerie Gains. Cherie could have changed her name, he mused. It could be her. But, why were her possessions inside a silver Cadillac? Was she living with someone else? He tiptoed up to the threshold of Apartment A, and rang the bell. He just had to see this lady for himself.

He heard a rustling sound inside, which got louder as the person approached the thin door.

"Who is it?" said a woman's raspy voice.

"Guess who, darlin'?"

"Why should I?"

"It's your Elvin, baby."

"Who the hell is Elvin baby?"

"Don't play with me, now, sugar. I don't blame you for anything." He pulled three twenty-dollar bills from his thinning wallet and slid them under the door. "Take it, honey. You probably need a little cash by now."

The money disappeared, and within seconds, the door opened, revealing a platinum blonde clad in a black negligee. Though it was still early morning, her face was fully made up, her full, red lips sucking on a fresh cigarette.

"You're right about that, Elvis."

"The name's Elvin."

"Whatever. I can always use some cash." She stuffed it in her bosom as she blew smoke into the air, flashing a bright smile. "Care for a drink?" The ashes crumbled onto the stained carpet. "You look like a beer man to me." She paused, watching for Elvin's reaction. "They're my favorite kind."

"You know, ma'am, this may sound a little funny to you, but I thought you were somebody else."

"Oh?" Valerie fluffed her rumpled hair with her scarlet talons. "Who did you have in mind?"

"It doesn't matter. Look, I'm sorry I bothered you so early in the mornin' and all. I'll just be going now."

"You say you're looking for a lady like me, are you?"

Elvin was hooked. "Yeah, that's right. Look, I said I was sorry."

Valerie took his hand, caressing his fingers with her own. "You are?" She laughed. "That's too bad. For a little more of that cash, though, I might have seen somebody like that around here."

Elvin sniffed the air, his eyes watering at the thickening smoke. "You hustling me, lady?"

"Just selling what I got, Elvis. You buying or not?"

Elvin looked around. The hall was empty. He could handle this woman, he felt sure of that, but he didn't want anyone to know he was with her, whatever she was. "Okay, I'm buying," he said, pulling out two more twenties. "But, let's hurry things up. I ain't got all day."

"I don't need all day." She snatched the cash and opened the door all the way.

He stepped into the living room, dodging the dried bloodstains. "I guess it's none of my business, but how did you get all these spots on your rug?"

For the first time, Valerie fidgeted, avoiding his gaze. "I-I need to get it cleaned up, I know."

"But how'd it get that way?" Elvin feigned ignorance. The smoke choked him and he coughed.

"Had an accident in here a little while ago." She stared at the stains as she spoke.

"Accident?"

"Yeah, accident."

"Must have been some accident. Almost looks like somebody was stabbed to death or something." He never took his eyes off of Valerie's face.

She stepped back from him, and the atmosphere between them grew chilly. "You a cop?"

"No. Right now, I'm just looking for somebody. Why don't you want to talk about the accident?"

"You act like a cop."

"How does a cop act?"

Before Elvin could answer, the smoke billowed from the back of the apartment, and the smell of flaming grease penetrated the front rooms.

"Jesus, God!" Valerie wailed, rushing into the kitchen. "I left the damn stove on!"

She ran away, dropping her burning cigarette on the rug. As

Elvin stooped to retrieve it, his eye caught a glimpse of a too familiar object behind the recliner. It was Valentino's black book.
While Valerie scraped singed sausage from her blackened skil-
let, Elvin stuffed the book into the back pocket of his jeans, and
waited for Valerie's return. In his heart, he felt that Valentine
wouldn't be coming back for it; just like he knew that a hooker
shouldn't learn the secrets scrawled across its tattered pages.

Eighteen

Di had awakened, but just barely, with a fierce migraine headache. The pressure over her left eye was like a hammer pounding a nail into the side of her head, threatening to splinter her
skull. She had just taken a prescription painkiller and sipped a
little orange juice when the phone rang. She didn't want to talk
to anyone right now. She let it ring five times, each ring pulsing
through her body like white heat, as she begged for the noise to
stop. When it didn't, she reached for the receiver with a clumsy
hand, a pillow held over her head with the other one.

"Hullo," she mumbled, her voice cracking with sleep.

"Hey!" said a woman's voice. The accent sounded oddly like
Elvin's, thought Di, while she struggled to sit up in the bed. "Could
I talk to Elvin Suggs?"

"Who is this?" Di pressed the pillow against her left eye.

"Who are you?" the woman retorted. "I need to speak to Mr.
Suggs. I was told I could reach him at this number."

The medication had caused Di's thinking to become fuzzy.
Nevertheless, she thought the voice on the other end sounded familiar, though she couldn't place the identity of the caller. "Who
gave you this number?"

"Who the hell is this?"

"I'm a friend of Elvin's."

There was a lull on the other end of the line. "Is he there or
not?"

"He doesn't live here, but I could get a message to him for you, if you want."

"You could? You know where he is?"

"Sure."

The woman on the other end took a deep breath. Di thought she heard men talking in the background. "Could you tell him Cherie called? I-I need to talk to him. Tell him it's urgent. Will you?"

Di felt her temperature soar; no, it was raging through the roof! How dare Cherie call Elvin after what she'd put him through? "Do you have a number where he could call you?"

Again, there was a slight pause. "N-no. That wouldn't be a good idea," replied Cherie. "Tell him I'll call him. Tonight, at this number, about 11:00." She hesitated for a moment, and Di heard a door slam in the background. "I'll be by myself then. Tell him for me, okay?" The line went dead.

Di hung up the receiver and glanced at the clock—8:30 a.m. She pulled the nightstand drawer out and fumbled for some note paper and a pen, but neither was to be found. Oh well, she thought. She laid her throbbing head on the mattress and sheltered it with a pillow. She'd remember to tell Elvin. The sound of buzzers and bells blared from the television next door, while Edith Mars savored the morning game shows. Despite the noise, Di slipped into a drugged, foggy sleep, oblivious to the activity surrounding her.

Upstairs, Rose was busy with the endless routine of caregiving, while Annie Silver nursed another hangover. Once again, she was unable to report to work, a fact that she successfully concealed from her husband, who had spent the night on call at the hospital. Both conditions were becoming more frequent.

Alone, Dent scoured the personal ads, hoping and searching for the ideal companion. Myles La Mour was finally meeting with Tasha Weeks at his office, though he had to admit, Parry's case did not look promising. It was to be a very short meeting. Elvin had returned to his apartment to finish going through the mail.

Around 10:00 a.m., Valerie Gains was wakening once again to face a new day. She was dying for a cigarette, but decided to put on a robe first. Despite her extensive wardrobe of showy lingerie, she slept without it. She simply couldn't stand the feel of it against her skin when she was asleep. She had just lit up and poured a glass of tomato juice when she was startled by men's voices in the apartment next door. She wasn't used to any noise from B. She went over to the far wall of her bedroom and put her ear against it.

At first, it sounded like only two men. The conversation progressed, and Valerie became aware of at least two additional people. She took a long drag of her cigarette, puffing smoke towards the high ceiling. She didn't really know why she was interested in what they were saying. She supposed it was because she didn't know who they were; and, new men always intrigued her. She grabbed an ashtray from the nightstand, and sipped at her tomato juice, snuggling closer to the plaster wall.

"I say we pull out, Wally," drawled Arnold. His fatty hand fumbled in a bag of peanut M&Ms and emerged with a fistful of multicolored candies. "Take our business to Kansas City, maybe someplace in Oklahoma. Y'all ever think 'bout Tulsa?"

There was a low buzz of conversation before Walter's calmer voice objected. "St. Louis is a gold mine, brothah. Don't tell me you're scared now. What are you afraid of?"

"I seen him the other day, Wally. I seen Elvin Suggs pokin' 'round your car in the rain. The man's a dick, for Chrissake! He busted the Pone gang in Memphis 'bout six months ago. It was him, Wally. I know it was Suggs."

"Why he wanna mess with my car, brothah?"

"Don't rightly know. But it was him alright, checking out all her stuff in the backseat." Arnold pointed an accusatory finger at Cherie.

"Elvin? You saw Elvin?" piped a childish voice. Young sounding, at least, it might have belonged to a very young female.

"It's nothin', sugah doll, nothin' at all."

"It was him, Wally, shore 'nuf. Kept me waiting in that rain just so I could get in my own damn car without him seeing me. Stupid. Jus' plain stupid."

"Maybe he live here," said Redman.

"Now, Redman, why would Elvin Suggs be living here? It couldn't have been him. He got no reason to be up here in St. Louis," said Walter.

"'Less he be following you," said Redman. "'Cause that's what it look like to me."

"That's it, Wally. He's following us."

Walter chuckled in amusement. "Now, why would he do that, brothah?"

"'Cause we got his wife with us, that's why. I knew it. I just knew it."

There was a pause in the conversation. Valerie stubbed out her cigarette in her souvenir ashtray from the Sunset Hotel. Within seconds, a woman began to scream. "Walter, stop him! You wild pig! What are you doing to me? My husband will get you for this. Elvin can find anybody."

There was a popping sound that reminded Valerie of a cork being pulled out of a champagne bottle, and the woman's shrieks ceased. The door to B slammed shut and the voices faded. Valerie poured herself more tomato juice, this time adding a generous shot of vodka. She settled back into the propped up pillows on her waterbed, and lit another cigarette, and considered the ways in which she might spend her day. She had heard of an audition in the afternoon, but it was for a musical. She sighed. Musicals just weren't her style. She'd almost rather do a dog food commercial.

Startled, she jolted forward, spilling tomato juice on her black satin robe. There were the voices again, out in the hall, passing by her door.

"I told you that gal was dead weight, Wally."

"Not now, brothah."

"Hope you two know what you doin'. I think we shoulda carried the body out."

"If Suggs is around, it's better if he finds her himself. Let her deliver the message in person."

"You said it, Wally," the other man guffawed. "I know he's around."

The front door banged and Valerie rushed to the front window. The living room was dim, but she didn't dare switch on a light. Peering through the wide slats of the blinds, she saw three men: one old, one fat, and one that was both thin and young. The fat man tossed what appeared to Valerie to be a large plastic trash bag into the trunk of the car. It was bulging at the seams, and ripped at the end. Something orange and gold protruded from the gaping hole. Then, all three piled into the car, that squealed away from the gritty curb, while the sloppy driver munched on a Twinkie.

Valerie didn't know any of them, but she knew one thing for certain: she had heard a woman scream in the apartment next to hers, and those men left without her. Suddenly, the popping sound registered in her mind. The building was deathly still as Valerie stood alone in her living room, clad only in her black robe, her lips trembling. She wasn't the type to get involved in other people's problems; she usually had too many of her own to care. Yet, something in the woman's voice haunted her. She herself had been with frightening men, but she had always known how to handle them. Someday, her own luck might run out.

She dialed 911, but when it rang the first time, she hung up. She bit her lip and glanced toward her bedroom. She didn't even know the woman. Besides, those guys sounded dangerous. Hell, they'd shown her as much.

She couldn't stop herself. Without hesitation, she redialed. "Operator," she blurted out, "send an ambulance to the Jewel Arms, Apartment B. No, not A. I said B. It's an emergency."

It was almost 8:00 that morning when Reggie pulled his car up to curb in front of Valentino's apartment building. As he strolled along the sidewalk in the dewy morning air, the sight of Valentino's car caused him to stop and stare in horror. The vehicle had been carelessly parked at an angle, its right headlight hanging by a mass of wires. The left taillight had been smashed and a major dent marred the rear bumper. Reggie could only hope he had the wrong car.

He stepped up his pace, jogging to the front door, and, after a quick check of the mailboxes, took the steps two at a time up to Apartment 2C, the last one on the end. The dim hallway was as quiet as a church. He punched the buzzer and waited.

The brick building was so solid that he couldn't even hear the rumble of rush hour traffic on Hampton Avenue as commuters fought their way to work. A couple of minutes passed, and still no one answered, despite Reggie's repeated knocks.

He had to be in there, thought Reggie. His car was outside, but, if he was in the same shape as that car…

Reggie pulled out his cell phone and punched Valentino's number. It rang five times before the detective's slurred voice came on the line. He sounded as if his mouth was full of marbles. "Whadya want?"

Reggie frowned. "Valentino? That you in there?"

There was a pause while Valentino seemed to consider the answer to the question.

"Valentino?"

"Yeah?"

"Are you alright in there?"

"Who's there?"

"It's Combs. I'm out here in the hall."

"Hi, Reggie." Valentino giggled like a schoolboy.

Reggie felt like crying. This was the day he prayed would never come; Valentino was drinking again. Time for a new approach. "Rick, open up. I'm outside your door."

"What you doing out there, Reggie?"

Reggie checked on either side of him, hoping no one could hear; or worse, hear him saying these stupid things to a hung-over detective.

"Rick, walk over to the door and let me in."

Reggie heard the rustling of sheets and crossed his fingers. Any minute now, he thought. That is, until heard the crash of shattering glass.

Instinctively, he covered his face. That's it, he decided. "Man's too damn drunk to help himself," he mumbled as he reached for his Swiss army knife. It took him all of a minute to pick the lock. That was the easy part. It was when he had to force himself to cross the threshold and confront the disastrous mess that seared his soul as if it were flesh. He wished he hadn't come. He wished he didn't care about Rick Valentino.

Splats of half-wet blood formed a trail to the rear of the apartment like some kind of inkblot test. Reggie dodged the overturned coffee table and straight back chair that lay on the living room floor. Bills and papers were strewn about like a ticker tape parade had passed. As he poked his head into the narrow galley kitchen, he glimpsed the thing that triggered his inner alarm.

A bloodied carving knife lay resting in the stainless steel bowl of the kitchen sink. Pink droplets of diluted blood stained the white porcelain counter beside it, trailing to the gray linoleum floor. Reggie squeezed his eyes shut, hoping to open them to find the blameless kitchenette of a colleague. He was afraid to proceed into the bedroom. What did the knife mean? He pulled his pistol from its holster, his natural guard aroused. Was Valentino dead—or alive?

Outside, an ambulance wailed. In the apartment next door, a baby cried. As he crept out of the kitchen and into the bedroom, a ticking clock measured his steps. The whole place smelled like beer. His cell phone rang. He ignored it, his mind focused on the job.

"Rick?" Reggie slowly made his way down a short, narrow hall. There was no reply. He stood next to a cramped, closet-like bathroom. He flipped on the light above the mirror. It didn't appear to have been touched. Reggie glanced in the chipped mirror of the medicine cabinet. Valentino's face smiled back at him. Reggie's hand tightened its grip on the Beretta.

"Hey, Reg," he said, his eyelids drooping. Barefoot, clad in a bloodstained undershirt and boxer shorts, he was undeniably hung over. His head leaned to one side, his hair matted and disheveled. "Want a beer?"

Reggie studied his friend's face, plotting his strategy. On one hand, Valentino was going to be tough to deal with, but on the other, he would be easier to manipulate.

"Got any coffee?" Reggie watched for his reaction. His cell phone rang again. He ignored it.

Valentino frowned, grabbing his head as he winced. "I don't know what I've got. How'd I get back here?"

Reggie relaxed—a little. "Want to go in the kitchen with me, Rick?"

Valentino gawked at the broken chair in his living room. "What happened in there?" Suddenly, his noticed his bloodied attire. Speechless for a moment, he exclaimed, "I'm covered in blood!"

"Yeah," Reggie muttered. He paused, his hand still on the revolver. "Want to tell me about it?"

The detective's lined face bunched into a mass of wrinkles, and he rubbed furiously at the bloodstains on his arms with the frayed edge of his undershirt. "Get 'em off, Reg!" he yelled. "Get 'em off!"

Reggie remained on guard. He didn't want to startle Valentino. He was already unstable enough, all by himself. "Rick," he said gently, as he hooked his fingers around the detective's elbow, "let's get you some clothes, my man."

"I got to get out of here." Valentino's voice cracked with hysteria. "I need some sleep. I need some food."

"You need clothes," repeated Reggie. "Now you stay right here." He patted his arm. "I'll go back and get you a few things to wear. Stay right there, man." As Reggie made his way back to the darkened bedroom, he checked the doors, the walls, the carpets—for signs of a break-in, signs of a scuffle. Past the living room and kitchen, there was nothing.

The bedroom was located at the end of the hall. It was a plain, dingy affair—the bed covered with plain white sheets that looked and smelled like they'd been around for months. Valentino's clothes were dropped in a heap next to the bed. A couple of empty beer cans cluttered the nightstand. On the edge, was a half-full ashtray positioned next to the telephone. The television in the corner was still going, playing a commercial for an antacid. Reggie mumbled as he scanned the musty closet for some slacks.

"Yeah, I could use something for stomach acid right about now," he muttered, as he grabbed a pair of khaki pants and a black knit shirt. His cell phone rang once again. This time, he answered it. "Combs."

"Reggie," said Pearl, "when you comin' back? I'm running out of answers for these people around here."

"I can't talk now," he whispered. "I'll be back in a about half an hour. What's the problem?"

"You're not gonna like this one."

Reggie shook his head. "It doesn't matter right now. It just doesn't matter."

"There's been another murder over at the Jewel Arms."

"What?" Reggie studied the clothes in his hand as he digested the news. "The damn sky's falling! Okay, I'm on my way over there now. Send back-up."

He clicked off the power and rushed to clothe his dubious assistant. Were it not for the bloody knife, he would have left Valentino right where he was; but this whole thing was getting too weird. He wasn't sure what he'd do with him when he got to the Jewel Arms, but he wasn't leaving him alone.

As he helped the fallen detective into his clothes and led him down to his car, he decided that in the future, Valentino wouldn't be working alone. In fact, he might not be working.

Nineteen

At 7:30 that morning, Annie Silver woke to call her supervisor. Mrs. Gatz advised her she had two sick days remaining—no more, no less. Annie recalled the stern tone in her voice and winced.

When Annie Silver opened her eyes again, it was 11:00 a.m.

She rolled over and tried to sit; she moved, and her head split from the sharp pressure over her eyes. Even the dim light that filtered through the Venetian blinds made Annie wince in agony. That supervisor didn't understand. If this wasn't an illness, it would do until one came along.

Without warning, bile rose in her throat. Her face grew clammy, and her eyes strained in their sockets. Sweat bubbled from her pores. She stumbled to the bathroom, hand clamped firmly over her mouth. She barely made it before she retched weakly over the toilet bowl. For once, she was glad Ben neglected to put the seat down.

Clad in the soiled T-shirt, she collapsed on the cold tile of the cramped bathroom. Annie couldn't make herself stand. She simply didn't care if she lived or not. She'd been drinking too much—Ben mocked her regularly for it—but it had become the only thing she looked forward to all day, everyday. *Take that away, and it's over.* The thought of not being able to get drunk frightened her in a way she didn't understand.

There was one thing she *did* understand very well, she no longer controlled her life. She no longer made choices for herself.

Ben listened to her phone conversations, opened her mail, scheduled her free time, ordered her food in restaurants. If he called the apartment and she was out, he demanded an explanation. She couldn't remember how happiness felt. The only thing that killed the pain was a pint of bourbon, a bottle of wine, a six of beer—or something else. It didn't matter what, so long as the dreary stretches of time passed, the minutes of her life ticking away in days and nights, weeks and months. Lately, she couldn't decide what was worse: being alone, or being with her husband.

Mired in despair, Annie didn't register the persistent knock at the door until it became quite loud. Startled, she rose from the floor, steadying herself on the old porcelain sink. She caught her reflection in the chipped mirror: face flushed and mottled, the whites of her eyes now pink, her nose swollen and red. She was in no shape to answer the door, and yet, she was curious. Curious and lonely.

She threw a bulky sweater over her thin body, and tiptoed barefoot to the door. "Who is it?" she asked, somewhat hoarsely.

"Elvin Suggs, ma'am, from next door. I believe I got some of y'all's mail yesterday by mistake."

Annie cracked the door just a bit, and Elvin handed her an envelope and a few catalogs. The sight of her ashen face alarmed him. "You okay there, Mrs. Silver?"

"I-I'm fine," she stuttered, avoiding his gaze. Elvin lingered for a moment, expecting her to continue. When she didn't, he added, "Well, I'll be next door for awhile if you need anything. Just give me a holler."

"Mr. Suggs?" Annie opened the door a little more.

"Ma'am?"

"To tell you the truth, I-I'm not feeling well at all. I'm a little dizzy." Annie suddenly felt self-conscious as she sensed Elvin's surprise at the sight of her stained T-shirt.

"What can I do for you, hon?" Elvin hooked his thumbs in the pockets of his jeans.

"I stayed home sick from work today. Would you sit and visit with me for a little while? I mean, if you aren't too busy."

"I don't know how that would look, even though I'd like to help you. I mean, you're not even dressed, really."

"Look, I'll go throw some jeans on, if you'll just sit with me for awhile." Annie didn't understand it, but her spirits lifted at the thought of a visitor she hardly knew—anyone that could distract her from her personal reality.

Elvin inspected the empty hall. It was eerily still. A roach crept across the baseboard, disappearing into a crevice. He decided he could use a lift himself right now. "Okay, I'll come in, but, just for a little while. I promised Vanna a walk and a cheeseburger. She really looks forward to getting out, you know."

"You married, Mr. Suggs?" Annie emerged from the back bedroom. Her voice sounded almost childlike—almost.

At the painful reference to marriage, Elvin dodged the question. He simply couldn't discuss it. "Vanna's my dog," he said, venturing into the small living room.

"That's right, now I remember. Ben and I found that out the first time we met you, didn't we?"

Elvin focused on the pictures on the wall above the sagging couch. A portrait of the Silver's wedding caught his attention. "You two really look happy in this one." He pointed to the picture, edged in a gold gilt frame. Obviously, it had been a source of great pride to Annie, at least at one time.

She pursed her lips and turned away from her guest. A tear dripped down her ruddy cheek. She said nothing, but her silence spoke volumes.

"Did I say something wrong, hon?" Elvin faced her, puzzled at the distraught blonde amid the helter skelter mess. From the corner of his eye, he glimpsed the telltale signs of another lonely night: an empty wine bottle and solitary goblet positioned next to three empty beer cans. A rumpled pillow remained at one end of the sofa.

Shifting from foot to foot, she appeared clumsy and embarrassed while she struggled to compose herself. Her face looked deathly pale. She clutched the sweater around her slumped body, and sniffled back her tears. "You never said if you were married or not, Mr. Suggs."

"Call me Elvin, will you?" he said, chuckling. "You're making me feel old, calling me Mr. Suggs like that." Then, he grew serious. "Listen, no offense, but I don't want to discuss my private life right now."

"Annie."

"What?"

"My first name's Annie. I didn't mean to pry. It's just that I don't think a single guy could really understand how I'm feeling right now. I'm not even sure I understand how I feel."

Elvin said nothing. The only sound in the apartment was the hum of the old refrigerator in the kitchenette. When he didn't reply, she rambled on, despite her original hesitation. "I mean, how could a guy like you understand what it's like to be taken for granted? I go to work, I come home and work some more, and I don't have much to show for it, do I? Ben doesn't even know I exist, except when he wants somebody to do the dirty work—or kick around." Annie trembled, even as she wrung her long, thin fingers into a ball of knots.

"Why do you stay?" asked Elvin, almost in a whisper.

Annie took a deep breath and her jaw stiffened as she declared, "I believe in keeping my promises."

"But you're so unhappy."

"I made the wrong decision. Maybe I deserve to be unhappy."

"Don't say that. Everybody deserves to be happy. Everybody makes a little flub now and then."

Annie shook her head. "See? Sorry, but you just don't get it. I'm stuck."

"So, what are you going to do with the rest of your life? You're a young gal." When Annie didn't answer, Elvin said, "You know what I think? I think there's something you're not telling me." He held up his hand to silence her objections. "That's alright, just keep it to yourself. But, I understand more than you think I do." He turned to open the door. "I'd best be going now."

"Elvin?"

"Ma'am?" Elvin's hand was still on the doorknob.

"He'd kill me if I left."

"Did he tell you that?"

"No. But, I know that he would. H-he killed my cat, you know."

"What?"

"Look, I've said too much already. I just didn't want you to think I didn't have a good reason for staying here."

Elvin folded his arms across his thick chest and said, "Fear isn't a good reason for staying with anyone, Annie. If you ask me, that's a good reason for leaving."

Annie shook her head. "You just don't understand. It's not that simple."

Without a word, Elvin opened the door and slipped into the hall, just as Dent stepped out to grab his newspaper.

"Hey there, Elvin! Been a busy morning around here, hasn't it?"

Elvin didn't respond, fearing Dent misinterpreted his presence in the Silver's apartment.

"Well, it sure has been noisy down there. Want to join me for some coffee?"

"Not today, Dent." Elvin inserted his key into his apartment door.

He latched Vanna's collar onto the leash, and wondered if he should have divulged more of his personal life to Annie. Maybe if he had told her about Cherie—how he had been taken for granted, how much he still loved her, and yes, all the broken promises in his own life—maybe he could have helped her. As he headed down the hall, he could only think about her last remark to him—that he didn't understand, that it wasn't that simple.

Suddenly, Vanna jumped forward, attempting to leap down the steps to the first floor.

"Whoa, lady, too fast," he corrected, jerking the leash. But the dog persisted in the tug of war. As they reached the first floor, however, Elvin spotted the reason for Vanna's response. The door to Apartment B stood wide open; uniformed police officers buzzed about like bees to honey.

"Back." Elvin coaxed the dog away from the scene. But as he waited for the hubbub to subside, his impatience grew, and he edged toward the doorway of the open apartment, all the while, holding Vanna close to his side. Craning his neck he pushed closer to the commotion, until he could overhear the muffled comments.

"Looks like they got her at close range."

"Must have been fast."

"Get these people out of here."

"Can you find any ID on the body?"

"Look for a purse somewhere, will ya?"

"Sir," a policeman approached Elvin, "you'll have to get that dog out of here." Vanna's whimpering and whining grew more intense by the second.

"Who was it?"

"You live here?"

"Upstairs."

The cop took a deep breath. "Ever seen a woman with blonde hair around here?"

Elvin nodded. "A blonde lives in A. Right there."

The cop looked hopeful. "Think you could take a quick look and tell us if this is her?"

"Sure."

"I'll hold your dog."

"No sir, she'll be fine." Elvin inched his way into the barren apartment. Nothing could have prepared him. Facing Cherie's corpse, Elvin's senses toppled like a smoldering skyscraper. His pulse stopped beating—or so it seemed to him—because he couldn't believe his eyes. Paralyzed by shock, breathless and heartbroken, retaliation was a distant daydream. For a guy who wished he could die, that dream made perfect sense.

"Sir, just tell us if you know the lady or not, and we'll take care of the rest."

When Elvin finally spoke, he felt as if he were floating up from the depths of the ocean, sputtering and gasping for air. "You don't understand, sir," he blurted. "It's not that simple."

Twenty

Reggie struggled to guide Valentino to his car, all the while suppressing his disgust at his comrade's condition. Dressed in wrinkled khakis and black polo shirt, wearing a pair of loafers with no socks, the detective looked nothing if not disoriented. His slicked back hair accentuated the gray circles beneath his eyes.

"Need a beer," he sighed. "Mouth as dry as cotton."

Reggie eased him into the passenger seat and slammed the door. "No time for that," he snapped. Fuming, he slid behind the wheel and gunned the engine. In a flash, the car screeched down the car-lined street.

It was going to be another one of those St. Louis nights.

Two floors above Valentino's apartment, at the same end of the building, Redman peered through his Steiner binoculars, following the car until it was out of sight. Alone in his own apartment, he slumped into an overstuffed armchair and took a deep breath, reflecting that it might be a good time to lie low for awhile. He was always careful—in his line of work he had to be—but last night had been different from the rest. He might have crossed a one-way line this time. Just the thought of it raised goosebumps on his lanky arm. As the memory of it surfaced in his brain, he suddenly felt very tired.

It hadn't been his idea. It was that goddamn Arnold Hubble. Redman sat in the dark living room with the lights off and the drapes pulled tight. What the hell was he going to do now?

No use complaining to Walter 'bout his fatass brother. He'd already tried that. Those two were thick as peanut butter. When Arnold tells Wally, leave that woman behind, Walter don't do it that easy. Naw. He do better than that. He bring her 'long an let Arno plug her.

Shit. He cursed the day he ever decided to do business with those two fools, and kneaded the back of his neck with both hands. The tension in his muscles made his head throb, thank you, Arnold. The fact was, he didn't care 'bout Cherry, Sherry, whatever the hell her name was. Just a sideshow bitch who talk too much anyway. Naw, what happened before Arno killed her nagged at his conscience like a bad toothache.

The worst part: he couldn't remember why they decided to go over to the Jewel Arms that morning. They made their drop, and stopped at Hardee's for some breakfast biscuits—those Southern boys got to have their biscuits in the mornin'—and before Redman knew what was goin' on, they were headed over to the Jewel Arms.

Redman fumbled on the coffee table for a beer. Damn. Bottle was empty. Gonna be one long damn night, 'cause he couldn't get that bitch outta his mind. A soft rain pattered on the roof and Redman felt a wet stain on his cheek. Aw, c'mon, dawg. He swiped the tear from his face and stared into the darkness. He hadn't cried since he was five years old. C'mon. Now, this crap. Now this…

"Where we goin', Arnold?" asked Redman. Arnold had just kept driving, staring straight ahead.

"Just going to check on my property," replied Walter. "We in no big hurry, are we, Redman?"

"Walter, I want to go shopping," whined Cherie, crossing her short but shapely legs. Redman recalled the pungent scent of her perfume had made him nauseous.

"Plenty a time for that later, sugah doll," said Walter as they slid up to the curb in front of the building. "Now, hush yo'self."

Redman saw Cherie staring across the backseat at him, confusion written all over her face. He had merely shrugged in response. At that moment, he knew no more than she did. He hadn't thought too much about the lady with the funny-looking eye either, as she passed them in the hall on her way into the building, dressed in her Sunday best. Nothing except she looked out of place in those fine clothes. It wasn't till she stopped before opening the door to her apartment, and turned to look at him, that he realized he knew her; and that she recognized him too.

"Dion! That you, Dion? Don't you know an old friend when you see one?" she exclaimed, and approached the foursome.

He recalled the way Arnold had nudged Walter. Walter gripped Cherie's fragile elbow in a way that she could not resist his strength; if he could have, Redman thought Walter might have plastered her mouth with duct tape.

"Naw, lady, you got the wrong guy," said Redman, even as the memory of Tasha and Antoine flashed through his mind. He hadn't seen her brother for years—they'd taken different paths—but he was the kind of friend you didn't forget.

Arnold simply glared at her as he inserted the key into the door of Apartment B, and the group huddled inside. Even after Arnold popped Cherie, Redman was feeling pretty together; a little shaken up, but he was cool with that. That 'ho was baggage, man, and gettin' too heavy. He didn't know this Elvis dude, but anyone the Hubble dawgs thought was bad—well, he just had to be the baddest ass in the city. Don't need that shit.

Redman shifted in the worn chair, upholstered in an orange and gold tweedy type fabric, somebody's cast-off he found in the alley behind his apartment. He struggled to erase the memory from his mind. A crackling noise made him pause to listen, but he decided it didn't matter. Maybe he just nervous, yeah. Damn, he couldn't let down.

He remembered feeling surprised that Cherie took the hit, yeah, but he could deal with that. He could even deal with leaving her body in that apartment. She was nothin'—to him. It was when they all walked out and into the vacant hall, when the two brothers looked at him in that determined way they had sometimes, that he sensed the pressure. Yeah, the heat was on.

"Listen up, Redman," Arnold said, leaning so close into his face that Redman smelled his sour breath, "you're gonna get us into that place." Arnold pointed to Apartment C when he spoke.

"What for?" asked Redman. "Let's get the fuck outta here."

"Unfinished business, my friend," Walter said. "Your lady friend in there knows you. And, she saw us."

"So?" Redman glanced wildly from one scheming brother to the other.

"So, we don't leave a trail," said Walter. "It's getting late. I want to leave as soon as possible, too, my friend."

"So," said Arnold, "who's it gonna be, Mr. Dion? Your lady friend—or you?"

Redman became speechless. His throat constricted. Redman, a cornered rabbit, a little cog in the big wheel, one more man to share the profits with: or one less, depending on how you looked at things. He had no choice. He stepped up to the scratched door of Apartment C and knocked. When Tasha opened the door, he would signal her—warn her in some way. He'd fix it, somehow, yeah.

But, she didn't answer. Damn, he thought, shifting from foot to foot.

"Step on it, Redman," Arnold threatened.

Redman leaned on the doorbell, the sound penetrating like a buzz saw. He heard the approaching footsteps, and the biscuits ballooned in his stomach.

"Who's there?" said Tasha.

"It's me. Redman."

Immediately, the door opened, and Tasha beamed a wide smile at her childhood friend. She reached out to embrace him and Arnold lunged at her with a knife, plunging it into her belly. Walter stood watch out in the hallway.

Redman would never forget the expression on her careworn

face as her body sagged, gasped for air, and finally slumped to the floor in a heap. She died with the knowledge that her trusted friend betrayed her. He would never get the chance to apologize.

He could not believe what Walter did after that. The soft-spoken gentleman strode over to the oversize kitchen trashcan and yanked the black plastic liner from its slimy interior. Together, the brothers wrapped Tasha's body in a faded afghan they robbed from the living room sofa, and stuffed the whole bleeding mess into the large trash bag, which now bulged conspicuously at the seams. They had not bothered to remove the knife.

"Move, Redman, move," hissed Arnold, as he hauled Tasha's body. "Give me a hand here!"

Redman felt sick and numb. Yet, somehow he managed to go through the motions. Walter ran ahead to open the trunk of the Cadillac. Around 11:00 a.m., they stalled at a stoplight, waiting amid the brisk Hampton Avenue traffic. Slumped in the backseat, with Tasha's corpse stashed behind him, he was certain the people in the surrounding cars knew everything. Yet, as he looked skittishly around, a young woman singing to the radio, a man lighting a cigarette, a young mother scolding two squabbling toddlers, Redman decided they didn't know they were within an arm's length of three murderers. He hadn't realized that himself, until about an hour ago. Dealing dope, sure, yeah. No big deal, but killing your friends...

The light changed, and Arnold pointed the Cadillac down an alley, passing a sign that read "One Way." A tear dripped from the corner of his eye, and he immediately smeared it away with the back of his hand. There was no going back now. He would never be the same.

"Where we headed, Arnold?" asked Redman in an expressionless tone.

Arnold glared at Walter, who nodded in the affirmative before answering, "We know where we going."

"But, this is my building!" exclaimed Redman. "For what you bringin' Tasha here?"

Arnold laughed, his flabby belly shaking behind the steering wheel. "Ain't just your buildin', fool. Other people live there too. You got neighbors, you know."

"Don't know any neighbors, man."

Walter turned around and faced him. "Ever heard of a guy named Detective Rick Valentino?" he asked, emphasizing every syllable of detective.

"Naw." Redman stared out of the window, a blank look on his face.

"Don't matter." Walter turned back around in his seat. "We gone go up to your place for awhile, anyway."

"What?"

"Got some friends coming by, do a little business," said Walter.

"At my house?"

Arnold cut the engine and turned around. The Cadillac was parked in back of the building in the rear of the alley. "You got a problem with that, Redman? Cain't have 'em delivering candy over to the Jewel right now, can we? Not with Cherie holdin' court in there." He laughed as he opened the ponderous door.

Redman became hysterical. He leaned forward and whispered, his muffled voice filled with panic. "What we gonna do with Tasha, man? Can't leave her here while we go upstairs."

"Why not?" asked Walter as he stepped out of the passenger seat. "She ain't goin' nowhere." He smiled at the young man. Clearly, he was toying with him, like a cat with a ball of yarn. "Come on, Red," he said, taking him by the elbow and guiding him along the sidewalk to the front door of his building, shorely you been in on other killin's before this. I'm sorry it had to end up that way, but you know we didn't get in this to get famous. Just rich. We been treating you right, now, ain't we?"

Redman nodded.

"Then forget about it."

"Yeah," repeated Redman as he pushed the front door open. Inside, there was a damp smell in the air, of mold and wet plaster. As he started up the stairs, Walter stopped him at the second floor, gripping his wiry upper arm.

"What?" exclaimed Redman. He was getting real tired of the boss about now.

"Lookie there, Apartment 2A." Walter pointed to a dark, thick, metal door on the end.

Redman held in his temper. "So?"

"That's where the detective lives, my man."

"So?"

Walter chuckled, his wicked laugh laced with evil. "We'll do our business first. Come on."

Walter motioned Arnold upstairs. He shoved the car keys in his pocket and jogged up the three flights of stairs to Redman's apartment. By the time the flabby man reached the landing, he was out of breath and dripping with sweat. Redman glared at him in disgust as he inserted his key into the rusty lock.

"What's your problem now?" Arnold mopped his wide forehead with a used handkerchief.

Redman shook his head, but remained silent. All the money in the world could never turn Arnold into a human being.

They had just finished take-out Chinese food when Walter checked his gold Rolex watch.

"Time to get up, boys." He cleared the bags and containers away.

"Hey, I was eatin' that fried rice, Wally." Arnold reached for the little white box with his chopsticks.

"It's almost 7:00, brothah. Time to go to work. We'll eat again later."

"Don't matter." Arnold, crumbled his paper napkin into a ball. He hobbled to his feet, and bits of sticky rice and fried egg roll tumbled to the linoleum floor. "Still got a box of Twinkies in the car."

At the mention of the Cadillac, Redman's mood torpedoed. "Walter, we got to move Tasha. It ain't right."

"You ain't gettin' soft on me boy, are ya?"

Redman's back stiffened. He spit his reply. "I ain't nobody's boy. I am an equal partner in this…business—whatever you want to call it—or I ain't nothin.'"

Arnold spat, "Cain't have no bleeding hearts workin' with us, Redman. We got a job to do, and we do it. Charge what the market will bear. Supply and demand, and all that shit."

Walter remained steady, his voice stern, but gentle. "We'll move the body, of course we will. But, we got to wait till it's dark. Cain't nobody see us. We done killed enough for today."

"Where we gone put her?" Redman was utterly confused. "She gonna start smelling like dead fish 'fore long."

Before Walter could answer, a short knock sounded on the hollow metal door. "Answer it." Walter clenched the butt of his pistol.

"Who's there?" Redman demanded, standing at the door-frame. Arnold shoved him out of the way.

"Wally said open the goddamn door." He yanked the tinny door aside, his hand on the dull brass knob. Redman had barely turned it before two people rushed inside. Instantly, the air turned hostile.

Though they were brothers, the two men were physical opposites—one short, pudgy man accompanied by a tall, skinny one. Their smooth skin reminded Red of a maple caramel. Tonight, they wore hockey jerseys bearing the name of the St. Louis Blues, though neither had ever attended a hockey game—ever. They each looked about fifteen years old, though the hardness in their expressions belied their age. The tall one had a large diamond stud in his left ear lobe.

"Hey, Loco," said Redman to the taller man.

"I got the word to meet you at your place. Who are they?" His finger jabbed the air, aimed at the Hubbles.

"Which one the boss?" asked the other man, called Popeye. As he turned to face the brothers, Redman noticed that Arnold seemed to be startled by Popeye's distinctive deformity: his right eye was stitched shut, lost in a shoot out. Redman began to feel like a referee.

"Man with the white hair," said Redman, almost in a whisper. "Get anybody a beer?" he asked, straining to ease the tension in the room.

"Shore," Arnold replied.

Loco and Popeye merely glared at him.

"Later," said Walter. "Got to keep a clean head right now. Same for brothah." Arnold hung his head at the admonition.

"Did you talk to him 'bout what we said the other night?" asked Loco, pointing to Walter.

Walter's hand twitched on the butt of his pistol. "What's all this about, Redman?"

"They want to negotiate a bigger cut. Feel like they doin' all the hustlin' out there."

Walter laughed, throwing his head back to savor a good, long laugh. Then, his face turned to stone. "You feel like that too, Redman? You think you doing all the work, do you?"

Redman shrugged. "It ain't easy out there. These people—these junkies—they do anything for their dope, you know that."

Arnold stood and positioned himself in the corner of the living room; Redman understood the strategy. Now, he was in a place where he could cover the threesome, and he stood directly behind Walter.

"Y'all lucky we mess with you at all." Walter pulled out his briefcase, and retrieved a thick envelope plastered with shipping labels, postmarked Los Angeles. "Brothah and me—you know, we could make a lot more money lots of othah places. This here, St. Louis—it's peanuts to us. Only reason we conduct any business here at all is the fine people we are privileged to associate with here." He gripped the envelope, holding it up for their inspection. "Y'all want a job this evening, gentlemen—or not? 'Cause if you don't, brothah and me be moving on." The static air crackled with electricity; the group considered the ultimatum.

Popeye shifted his weight, his feet clad in high top tennis shoes. Loco's deadpan face concealed his resentment. Again, Redman attempted to negotiate. He reached for the envelope, but Walter hugged it to his chest. "Not so fast, partner." His deliberate use of the word 'partner' seemed to please Redman. "This here candy comes C.O.D." He chuckled, joined by Arnold in the background. "Me and brothah short about $25,000 right about now."

Loco's head jerked at the mention of money. "Redman say 24 thou."

"A grand for our trouble, friend."

Loco nudged Redman. "What is this shit? I got to eat, too."

"Give it to the man, Loco," muttered Redman. "Jes' pass it along to the customer."

Loco hesitated. "C'mon now, we wasting time."

Popeye pulled out a bulging envelope from his pocket, and Loco counted out the additional thousand from his impressive personal stash.

Walter grinned. "I knew my partners would understand the cost of doing business. I'll take the cash right here." He tapped the scratched surface of the coffee table.

"Want me to count it, Wally?" asked Arnold.

"No brothah, only person count cash 'round here is me," said Walter as the envelopes changed hands. He nodded to Loco and Popeye. "Y'all have a good evening, hear?"

Loco merely grunted in response, leaving as quickly as he had arrived. Popeye raised his hand in farewell and followed him out. Redman locked the door behind them. Walter handed Redman a wad of cash.

"I think you'll find this to be satisfactory."

"Thanks." Redman accepted the money, before adding, "I got to tell you, Loco and Popeye's getting tired of the streets. They be wantin' to move up in the business."

"They ain't room for anymore at the top," said Arnold. "Right Wally?"

"Yeah, well, I tell them that, but you know…"

Walter had no interest in discussing promotions. He stood up, contented with the status quo. "It's dark enough now, I believe, brothah. Time to move the body."

Twenty-One

Rose stood alone at the kitchen counter in Apartment G, chopping half-frozen chicken breasts into strips with her new knife. The meat was firm and icy, and the blade slid easily through the flesh. She worked quickly, unsure of how much free time she could enjoy, her thick fingers growing numb. Belle had been tough today. Finally, she had fallen asleep.

Rose contemplated the possibilities that awaited her now that Mattie was gone, and about quitting this dead end job. Belle needed her, true enough, but it was only a job, and she hadn't promised Mattie she would stay forever. Belle could watch her wrestling in a nursing home just the same as she could here. Still, Matt had been generous.

She hadn't thought about Mattie for a couple of months now. It seemed that the interest in his murder had faded. Her thoughts were interrupted by a ruckus in the hall, a pounding sound followed by the echo of an angry voice. It was that doctor again, she thought, setting the knife in the sink. She wiped her plump hands on her sweatshirt and moved nearer to the door to eavesdrop. Again, the pounding persisted.

"Goddamn it, woman! Open the flipping door!"

Silence answered his request.

"Fine. Just fine." A tense undercurrent strained his voice.

Again, no reply.

"I'm going now."

Silence.

A doorknob rattled so hard she thought it would pop out of the door.

"You're going to pay for this, Annie. I'm coming back!"

The building seemed to vibrate; the front door slammed. Rose glanced through the misty window. The cloak of twilight had settled on the shoulders of night. Ben Silver roared off in anger to the screech of tires.

"Rose!" whined Belle from the back bedroom. Rose felt irritated at the intrusion, though she couldn't say why. "Yeah, yeah, keep your shirt on," she huffed, starting back to the stuffy room.

She had barely turned on her heel when the buzz of the doorbell stopped her. If she hadn't just heard Ben Silver leave, she wouldn't have answered it. Hell, she wasn't afraid of anybody. She pulled the door open, and faced a frantic Annie Silver, dressed in a rumpled white T-shirt and orange jogging shorts. Drops of blood trickled from her forehead onto the shoulder of the shirt. Her legs were visibly shaking in her battered jogging shoes.

Rose frowned, and Annie began to babble. "I'm-I'm Annie Silver, from across the hall. Y-you don't know me."

"I've seen you around, sweetie. I've certainly heard enough of you and that husband of yours. He is your hubby, right?"

Annie studied her shoes. "Yes." She resumed her babbling. "I-I wonder if I could borrow a beer— or two?"

Rose laughed. "That sounds good to me about now, too."

"Rose!" cried Belle. "Rose, I need you."

Rose's shoulders slumped. She stepped aside, gesturing to Annie with a wave of her hand. "Come on in. I'd love some real company tonight."

"So would I," said Annie.

Rose glanced back at her as she turned to make her way to the back bedroom. "Sounds like you got rid of yours for awhile, sweetie."

"Rose!"

Rose sighed. "Have a seat. Beer's in the fridge. I'll be right back—I hope."

As she hustled back to help Belle, Rose considered the bloody gash on the side of Annie's face. Her anger swelled like a blaze of fire. She always figured that guy was the physical type when he got mad. Switching on the bedside lamp beside Rose's double bed, she was greeted by the sight of the shriveled old woman, tangled in a web of ammonia soaked stench. The flowered sheets clung to her bones, so wet they were almost transparent.

"I hope I've got another set of clean sheets, sweetie. We've gone through three today already."

Belle just smiled at her. "What's for dinner, Rose?" she asked.

Rose worked in her brisk manner, extricating Belle from the sticky mess, filling a basin with soapy water.

"What's the hurry, Rose?" asked Belle.

"We've got company," whispered Rose, as she gently sponged Belle's paper-thin skin.

Belle fluttered her eyelids in excitement. "Company, Rose?"

"Tell you what. Why don't I move you to the living room and you can visit with our guest, Annie. Let me get you a pain pill first," she added hastily.

At the mention of the painkiller, Belle stiffened in resistance. "I don't like those. They make me sleepy. I tell you all the time, I don't have any pain."

"Okay, okay," said Rose, grunting as she hoisted the old woman into her arms.

"At least go talk to her while I clean up."

Annie stood up as they entered the living room. Two empty cans of beer were already on the coffee table in front of her, another half-empty in her limp hand. "I should go," she said hesitantly, one eye on the door.

"No, no," said Rose. "We had a little accident, that's all. No reason to leave.

As she set Belle on the afghan-covered sofa, Belle cried out. "Oh, Rose, be careful! Remember my back!"

Rose shook her head. "I told you that you needed a pain pill before we came in here," she said, turning to retrieve one from the assortment of medications in the bedroom.

"No, no, Rose," Belle countered. "Those are too strong. I can't think when you make me take those."

Rose appealed to Annie. "Tell her for me, won't you? Tell her that people who are in pain don't need to think. First, they need to make the pain go away. Then, they can think."

But Annie didn't answer. The beer was kicking in, and Rose's words seemed to disturb her.

"Annie?" said Rose. "What's wrong, sweetie?"

Annie lifted a hand to her temple, fingering the dried blood from the gash. "I'm okay," she said. She bit her lip, and Rose thought she would cry any minute. Annie surprised her when she said, "You're right about making the pain go away, Rose." She paused, pushing some stray hairs away from her face. "But, when you're in pain, you need to think—think about why you're hurting, you know. Like-like, I blame myself for my own pain."

Rose remained silent struggling to digest Annie's viewpoint. Belle smiled at her, slowly tipping her head from side to side in agreement.

"If you're blaming yourself," Rose moved closer to Annie, "then you need to do what it takes to get rid of that pain." Her expression grew hard as she emphasized, "Whatever it takes, girlfriend." Glancing across the room at the kitchen counter, she noticed the chicken strips, still waiting on the cutting board, the knife resting in the slimy pink juice.

"Sit down, sweetie," she coaxed, smiling as she opened the refrigerator door. "How about another beer?"

The moment she saw Elvin's face, Di knew. She knew it the moment she opened the door, and the unflappable hunk fell into her arms, that Cherie was dead. There were two puzzles Di knew she might never solve: why Cherie called to talk to Elvin that morning, and the most baffling riddle of all, why Elvin still loved that bimbo. She had never understood the attraction, and now, she probably never would. Meanwhile, Vanna enjoyed her fill of the candy dish, her master in no condition to restrain her.

Still, Di asked the loaded question. "What's wrong, El?"

At first, he merely shook his head, his mouth sealed by the tears of a man who never allowed them, his shoulders trembling from the strain of self-control; and then, his grief erupted like a volcano that has been waiting to vent its force. "My wife's g-gone," he said, struggling to compose himself.

"She left awhile ago," replied Di.

He blinked, his mouth rigid as he spoke. "She's dead, Di."

A gap of time elapsed, Di didn't know exactly how much, but it seemed like an eternity, as she fumbled for the right words, the right sentiment to express. Here was the dearest friend she had, mourning the loss of someone she hated so much there had been a time she could have killed her herself.

Suddenly curious, she asked, "When did it happen?"

Elvin frowned. Clearly, that was not the reaction he anticipated. "Sometime today, I guess. Why does it matter? She's dead."

Again, his handsome face contorted into a mask of pain. Now she'd done it. She hated the way she always talked herself into a corner. Should she tell him about the phone call?

She decided Elvin was right. Cherie was dead. She barely recalled the conversation anyway. There was no reason not to tell him now. Whatever there had been between them was over—forever.

She scratched the top of her head, still hesitant to divulge the information. She knew Elvin watched, waiting for her to be a friend. This wasn't a time to play games. She steeled herself for his reaction as she told him Cherie had called that morning around 6:30 or so, looking for him.

"Where was she when she called?"

"Look, El, I've been sick with a migraine all day. I was when she called, and…"

"Did she leave a number? Why didn't you call me?"

Di took a deep breath. "That's just it, right there. She didn't leave a number because she didn't want you to call, wherever she was. I heard voices in the background, so I think someone was listening. She said she'd call back tonight around 11:00 or so. She thought she'd be alone then."

Elvin covered his face with his hands, as he sank into the sofa. "This is too much, man, too much." Suddenly, he burst into anger. "You knew she was in trouble, and you didn't tell me? I know you didn't like her, but that's no reason..."

"She didn't say she was in trouble! If she had, I would have looked for you right away. She didn't say what she wanted—only that she needed to talk to you. And she wasn't very nice about asking either, not that it matters now." In an instant, she wished she hadn't added that last comment. "Look, she must have been under a lot of pressure. I didn't know it at the time."

Elvin had just opened his mouth to speak, his index finger poised in mid-air, when the doorbell buzzed. Vanna charged to the door, knocking the rest of the M&Ms to the floor.

"No, Vanna, no!" Elvin said as the fuzzy dog burrowed its black nose among the multicolored discs. As he hustled to retrieve the chocolate candies, he called through the door, "Who's there?"

An unfamiliar voice replied, "Sergeant Combs, St. Louis Police. Like to ask a few questions, sir."

Still on his knees, Elvin turned to Di and whispered, "You know anybody named Combs?"

"No."

Again, the buzzer rang. Elvin grabbed Vanna and opened the door. "Valentine!" He resisted the urge to stare at the detective's rumpled appearance.

"You know these people, Rick?" Reggie asked. To Di it seemed the sergeant was amazed at the apparent rapport between the tenants and his companion.

"Sure, I know them," slurred Valentino. "How the hell are you guys, anyway? Say, Mrs. Redding, you wouldn't happen to have a beer around anywhere, would you?"

At that moment, Vanna stuck her large skull around the corner of the door to meet the visitors.

"Aaah!" screamed Reggie, as the Airedale growled and drooled on his shiny black shoes.

"Back, Vanna." Elvin grabbed the dog by its thick leather collar. He displayed a weak, embarrassed smile. "She really loves people."

"Some people," Reggie said. "Could I talk to you two for a few minutes? It's urgent."

Di didn't want Valentino in her apartment and she sensed Combs knew it. She didn't care what he thought of her; he was right. For once, she agreed with Vanna.

As the two men entered the apartment, Di said to Elvin, "Put Vanna in the back bedroom, and make sure you turn on the radio." As he disappeared into the hall, Di whispered to Reggie, "I know why you're here. The dead blonde was Elvin's wife. I just thought you should know." Then she turned to Valentino and said, "Just don't say anything stupid. He's upset enough."

"Did you say you wanted a beer, Valentine?" Elvin said as he entered the living room.

"He's working tonight." Reggie's hasty response was not lost on Di.

"How about some candy instead?" She offered the salvaged M&Ms to the detective.

"I'm flattered." Valentino helped himself to a fistful. He turned to Reggie. "She never offers anybody any of this candy, Reg." He chewed with his mouth open, the shells cracking between his teeth.

Reggie cleared his throat, attempting to ignore him. "Let's get down to it here. We've got lots of folks to talk to yet. First of all, let me offer my condolences to you, Mr..."

"Suggs. Elvin Suggs. That's—"

"S-U-G-G-S," spelled Valentino.

"Thanks, Rick," Reggie said. "We'll let Mr. Suggs talk for himself tonight." He settled back in the chair. "Perhaps you could elaborate on the nature of your recent relationship with the deceased; for the record, you understand."

"Just what are you gettin' at, Sergeant?" asked Elvin.

"El, calm down."

"I don't like the tone of his voice. I would have been there for my wife if I'd known she needed me." He pounded the end table with his fist. "Count on it."

Di turned to Reggie and Valentino. "Look, he's upset—"

"Upset? Upset? Why should I be upset just because my wife—by the way, we were not legally divorced yet—why should I be upset because my wife was murdered right under my nose? I can't think of a good reason, can you, Valentine?"

"I'm outta candy."

Di thought she had never seen such a pitiful excuse for a detective in her life. Elvin grabbed Valentino by the front of his shirt, yanking him to his feet. "Get this loser outta here," he said to Reggie.

Reggie stood. "I understand. This is not a good time for questions. You need privacy. We'll just come back later."

"No." Elvin poked his finger into Reggie's face. "You don't understand. I don't want privacy, and it's the perfect time for questions. Only this time, I'll be the one doing the asking."

"What? Look Mr. Suggs, we're trying to solve this murder. This one—and the others that came before it."

"That's my point exactly. If you had solved those, maybe my wife would still be alive."

"Maybe, maybe not. We don't know what we're dealing with here. You don't have any business getting close to this one."

Elvin straightened his back and his jaw jutted with rage. Di thought she had never seen this version of Elvin—Suggs, the raging bull, Suggs, a formidable warrior.

"I want to get so close he can feel me breathin' down his neck, right before I—"

"Elvin!" Di stopped him from completing his threat.

He didn't seem to hear. "I want to get this one myself. And I ain't waitin' two months either."

"I assure you, we are doing everything in our power to find this killer—whoever they are. We're just not sure if it's one person or three."

Elvin remained silent for a moment, pondering the suggestion.

"I hate to say this, Mr. Suggs," continued Reggie, "but under the circumstances, you are considered a suspect in the murder of Cherie Suggs."

"What?" Elvin was on the verge of hysteria.

"Now, if you could just answer a few questions…"

"Get out!" Elvin shouted.

"Sergeant, if you could just come back later," urged Di. She could see Reggie's back was up.

"Yeah, Reg, that's a good idea," Valentino said. "Let's move on."

Reggie looked at Di. "I'll be back." He made his way to the door. "Next time, I'll expect some cooperation."

"By the time you come back, I'll have the sonofabitch waiting for y'all." Elvin slammed the door behind them.

Twenty-Two

Ben Silver pulled up in front of the Jewel Arms and noticed the unmarked police car. He'd always been good at spotting one, ever since he got a driver's license. That's why he was where he was today. He congratulated himself smugly, and stepped into the brisk night air. *Pays to know how to play the game. Got to know the rules to break them.*

The moment he cracked the front door, however, he knew why the car was there. A strange smell saturated the stuffy air in the foyer. He sniffed. Almost like alcohol and dust, he observed creeping through the downstairs hall to the stairs. The smell seemed stronger as he passed Apartment B, but he didn't stop. It was almost midnight and he was exhausted.

As he climbed the wooden stairs, the brittle rubber treads crackled underfoot; he consoled himself that he wouldn't be living there much longer. About six months from now, after graduation, he'd be golden. The world would be his oyster. He'd get a new car, new apartment—who knows, maybe even a house—and then, there were the women.

Ah yes, the lovely ladies who would throw themselves at his feet. That nurse at work, the blonde that just got the boob job, she'd been coming on to him for months. He fumbled in his back pocket of his pants for his keys. In fact, as he recalled those bouncing boobs, he didn't know what he was waiting for. He'd ask her out tomorrow, he decided. Tomorrow.

"Hey, buddy!" said a voice behind him. "Can I help you?"

Startled, his mind focused on his fantasy, he turned to see a barefoot man clad in a white terrycloth bathrobe. The stranger smiled broadly, the whiteness of his perfectly capped teeth almost blinding in the shadows.

"I live here, dumbshit." His mouth curled into a snarl.

"Hey, so do I," said the man, extending his hand. "Dent Smith, Texas."

Ben recoiled from the gesture. "I'm going to bed," he said, slipping into the voice he reserved for patient contact, "and I'd advise you to do the same."

Dent shook his head. "Been a little hard to sleep tonight, buddy."

"Yeah, well try." Ben strode off toward his apartment, leaving Dent in the doorway of his apartment. He waited for a few moments before closing his door, and Ben got the feeling the man watched, although he couldn't imagine why. Lonely, he decided, but he found him incredibly irritating.

"I hate people, I hate people, I hate people," he chanted and inserted the key into the lock of his apartment door. He hoped Annie was asleep, or passed out. The last thing he wanted was another fight with that whining bitch.

As he entered the living room, he was surprised not to see her on the sofa, her usual spot, keeping company with her bourbon and beer cans, the damn television going and nobody watching. Didn't look like the kitchen had been used, either. He tossed his white coat on the sofa, the stethoscope trailing from the pocket. He grabbed a soda from the refrigerator and flopped down beside it to watch some no-mind rerun—anything to unwind.

A pillow stuffed beneath his head, he threw the coat on the floor, and propped his feet on the shabby arm of the couch. The remote control in one hand, soda in the other, he flipped through the channels before settling on an old episode of MASH. Two sips of Coke later, he was asleep.

Elvin stormed out of the building around midnight, taking

Vanna with him. He desperately needed to be alone. The sky was black and clear, the air cool and clean. As he looked up at the stars, Vanna beside him, he wondered where he should go, what he should do. A free man, his fate had been rerouted by something in those twinkling stars. At over fifty years old, he stood at a crossroads.

He jogged to his car. Tonight, it didn't matter where he went, or what he did. For a fleeting moment, as he slid behind the steering wheel, he realized that if he decided to drive to Canada, it wouldn't matter. Cherie was dead, along with any part of his past that he cared to remember. The rest you could keep.

The streetlamp cast a soft glow on the rough city streets, resting in the eerie silence. Numb and weary, he cruised the slumbering neighborhoods. The "Closed" signs on the shop windows reminded him that other people had regular jobs, with predictable schedules, and places they called home. His eyes filmed over, until blinking no longer controlled the salty tears, and he searched for a place to park the Caddy. His body ached with fatigue, yet he knew he wouldn't sleep. He just needed to get a hold on his emotions. Just for a minute, he promised himself, then he'd keep moving. That's all he really needed to do. Just keep moving.

He reached a stoplight at Jamieson and Fyler and waited for the light to turn green. The only car on the street, the silver Caddy gleamed in the winter moonlight. It was then he saw him, huddled against a newspaper stand, a plaid blanket wrapped around his stooped shoulders. The street lamp shined on his weathered face. His bumpy nose was a prominent feature, even in the dark. Elvin probably wouldn't have noticed him during the day, but now, the man was the only available distraction. One thing Elvin needed at that moment, a distraction.

"Hey!" Elvin yelled out the window as he rolled it down. "You like coffee?"

At first, the man did not respond. Yet, Elvin didn't think he slept. Instead, he sensed fear—fear and despair.

"What the hell," Elvin muttered under his breath. He needed

to talk to somebody tonight, almost as bad as he needed rest. "Hey!" he repeated. The man looked his way, his black hair graying at the temples, his dark eyes small and suspicious. "Want to get a burger or something?"

The man stood up and approached the car, still gripping the blanket around his compact body. His dark beard was flecked with gray. As Elvin leaned out the window he got blasted by the odor of a man who had not bathed in months. Strangely familiar in a déjà vu kind of way. The last time he encountered it was in Vietnam, in Khe Sanh, where he'd been that dirty himself, fighting right next to another dirty guy; mud, sweat, and bugs all around. It didn't bother him then, and it didn't bother him now. When their eyes met, though, recognition appeared in the stranger's face. "Suggs!" he said in disbelief, "is that really you, Suggs?"

Elvin struggled to place the man's face. He couldn't. He didn't know anyone who slept on a street corner in St. Louis, Missouri. "Sir?" he said. It was the only reply he could muster.

"Suggs? Don't you know me, man? It's Cobra." The man's lips quivered, and he tried to smile, revealing decayed, brown teeth. It seemed to Elvin that he hadn't done it for a while, but he hadn't quite forgotten how—not yet.

Elvin squinted in the darkness, searching the shell of this human being for the spirit of the Cobra he'd once known. Could it be? Then, he remembered the tattoo.

"Show me your arm, friend," he said.

"It's you alright." The stranger laughed. "I knew you were Elvin Suggs."

He dropped the blanket on the sidewalk and hurriedly rolled up the sleeve of his stained fatigue shirt. The arm underneath was pasty and wasted. Elvin chose to ignore the needle tracks he thought he saw on the pale skin. All that mattered was the sight of the coiled snake on the man's forearm: his old friend Cobra's distinctive trademark. In spite of his personal devastation, Elvin felt elated. Maybe something from his past was worth remembering after all. Cobra saved his ass more than once in '68. That was worth at least a burger and fries now.

"Get in, Cobra! I don't believe this!" said Elvin. "What the hell are you doing here?"

"I live here. Always did. Got a cigarette, Suggs?"

"Nope, don't smoke no more. Got healthy, you know. Still like beer, though."

Cobra looked out the window. Elvin turned onto Chippewa Street.

"What are you doing in St. Louis, Suggs? I mean, I'm glad you are, but this is too weird, you know?" Cobra began to hack up some mucous, which he spit into a torn handkerchief.

Elvin pulled into the drive-thru lane at McDonald's at the corner of Hampton and Chippewa. "This okay by you?"

"Sure." He paused. "You didn't answer my question. Not that it's any of my business. Probably isn't. Just forget it."

"Let's get some food and head on back to my place, Cobra. I'm beat."

Cobra simply shrugged in agreement. Elvin was relieved. He'd had enough surprises for one night.

Around the same time Elvin returned to the Jewel Arms with Cobra, Reggie personally delivered Valentino to his apartment on Hampton Avenue. Things had not gone well at the Jewel at all, interrogation-wise. Edith Mars had been unwilling to provide any information besides her name. The lady named Rose Honeycutt had been downright hostile, and no one else even answered their door. The only real source of information had been the man from Texas that lived upstairs, but Reggie didn't trust people who talked so freely.

Something about the Jewel Arms he didn't understand at all. For a place with so much going on all the time, no one ever seemed to be at home. At least Valentino was beginning to sober up a little. He watched his partner open the vault-like door to his building. He was beginning to feel like a babysitter, and didn't like it, not one bit. He wasn't sure how he'd do it, but as soon as things settled down, he would convince Rick to get help; maybe even retire on disability pay. As much as Reggie hated to admit it, Valentino was still an alcoholic. That stint in rehab five years ago had helped for the past five years, but Rick needed a more permanent solution.

"Well, I guess I'll be by tomorrow morning, then," said Reggie, as Valentino shoved open the door. "About 7:30 or so."

"7:30? Can't you make it a little later? Say 8:00? How about 9:00?"

"7:30. Keep complaining, and I'll make it 7:00."

"Thanks." Valentino entered the apartment as Reggie began to leave. He hadn't taken five steps before Valentino stopped him. "Reg! Come back, will ya? Somethin' stinks in here."

"What in the…" Reggie was tired, disgusted, and irritated, and now, Detective Valentino thought he smelled things. Great. He stepped into the apartment, pushing the door wide. The odor doubled him over. He jerked the refrigerator door and found an open package of hot dogs, one aging tuna casserole, which he removed and put in the kitchen sink, and a week old carton of milk. He threw that in the Rubbermaid trash can by the phone. "Okay, get rid of that moldy casserole, and your problems are solved." Reggie looked around him. "Rick?"

Valentino had moved down the hall, into the bedroom, his footsteps audible from the kitchenette.

"Rick," he said, as he followed, "it's been a long day, and I'm…" As he walked past the bathroom, the odor grew stronger, and even more distinctive. Yet, the source eluded him.

"Smell that?" Valentino rummaged through the closets. Reggie stood motionless, cataloging the condition of the bedroom in his mind. It did not appear any different from the last time he had seen it, but still, he had that nagging feeling someone had been there while they were gone. Valentino reached to open a dresser drawer, and Reggie stopped him.

"Don't touch it."

"I live here. This is my stuff."

"I don't care." He approached the closets, putting his head low to sniff the contents. There wasn't much to inspect: just pairs of hanging slacks, a few shirts, one suit, a few ties, and two shoe boxes.

"You're not much of a pack rat, are you?" Reggie remarked.

"No. What the hell are you doing?"

"Somebody was in here," said Reggie. "Anybody else have a key?"

"Are you kidding me?"

"Who else would have a key, Rick?"

"Landlord, I guess." He threw up his hands. "Why do you think anybody was here? Nothing looks any different to me."

Reggie paused. He scratched his head, as if he was looking for just the right words.

"Well?"

"It's the smell. Don't you know that smell?"

"Okay, I'll throw out the tuna casserole while you wait. Happy?"

Reggie's expression remained somber. "Smells like a dead animal."

Valentino chuckled. "So, you're saying a dog or a cat or something came in here tonight, and died? Is that what you're saying?"

Reggie walked over to the bed and lifted the blanket, peering under the mattress. Nothing. He shook his head.

"I can't help it. Something just doesn't feel right to me, Rick." Again, he sniffed the air. "I tell you, I know that smell."

Valentino frowned. "You want to call for backup?"

"No." He left the room, slowly inching his way back up the hall. He flipped on the bathroom light and paused. The shower curtain had been disturbed, he could tell. It had that subtle difference found in a perfectly organized bookshelf in which a book had been removed, and carefully replaced. It was never the same as the untouched version.

Reggie moved closer, the rotten odor causing the bile to rise in his throat. "You keep trash bags in your shower?"

Impulsively, he yanked the plastic curtain aside and revealed a mangled black trash bag, twisted around a bloodied orange and gold afghan. A woman's head protruded from the top, a lifeless brown arm poking through a hole in the side. One dark eye was open, staring helplessly at Reggie, her sticky black hair matted with her own blood.

Reggie was relieved that the toilet was close by, as turned to involuntarily retch.

Valentino stood in the doorway, dumbfounded.

"Just tell me one thing, Rick…" Reggie wiped his face with his handkerchief. "Tell me you never saw this woman before in your life."

Twenty-Three

Walter reclined in the plush easy chair. The Executive Suite at the Sunset Hotel suited his taste just fine. "Now this is more like it," he drawled, filling a tumbler with ice and premium Scotch. "Only thing is, I miss Cherie, just an eensie-weesie bit."

"Christ, Wally," said Arnold, "how can you say that? Woman liked to drive me crazy." He jammed his fist into a crystal bowl of mixed nuts, popping them into his mouth. He chewed voraciously, like a ravenous, wild animal.

Redman couldn't face him, though his convictions compelled him to speak. "If you want my opinion on all of this, Walter, I'd say it's time we moved on."

Arnold glared at him with silent venom. Walter spoke in his soft Memphis drone. "Your opinion is welcome, Redman. But this time, y'all are wrong. In fact, you know, boy, I been thinkin' a lot 'bout Loco and Popeye. I do believe it's time you ordered up a couple 187s for your friends."

Arnold continued to gorge himself on nuts, crunching loudly in the background.

Redman's jaw dropped. He sat motionless for about a minute, contemplating Wally's proposal. 187s on Loco and Popeye? Naw. Not after Tasha, no way. He'd promised himself now: Redman was a brand new man. He rubbed the back of his neck, wondering how to tell Wally he couldn't order no one to kill nobody, especially his friends, ever again. He'd have to get somebody else.

Walter swilled his scotch in his jowls before swallowing. "So, what'll it be? Don't tell me you're thinking 'bout backing out. You're my enforcer, now."

Redman glanced at Arnold, stuffing himself from a box of jelly donuts. Droplets of red jelly dripped from his chins while he swallowed. Redman had to avert his gaze. He thought he would never touch another donut in his life.

"How about Arnold?" he asked, his voice tempered with caution. "Maybe he could take them out."

For once, Arnold stopped chewing.

"What you mean, Arnold? I'm the brains of this operation. Plus, I do all the driving. Least I don't have to put up with that girlfriend no more."

He wiped sugar crystals from his lips with the back of his hand.

Walter finished his drink and placed the empty glass on the nightstand beside him. "I'll give you a little time to make your move, don't worry none 'bout that. Just keep in mind, that's two less partners to split the profits with, and one more thing—I ain't asking you. I'm telling you, hear?"

Redman stared back, barely nodding his head in agreement. He knew he usually ordered the 187s, sure, but this—this was too much. Not Loco and Popeye. He couldn't do it.

"Which brings me to my other problem," Walter continued. "Which is, the title to the Jewel Arms."

Arnold popped a beer can. "I don't follow you." He threw the empty donut box into the trashcan beside his sagging chair.

"Fact is, before Cherie's death becomes public knowledge, I need to put that place in somebody else's name, preferably a female. Wouldn't hurt if she was blonde, neither." He raised an eyebrow suggestively and smirked.

"I don't see why you can't leave it in Cherie's name," said Redman. "You own the building. You can do what you want with it."

"Ain't nobody but us know that. Don't want nothin' traced back to me—and my money."

Arnold guzzled the rest of his beer, crushing the empty can in his meaty fist. "For the record, Wally, I am completely, absolutely, and totally against you bringing another girlfriend into this organization. We just got rid of one, and I am telling you, I am one happy man."

Redman shifted uneasily in his seat, crushing the plush blue carpet beneath his tennis shoes. He was still pondering the 187s.

"What you think, Redman?" asked Walter.

Startled, Redman fumbled for a reply. "You say something 'bout a girlfriend or somethin' like that?"

"Yeah," said Arnold in mock disgust. Ain't you been listenin'? This here's a business meetin'." He popped another beer, pouring half down his throat. "You know, this St. Louis beer is pretty damn good."

"So," continued Walter, "what you think, Redman? I was thinking a little bit 'bout that blonde living in A."

Redman shrugged. "Don't know the girl." He paused, reflecting that he could have asked Tasha about her—if Tasha was still alive, which she wasn't. He was beginning to feel like maybe he wasn't. *Maybe all this just didn't matter.* "Go on, boss. Whatever you say is fine with me. What have you got to lose?"

Walter had crossed the room to admire himself in the full-length mirror. He turned this way and then that, assessing his trim body, tanned skin, perfectly styled, full head of silvery hair. "What do you think, partners? Does Walter Hubble still have what it takes?"

Arnold finished his beer, belching loudly in reply before he turned away in disgust. Walter ignored him. He preferred Redman's predictable support.

"Redman?"

Redman shook his head. "Man needs a woman, Walter. 'Course you don't know if this lady have a man already now, do you?"

Walter threw his head back, laughing heartily. "Oh, you do

amuse me, you really do."

"What you mean?"

"I mean, my friend, that if I want a woman, I'm not going to let somethin' like another man get in my way." He grew serious, almost threatening, thought Redman, as he added, "I didn't let anyone stand in my way the last time, now did I?"

"I don't want you with me on this one, Cobra." Elvin sat across the breakfast table from his old friend the following morning, sipping coffee.

Cobra dunked a donut into his own coffee, contemplating the situation as he chewed. "Suit yourself, man. I'll be movin' on, then."

Elvin got up to leave. "Don't have to. Where you headed?"

"Looking for work again." Cobra shook his head. "You know, I get a job and things go okay for awhile, but then—"

"What?"

Cobra ran his hand through his shoulder length graying hair. "I get stressed out, man. I start hearing things. Noises really get to me—big ones, little ones—especially little ones. Vietnam really screwed me up. I haven't been right in the head for thirty years. I get these anxiety attacks…that's what the psychiatrist calls them. He gave me a prescription for some pills, but you know, I run out of money before the end of the month, and it's buy more damn pills or eat. It's tough to keep up, you know? I still got my pride, Suggs. Don't like taking handouts from anybody, especially the government. Don't trust them. I got to find work I can hang on to."

"You don't have anything to be ashamed of, man. You did what you had to do. We both did."

"Then why do I feel like I should go to confession for being a sniper in 'Nam, huh? Tell me why I sit and listen to the vets from World War II tell their Nazi war stories, and I don't feel like I have the right to tell mine?"

"You got the same rights they do."

"It doesn't feel that way. You know what I'm talkin' about." He looked away, biting his lip in resentment. The gray in his beard gleamed in the morning sunlight.

Elvin stood and wiped his mouth on a napkin. "I won't be long," he said, and walked to the door. "Take a shower, read the paper. Spend some time with Vanna. She's a great listener, aren't you girl?"

At the mention of her name, the Airedale perked up her ears. Cobra looked at Elvin with gratitude in his tired eyes. "You're a real friend, Suggs. I don't know how I can thank you for caring about me, but someday I'll make it up to you."

Elvin waved and walked out without saying a word.

Half an hour later, he was at the City Jail, waiting to visit Parry Leach. It was almost 10:00 a.m. when Parry slumped down on the other side of the glass. His hostility simmered in the air. "Thought you wadn't coming back," he mumbled, avoiding Suggs' gaze.

"I told you I would."

"Yeah. Well, I haven't seen you for a month, and Tasha missed her visit yesterday. She never misses on Sunday. Never. She slips me some of those cinnamon cookies too—have to share those with the guard back there—he even axed me where they were. Guess she be forgetting 'bout her old friend Parry. Got better things to do, yeah."

"Look, I apologize on my account, anyway. I should have been better about keeping you up on things, I know, but—"

"But what?" Parry pounded the table. "What's so damn important out there in your world, huh?"

"I don't expect you to understand. I'm not asking for that, b-but my wife was murdered yesterday."

Parry relaxed his shoulders and pursed his lips. He was still pouting, in his own way. "Sorry 'bout that, man. My sympathy." He scowled. "I thought you was getting a divorce or somethin'."

Elvin's jaw hardened at the 'D' word. "I loved the woman. She was my wife."

Parry looked away, hung his head. "Yeah." He paused, his lower lip quivering in embarrassment. "Well, you heard anything on my case?" He looked over his shoulder. "This lawyer they got me is selling me down the river. I'm just another number on his caseload."

"How do you know that?"

"He ain't never coming 'round no more, that's how I know. He don't care. I'm a black man with a record, and he's got better things to do than figure out who killed Torrez. They gotta pin it on somebody, and right now, I'm just the kind of man they be looking for." Parry nodded his head with certainty.

"Okay, I'm here, and I'm listening. I got a hunch that whoever killed Torrez is the same person who murdered my wife."

Parry's face brightened. "Yeah?"

"Yeah." Elvin leaned forward. "Listen, Leach, I'm not waiting for the police to figure this thing out. I'm going in on my own. I got a couple friends for back up if I need it."

"What can you do without the police, man? They got all the evidence."

Elvin pulled Valentino's black book from the back pocket of his jeans. "I got some of it right here. And, you could tell me what you know about Matt Torrez—before he died."

"Like what?"

"Like what was the man like? What kind of clothes did he wear, what food did he eat, what kind of women did he date? Anything at all, it all adds up to something. What can you tell me?"

Parry rubbed his forehead, and put his elbows on the counter before taking a deep breath. "See, the main thing about Torrez was that he liked status. He always wanted to be the big shot. He had that car dealership in the county, you know—"

"Yeah, I think I know the one."

"Okay, well I had some white friends working over there tell me he had a job open up, so I go over there, and he tell me, naw, he ain't got no job for me. I axed him three times. I woulda done anything he needed doing."

"You already told me."

"Yeah. Well, I know the reason he turned me down, and you do too. He don't want no black man with a record workin' for him."

"Yeah."

"Yeah. Well, I tole my friends 'bout him and they say he done it before. They didn't like him either, see. The man was cheap, wouldn't never go out to lunch. Made them pay for coffee by the cup. Say they hadn't had a raise in two years. Not even a damn Christmas party. One guy's mama died—didn't send flowers, no card, nothing."

"So why do they stay?"

"They got they reasons. But they looking to leave, I know that. They just didn't want him to know they was looking." He shrugged. "The man made his own enemies. What else can I say?"

"Strange."

"What?"

"What do you know about the diamond?"

"What?"

"When Torrez died, there was a huge diamond ring in the pocket of his coat. For a man that was so cheap, that seems strange to me."

"Big diamond ring? For what?"

"That's just it. Nobody knows. Thing is, he was trying to get inside A when he was killed. Hooker lives in there, Leach."

"Okay, so he wanna give a diamond ring to a hooker. Lots of guys do that."

"Didn't seem like he was that kind of guy, from what I hear."

Parry laughed. "And what kind of guy is that? Believe me, I seen all kinds of guys give diamonds to hookers. Rich, poor, old, young, dumb, smart, fat, thin. Don't matter, man, so get that outta your head." He shook his head again in amusement. "Shit."

"Leach, you said the guy was cheap. Not poor—cheap."

"He was!"

"I'm having trouble believing he'd spring for a rock that big—say, four or five carats."

"He wouldn't. No way. But he might. So, I'm saying, either it wasn't his to start with, or it ain't the real thing. I'm telling you, that's where my money is."

Twenty-Four

With a jolt, Ben Silver awoke to the buzz of the doorbell. Who had punched the damn thing? It must be—he looked at his Timex—Christ, it was already 7:00 a.m. He was late. Why didn't Annie wake him? That lazy broad. Bet she hadn't made breakfast yet, either. He stumbled to the door and looked into the hall. No one there. He almost slammed the door before he saw it. A small box placed carefully at the threshold. Ben looked up and down in the shadows—no trace of anyone. What was this, a fucking joke? He picked it up and shut the door. It was wrapped in brown paper with a small white card taped to the corner, simply addressed to Annie.

Annie? What the hell. Who would give her anything? He threw the box on the coffee table and began a search for Her Highness. She had some big time explaining to do.

As he made his way past the bathroom, he began to think she wasn't home. There were no sounds—no sniffles, no rustling of sheets, no running water. Maybe she was hiding from him. Yeah, that was it. She was hiding from him because she'd made him late for 7:00 rounds. Well, it was time for her to pay up. His temper rose with each step. And pay up, she would.

He tried to open the door and stepped in it—sticky blood pooled on the hardwood floor. The room was still dark, lit only by the shadows cast by the gray light of a November morning. As he forced the door the rest of the way, cursing the calamity, ever mindful that he would now be unforgivably late for rounds, it didn't occur to him that Annie would never get up again. Only that she was being damn inconsiderate, especially with the board exam coming up: she knew all about that, she had known for months, and now she pulls this at the last minute. Bitch.

The body, lodged between the mattress and the bedroom door, didn't respond to Ben's insults and demands. Huffing and puffing, he finally loosened the macabre trap and collapsed on his back. For a moment, he lay, fuming, in Annie's sticky, rotting blood. There, in the gray dawn, he cursed Annie, God, that fat gal across the hall, Dent Smith, and that big hick from Tennessee too, and anyone else he could think of who was going to pay Big Time and For Ever for this goddamn mess.

Back on his feet, his rumpled clothes stained in his wife's blood, Ben stood in the doorway to the bedroom, and fixated on the knife protruding from Annie's back. He speculated that it must have hurt to die like that, a big, sharp knife to the back—might still. Maybe he should remove it. He even reached out to touch it, but then, decided not to. He wondered how long she had been dead—there was no doubt in his mind that she was—and who he should call. Most of all, he was furious at having been deceived. Somebody had surely taken him for a fool. Well, they wouldn't get away with it. Nobody made fool out of Ben Silver.

He dialed 911 and reported an emergency, and then, called the medical school to tell the secretary he'd be late. She did not sound very understanding, and Ben sure hoped they didn't hold this absence against him. Well, it would be at least five or ten minutes before anyone showed up to clean up this mess. Might as well go in and open that package.

Elvin waited in traffic on Highway 44, and squinted at the bright morning sun. All he could think about was that diamond. Was it real? He'd have to talk to Reggie, probably Valentino too. Might be time to make a visit to that fancy car dealership, and mind Mattie Torrez's business. But first, he'd talk to Tasha. She'd told him that she was seeing La Mour about Parry's case. Maybe the background information on Torrez could help. Maybe she could tell him something about the relationship between Torrez and Valerie Gains.

As he attempted to pull up to the curb in front of the Jewel Arms, however, a cluster of vehicles prevented his approach. There was no place to park. He circled the block, finally locating a spot on a side street. He strolled up to the building, just in time to see a body being loaded into an ambulance. He jogged up to the front door, and saw Di standing there, watching the departing vehicle. She saw him, but didn't wave. She put her head down and folded her arms. Her emotions cautioned him.

"Di?" he said, stepping through the unmowed grass. "What's going on?"

She looked at him and burst into tears. From the look of her swollen eyes, Elvin was certain that they were not fresh ones. "It's Annie," she sobbed. "She was stabbed."

"Is she…" Elvin didn't want to say the last word.

"She's dead. Her husband found her this morning."

"I'll bet he did," said Elvin sarcastically.

"They took him in for questioning, but they said they'd be back."

"Who's they?"

Di shook her head. "Valentino again, but he's got a new guy working with him. I think his name is Reggie."

"Oh yeah, Reggie. I met him the other day." He paused. "I just got back from the jail—went to visit Parry Leach."

"What for?"

"I'm dealing with this thing on my own now. I think whoever killed Cherie probably killed this Torrez guy, maybe even Edward Mars."

Di frowned. "You know, I haven't seen Edith Mars around for the longest time. The last time I talked to her she told me she was going on another cruise. This time, it was the Bahamas."

"She didn't seem like the adventurous type."

"Well, she said now that Eddie was gone, she wanted to

travel. He never wanted to go anywhere, she said, and since she
had money now, she thought she might as well see a few things.
You know, it's a funny thing about her. She's even started wearing jewelry."

"So?"

"Well, it's just that she was such a plain woman while he was
alive. Doesn't matter, I guess."

Their conversation was interrupted when Reggie and Valentino pulled up to the curb. Valentino, dressed in a gray suit,
looked embarrassed at the sight of them.

"Looking a little better than the last time I saw you, detective," Elvin said.

"So are you, sir," Reggie replied. "In fact, you might be more
amenable to answering a few questions now. Would I be cor-
rect?"

Elvin bristled. "Sure, if that's what y'all want to do. I was on
my way in to talk to Tasha Weeks, but it can wait."

Reggie hesitated, licking his lips. He seemed to be waiting
for something. "Mr...Suggs, is it? Mr. Suggs, Miss Weeks won't
be talking to anybody."

"You can't stop me from talking to her."

Reggie looked up at the gray sky, shoving his hands deep
in his pockets. Finally, he took a deep breath, and announced,
"She's dead, Suggs."

Elvin looked as if someone had punched him in the stomach. "How do you know?"

"It's a long story, but suffice it to say that we found her body
today, and she is, without a doubt, dead."

"Where did you find her? In her apartment, I'll bet."

"We are not at liberty to say," said Reggie.

"That's five people what died in this building. When are you
gonna up and do somethin' about it?"

"Mr. Suggs. Perhaps we could begin with a few questions
about your wife. It's vital we follow proper procedure in this investigation."

At the casual reference to Cherie, Elvin's face reddened with fury. "You know," he said, jabbing his index finger in Reggie's face, "the whole problem with guys like you is that you're always worried about covering your behind. Forget about your procedures, Combs. It's time to find this killer before somebody else dies. That's what's vital." He turned to address Valentino. "Tell me something. Do you even know who owns this building? Because if you do, it's high time you let them know what's going on over here."

Reggie shuffled his feet restlessly, and Valentino glanced sideways at him, as if to ask permission to speak. "Perhaps we should go somewhere where we can talk privately, Suggs," suggested Reggie, as he looked over his shoulder.

"Do you want to step into my apartment?" Di asked.

"No," said Elvin. "Whatever y'all have to say, you can say it right here."

"We know who owns the building," said Valentino. "But, unfortunately, we will not be able to notify that person of the problems over here at The Jewel."

"Why the hell not?" shouted Elvin. "What does it take to get you guys to do something? All right, just give me the name and I'll tell the owner myself. I have the right to know who is collecting my rent check, don't I?"

Reggie heaved a sigh. "Pearl down at the office did some research for me, some asking around, you know, digging through microfilm, and—"

"Just spit it out, Reggie," said Valentino.

"What?"

"To tell you the truth, Suggs, I'm surprised you don't know who the owner is," said Reggie. "But I guess it doesn't matter if you know now. You'd find out anyway when it went through probate."

Elvin balled his hands into fists. The muscles in his forearms tensed. Sensing his frustration, Valentino blurted out the truth. "The title search showed that The Jewel Arms belonged to a Mrs.

Cherie Suggs of Memphis, Tennessee." He paused and then mumbled, "Sorry about that."

Redman sat in the tattered armchair in his apartment, trying to enjoy the chicken fried rice and eggrolls the Hubbles had ordered from the Shanghai Express around the corner. It was no use. With every bite, he found it hard to chew, and even harder to swallow. He was starving. Yet, his stomach wouldn't accept the food. He hated himself right now.

Arnold sat across from him on the leather sofa, cramming rice into his mouth from a little white box, the stray pieces dropping onto the coffee table in front of him.

Walter munched on an eggroll, sipping scotch from a glass tumbler. "What's ailing you there, Redman? You look like a hound that's been in the sun too long." He set the tumbler on the end table, the ice clinking against the sides of the glass.

Arnold guzzled half a bottle of beer, his blubbery chin quivering, before he finally glanced over at Redman. "Had to be done," he said, wiping his mouth with the back of his hand.

When Redman didn't reply, Walter leaned forward, speaking in a paternalistic tone. "We sorry 'bout your friends, partner, but you know this here's a business. Ain't no room for any more at the top." His voice hardened. "I do b'lieve they was shorting us on the candy money, and you know, Redman, we cain't have that."

Redman leaned back in the chair, and rubbed his drawn face with both hands. He shook his head from side to side. "It's just— it's just that first, we do Tasha, and then, it's Loco and Popeye. These were my friends, man! They weren't nothin' to you. Naw. You come up here from Memphis, and think you can buy me, buy my friends, and run us all like we was a stable of horses."

Walter laughed. "Fact is, partner, I do run you—and your friends, and your crappy little neighborhoods. I been damn good to you and your friends." He pounded the end table. "This is a business. We sell, they buy. Market price, supply and demand. It's as simple as that."

Redman curled up in the chair, and turned away. "Naw, it ain't that simple. I knew those three people all my life, man, and you used me to kill 'em. It ain't that simple at all."

Walter reached into his pocket and retrieved his wallet. "This oughtta make you feel better, partner." He peeled off a wad of hundred dollar bills, and held it out to Redman.

Out of habit, Redman started to accept the cash, but as he reached for it, he hesitated. "How much is that?"

"It's the usual. Three grand."

"Not bad for a couple days work," leered Arnold.

"So, I killed my friends for a thousand apiece? Is that what you're telling me?" shouted Redman.

Walter sat back in the chair. He took a sip of his drink, still clutching the cash in his hand. "Brothah, I b'lieve Redman here is getting a bleeding heart on us."

Redman's eyes grew wide. "Naw, I didn't mean it that way," he said, as he rose from his chair. He walked over to Walter and extended his hand. "Three thousand, did you say?"

Walter grinned diabolically, the ends of his mouth turned up in victory. "Count it if you want." He jammed the money into Redman's waiting palm.

Redman shoved the wad into the back pocket of his cargo pants. "Naw."

Walter rose to leave. "We best be going now, brothah."

"You gonna eat that?" Arnold asked Redman, gesturing to his uneaten rice and eggrolls.

"Naw."

"Good deal." Arnold gathered the leftovers into a white paper bag. "Y'all outta beer anyway, Redman."

"We'll be callin' later tonight." Walter opened the gray metal door. "Be ready for us."

Redman barely waved in response as the pair departed into the dusky twilight. He turned to face the row of empty beer bottles, and the single tumbler of scotch and melting ice; he didn't think he'd ever felt the way he did at this moment. It was a new sensation, and Redman didn't know quite what to call it. Only that he suddenly felt cheap. He shuddered. How could he feel cheap with three grand in his back pocket?

As he threw the bottles into the trash can, he tried to figure it out. He couldn't. It was when he picked up the slippery tumbler, the condensation running down between his fingers, that the revelation hit, and he understood what was new. "Fact is, partner, I do run you," echoed in his frazzled mind, and he realized he had just sold his soul—to a devil named Walter Hubble.

Twenty-Five

Reggie drove along Hampton Avenue, Valentino beside him. He wondered how to deal with the predicament. After all, he found a bloody knife in his sink, and a corpse in his shower, not to mention the trash bag, and now Rick had started drinking again. Yet, he believed him when he said he had no idea how the corpse landed in his shower, or the knife in his sink. The knife had been submitted for fingerprints. Might tell 'em something.

Fact was, he'd put a lot of time in on the Jewel Arms—he knew all those tenants, he'd studied the circumstances in the case, and believed he needed Valentino to find the killer. He'd covered for him before. Now, he was doing it again.

He pulled up to the curb and shut off the engine. Valentino began to step out of the car, when he stopped him. "Rick, sit a minute, there."

"You want something?"

Reggie looked straight ahead. "Yeah." The navy sky was starless as Reggie sat brooding behind the wheel.

"Mind if I smoke?" asked Valentino.

"Go ahead."

Valentino proceeded to light up as Reggie struggled with his feelings.

"Rick," he said, fidgeting with the steering wheel, "I don't think you should go home tonight." He glanced at the rambling apartment complex on his left.

Valentino sighed, as he blew smoke out of the half-open

window. "I know what you're thinking. I swear, I don't know what went on in there, Reg. You've got to believe me."

"I do, I do. The thing is I'm pretty sure no one else will." He turned to face Valentino. "Rick, you need help. You're slipping again, buddy."

"Don't tell me we're going to have this conversation again. Just because I had a few beers one night does not mean I'm slipping."

"One night?"

Valentino stubbed out the cigarette in the ashtray and lit another with his Zippo lighter. "Okay, a couple of nights." He frowned. "You been talking to Valerie?"

"Who?"

Valentino turned away. "Nothing."

"Look, I've been thinking about all of this, and I believe someone broke into your apartment when you were there—while you were passed out."

"Don't you think I would have known that? Jeez, give me a little credit here, will ya? I keep a loaded gun on the nightstand for just those occasions."

Reggie stopped, a look of panic crossing his face. "I didn't see it when I came in the other day, Rick. Where'd you put it that night?"

He stubbed out the cigarette, but did not light another. "I always keep it beside the bed." He patted his pocket out of habit, as if he might find the gun in his pocket.

"Do you know where your damn gun is now?"

Valentino hung his head. "No." He took a deep breath and exhaled loudly.

Reggie sighed and looked at the complex again. A group of teenagers were entering the building. "They picked up the woman's body this afternoon. They'll know more by tomorrow." He hesitated. "You want to stay at my place tonight?"

"Did they know it was my apartment?" asked Valentino.

"I didn't include your name in my initial report. But it isn't going to be long before they put two and two together. We need to find the killer before somebody decides you killed her. You better think about getting yourself an attorney, my friend."

Valentino took another deep breath and opened the passenger door. "I'll see you tomorrow, Reg."

"I don't think you ought to go up there tonight."

"I can handle myself just fine, think you very much."

"What about your gun?" Reggie called after him.

"It's up there somewhere, don't worry."

Reggie sat in his car, watching Valentino stride up to the massive front door. The streetlamp above had kicked on, shining directly on his face. Time to go. As he pulled away, he worried about Rick—and his gun. The man just wasn't careful. Somebody needed to do his worrying for him.

Valentino had just finished climbing the two flights of steps to his apartment. As he stood huffing and puffing, fishing for his keys, he thought about what a good thing it was that he lived at the end of the hall, close to the stairs. Saved a lot of walking. He had just inserted the key when he felt someone behind him, and turned to face a tall, black man he estimated to be around twenty years old.

The young man shuffled his feet and stared at the floor before he began to mumble in a low voice. Valentino didn't feel threatened.

"Mister?" he said, barely raising his head.

"Yeah? You want money or something like that?"

"Naw." He looked over his shoulder and jerked his head toward Valentino's apartment. "I got to talk to you."

"So talk."

"Naw. Let's go inside."

Valentino pushed the door open, painfully aware that he didn't have his gun. It wasn't often that he followed his gut instinct, but this was one of those times. Who the hell was this guy?

Once they were inside, he closed the door and faced him,

remaining close to the door.

Redman spoke first. "I know who put that dead lady in here. They got your gun, too."

"Who are you?"

"Don't matter, man. I'm sorry I tole them where you live. You got to get out of here. They be coming back tonight."

"Wait a minute. Who was that in the trash bag?"

Redman shook his head. "She was my friend—my good friend. Now listen to me—get out of here."

"Get my gun back."

"I can't." Redman pushed his way to the door. "I got to go, man."

"But—"

He was gone before Valentino could stop him. He stood with his back to the door, digesting the urgent message. He looked at his watch. Ten o'clock. Where would he go this time of night? He'd already bothered Reggie enough, and besides, he didn't want to listen to any more of his preaching about a few beers now and then. Before he could consider his options, the shot exploded. He hit the floor. As he slowly rose to examine the door, however, he realized the bullet had not penetrated it—at least not this time. He wanted to open the door, but didn't dare. Time to call Reggie, he decided. He punched the number into his cell phone and waited.

"Reg?"

"Yeah."

"Somebody just got plugged out in the hall. Where are you?"

"Still out in front, man. Told you I had a bad feeling. Stay low. I'm coming in."

The traffic on Hampton Avenue whizzed by as Reggie sneaked up to the front door. He didn't like going in without backup. He considered calling for some, but decided it would slow him down, or worse, call attention to him.

He figured the back door was locked. Using the overgrown bushes as camouflage, he approached the wide front door and slipped through, immediately darting to the left of the foyer, his back pressed against the cold mailboxes on the far wall.

He stood in the shadows and listened. The sounds of an aging building serenaded him: the clanging whistle of steam radiators, creaking floors, and crackling plaster. The pungent smells of dust and cedar, of musty rugs and greasy stoves, tickled his nose. With no windows in the foyer, he resisted turning on a light, for fear of announcing his presence. Instead, he chose to grope his way in the night, negotiating by touch.

As he ascended the stairs one by one, probing the foreign blackness, his ears strained for warnings, for clues. Anything that could whisper a signal. There was nothing but the silence of the building as it breathed.

He passed the second floor, and glimpsed into the open doorway, before staring up the third flight. The scarlet glow of the exit sign lit his path, and he moved a little faster, more certain of his steps. On the landing outside, however, he stopped. The metal door was not only closed; when he tried it, he found it was jammed.

Reggie gripped his pistol, plastering himself against the wall outside, even as he tried the doorknob with the other hand. It turned. Reggie was certain it wasn't locked. His pistol cocked and ready, he rammed the door with his body, finally forcing his way into the darkened hall. He lost his balance in the thrust, and landed face down, not on the terrazzo floor, but on something lumpy and soft. Reggie was grateful something had cushioned the fall—something that, at first, felt like a pile of clothes. That smell, though—Reggie didn't trust that sweaty odor. He would have sworn he could smell fried eggroll, too. He groped for his flashlight and flipped the switch. The flat, lifeless eyes of Redman stared back at him.

Cobra lounged at the breakfast table, and munched a cinnamon-sugar Pop-tart. The soft rain pattered on the slate roof. Across from him, Elvin sipped coffee and read the sports page, while Cobra read the Want Ads.

"These critters are pretty dang good," Cobra said. He popped a corner of the pastry into his mouth.

"They're my favorite," said Elvin. "Vanna's too. Say, what kind of job you looking for?"

Cobra folded the rustling paper and sipped his coffee. "That's just it. The kind of skills I have, nobody advertises for. I mean, who says they're looking for a sniper?"

Elvin laughed. "True enough. But listen, I got an idea. How about you become a decorator consultant? They seem like they're pretty happy people. Maybe a little too happy, if you ask me."

"Why would you say a thing like that?"

"Like what?"

"Like why don't I be a decorator? Really, Suggs. Are you crazy? I think you are. Yeah, that's it."

"No, I'm not. I mean, those red beady things you hung from the ceiling look pretty good. I thought this place was going to look like the Saigon Red Line, but no, you did good. You really got a good eye for fashion."

"You're mocking me, Suggs. I'm going to take my beads someplace else, that's all there is to it. For the future, that bead curtain was a gift from one beautiful lady I knew very well. She said it was the gateway to heaven."

"Go on, I'm with you."

"Nope. But, it's enough to say that wherever that bead curtain hangs, she's with me. That's enough of my love life for now."

"Wow. Didn't know you had one. That's all. Anyway, I have a question for you. Say you thought somebody stole a diamond ring from someone, and was gonna give it to someone else?"

Cobra nodded. "I'm with you, so far."

"Okay. But, when you checked out the diamond, you found out it was a phony."

"I would say it means the stolen ring was fake, that's all."

"Yeah, but knowing the owner had a lot of money, that just don't seem right to you."

"Well then, there's only one way to know. Go back to the owner and ask if it was a real diamond."

Elvin's face brightened. "I shoulda thought of that myself. With Cherie and all, though, I haven't been thinking clear. Today's Tuesday, ain't it? According to Valentine's little book, that means that Rose will be going to the beauty shop around 1:00. Probably be back around 3:00. I could go across the hall sometime in between."

"Want me to go with you?"

"No, Vanna would appreciate the company here. Anyway, I don't want to startle the old lady. I'm gonna ask Di to get the key for me, though."

A few minutes later, Elvin strolled down the hall, on his way to Di's apartment, and almost collided with Myles Lamour. "Well, look who it is! Haven't seen you around for a long time, buddy."

Myles laughed. "Well, you know, I do work a lot, and then there's the weekends."

"You like the ladies, don't you?"

"I've got my favorites." Myles hesitated, and his mood grew somber. "I guess I can say this now that Torrez is gone."

Elvin frowned. "What?"

"Well, I miss the referrals, if you know what I mean."

"I got no idea what you mean, cowboy." Elvin stepped a little closer.

"Well, like I said, Torrez sent me girls from time to time."

"What kind of girls are we talking?"

Myles shook his head, as he chuckled. "See, Suggs, the thing you need to understand about Torrez is that he was always, you know, 'looking for love in all the wrong places,' like the song says. One minute, he'd be telling me how he wanted to settle down with a wife and kids, and a home cooked meal, and that very night, he'd be out with a lady like that Miss Gains down in A. I don't think he was ever with a lady longer than one, maybe two nights at the most, and believe me they liked to help him spend his money. Then, he'd send them my way. All of them nice girls, matter of fact. Only one he seemed to stay interested in was Valerie Gains, and believe me, Suggs, she is not interested in settling down any time soon."

"Yeah, I hear you on that. Why didn't you tell me all this before now?"

"Didn't want you to think I knew too much about Torrez, I guess. But, it doesn't matter now. I'm sure they've got Parry Leach fingered for this one, don't you agree?"

"Where did you hear that?" Elvin was surprised at Myles' conclusion.

"Listen, I'm late for work," replied Myles, dodging the question. He took a few steps forward, stopped, and turned to face Elvin. "Hey, did you know that another car just like yours is hanging around out front these days? Has Tennessee plates, too."

"Yeah, I saw it the other day. Same day my wife died."

Myles breathed an embarrassed sigh. "Hey man, I was meaning to tell you I'm sorry to hear about that." He paused. "No, uh…connection, was there?"

"What do you mean?"

"I mean, does the owner of that other car know your wife?"

"I don't know. My wife knew a lot of people, for sure. I've been too rattled to ask questions."

"The cops are working on it, right?"

Elvin rolled his eyes and looked to the heavens above for an answer to that question. "Lord knows."

"Well, I've really got to go. We need to get together sometime for a beer."

"Shore 'nuf." Elvin descended the stairs past Apartment C, and then B. The closer he came to the end of the hall, the more agitated he grew. The clues had been in front of his face.

He'd lost his focus. His edge was dull. He'd gone soft. Elvin banged on Di's door, and felt his adrenaline surge. He grinned at the rush.

It was good to be back in the saddle.

Twenty-Six

Reggie sat at his desk and scanned the murder report from Valentino's apartment. For at least one thing, he was grateful: the fingerprints on the knife in the sink did not belong to Valentino. The body in the trash bag had been identified as a female with a lengthy criminal history, a Miss Natasha Weeks. For Reggie, however, the most upsetting detail was her Jewel Arms address.

He sipped hot chocolate, and his mind wandered. The victim in the hall had also been identified. Known simply as *Redman*, he was a local drug dealer. The fingerprints on the knife belonged to him. Up to this point, thought Reggie, everything fit together quite nicely. When Valentino told him of Redman's warning before his untimely death, he had tainted the entire case.

In the worst way, Reg wanted to trust Valentino. Yet, Rick was bumbling this investigation with both hands. He had never been certain of Parry Leach's guilt in regards to Matthew Torrez's murder, not in the way Valentino had been. The evidence was purely circumstantial, in his opinion. And everything that happened since then only convinced him he was right. Valentino was getting in his way. Hell, he was getting in his own way. At that moment, Reggie decided he would finish this investigation alone. If Valentino was guilty, Reg wanted to be the first to know.

"Reg!" called Pearl from her desk. "You still owe me that lunch, remember?"

"Yeah, I know." Reggie shoved his pistol into its holster.

"Today would be good for me. I'm broke."

Reggie slipped her a ten-dollar bill as he passed her desk. "Not any more. Cover for me, will you?"

"Where you going?"

"Over to The Jewel Arms for a little while."

"Again?"

"Again."

Elvin was about ready to give up when Di finally opened the door. "What's up?" To him, she appeared hungover. "It's just another migraine, El. Come on in."

She ushered him into the cluttered apartment. "Coffee?"

"No. I'm kind of in a hurry."

Di rubbed her temples and frowned. "Hurry?"

Elvin remained standing, and spoke in a low voice. "I'm wanting to talk to Mrs. Torrez, up in apartment G."

"So, ring the bell and talk."

"No, I mean, without that nurse listening in."

"She is a snoop, isn't she?"

"She's going out for a little while today, and I was wondering if you'd get me the key…"

"From Mrs. Mars?" Di grabbed her head as if it had begun to throb again. "She gave me such a hard time about it last time, El. I don't think she believes Rose really asked me to check on her when she's out."

"Why?"

"I don't know. I just get that feeling. Why don't you ask her yourself?"

"She won't give it to me. She doesn't like me. She says she doesn't like my dog."

"Imagine that, will you?"

Ten minutes later, Di emerged from Edith Mars' apartment with the key to apartment G. Elvin waited in the hall. "Come on," he whispered. "Rose goes to get her hair done on Tuesdays, but she's never gone for long." Di shot him a puzzled look. "Don't look at me like that, I know what I'm doing.

I really believe I'm onto something here."

"I just don't feel right about breaking in to her apartment."

"We ain't breaking in." Elvin slid the key into the lock. "We're just going visiting."

He barged through the door and startled Rose, who emerged from the back bedroom with a tray in her dimpled hands, laden with spoons, glasses, and pill bottles. The expression on her face was hard, yet her voice remained congenial. "I believe you live across the hall, Mr. Suggs."

"Ma'am?" Elvin masked his intention with his best "rope-a-dope" smile.

Rose set the tray on the coffee table. Elvin noticed that a few of the pill bottles were empty. "I said, I believe you have the wrong apartment."

"I just thought I'd come up and check on Belle," said Di, glancing toward the hall.

"With him?" asked Rose. Elvin sensed the suspicion in her voice.

"Would it be alright if we visited with her for awhile?"

"No, it would not," said the husky nurse. She snagged a cigarette from the pocket of her jeans. With the crack of a cheap plastic lighter, her trembling hand lit the end, and the chubby blonde sucked a long drag. A puff of smoke wafted into the dim hall. "Belle is very bad today. She's on oxygen." She paused. "That's the reason I wasn't able to keep my appointment at the salon." Her mouth curled in a diabolical smile. "I suppose you thought I'd be gone, did you?"

"If Belle's on oxygen, as you say she is, I don't think I'd be smoking in that apartment today—or ever," said Di. "It isn't good for Belle or you. And it certainly isn't safe for anyone else that lives here."

"Like I care? You have no idea what a day with Belle is like for me, lady. Don't come around here telling me how to live. I'll smoke a whole carton of these dags if I want to."

"Don't matter, Miss Honeycutt," said Elvin.

"Did Edith give you the key again?" asked Rose. When neither Di nor Elvin replied, Rose snickered. "As you say, Mr. Suggs, it doesn't really matter, does it?"

"Could we wait to talk to Belle?" asked Di. Elvin watched while she started to tiptoe down the hall.

"No! You can't go back there!" cried Rose. "Belle can't be disturbed." The nurse dropped her burning cigarette on the rug, smashing it with the fat heel of her Keds tennis shoe. "Don't you have any manners? Get out of here! I've got everything under control. I don't need your help, you nosy busybody."

"Shore 'nuf, Miss Honeycutt. C'mon Di, Vanna needs feeding."

Di laughed. "You're better at that than I am, El. I'll be over in a few minutes. You don't want to keep Vanna waiting for anything or anybody, especially you."

Elvin stared at Di, and then at Rose, and then, back at Di once more. "Okay, girl. Then, don't keep me waiting on you. I'll be around, hear?"

Twenty-Seven

Vanna paused by the front door of the apartment and snarled. She barked, and snarled, and lunged forward and backward, and whined…and snarled. Elvin wondered if she was sick.

"Vanna, sugar, why don't you sit yourself down by me and have some popcorn? You know it's too early for lunch yet. Besides Baby Girl, '*Nam and Me* is on the TV." That's when Elvin heard the cheap chime of the doorbell. "You expecting company, Vanna?"

He peeked through the hole in the door and saw two well-dressed men. One of them looked very familiar, but Elvin couldn't place him. He decided to open up and see what they wanted.

"Mr. Suggs?" said a distinguished looking man with a thick head of slick white hair. "We would like to discuss a business opportunity with you, Mr. Suggs. It concerns your ex-wife Cherie."

"You mean, my late ex-wife."

"Whatever," said a fat man on his left.

"How do you know who I am?"

Walter threw his head back and laughed, long and hearty. "I b'lieve you knew a little gal named Cherie mighty well, didn't you?"

"You knew Cherie?" At the mention of his wife's name, Elvin's weathered face became grim.

"Shore did," said Arnold. "And a real pain in the ass she was, too."

"See Suggs, your wife and I, we got to know each other real good. So good, I got a little bit careless, you might say. You ever heard her talk about Walter Hubble?"

Elvin's mind returned to that fateful Memphis day—the day Cherie left him. It was the same day her purse spilled and the Visa card tumbled into the wet grass. He remembered now—the card was embossed with Walter Hubble's name in tiny gold letters. Was this *the* Walter Hubble?

"What do y'all want with me?" His voice cracked with emotion, but Elvin knew he had to control himself. He had to maintain, is what he liked to say in situations like this.

"This here's my building, Suggs. As you may or may not know, it's in your wife's name. I done found out y'all weren't divorced yet when she died, and now it seems you could end up with my building. That is, unless we reach an understanding, which, of course, I'm shore we can."

Elvin's eyes narrowed. "You know who killed Cherie?"

Vanna growled. Neither Arnold nor Walter answered.

"Who killed her?"

"Now, I came here to make you a deal, Suggs," said Walter. "Just you and me, man to man. But, I see you don't understand business too well." He paused. "And that is a shame."

"Told you," said Arnold.

In that moment, Cobra thought he had died. The warm sunlight that streamed through the dewy leaves beside his open bedroom window almost convinced him he was in Heaven. One big thing told him he wasn't: heaven didn't have Huey helicopters, which sounded like they were taking off or landing in his living room, to the music of Credence Clearwater Revival's "Fortunate Son."

He turned on his side, and punched his pillow. Elvin must be watching some show on 'Nam again. Why did he do that? Himself, he couldn't tolerate the thought, sight or sound of that war. Since those days, his life had never been the same. He guessed it never would be, unless he could get the anxiety and his panic attacks under control.

That was one big *if* in his book. It loomed large enough that he just couldn't see how that counselor at the VA Hospital expected him to give up cigarettes and weed at the same time. Well, he just couldn't, that's all there was to that. Hell, he'd already cut the coke—what else did they want from him? Next, they'd want him to eat organic veggies or something, maybe even oatmeal. Give up potato chips, Hershey bars, pizza, burritos…he could hear it now…

"I'm a busy man, Suggs," said Walter. "Now what'll it be? Do we have a deal?"

"I don't deal with pond scum."

"Told you," said Arnold, drawing his nickel-plated Taurus revolver. At the sight of the gun, Vanna lunged and crunched her pearly teeth into Arnold's ankle. The blubbery mound tumbled to the floor.

"Vanna! Release!"

Vanna's clenched jaws were stubborn steel. A shot rang out, and Elvin roared in pain and grief.

Walter had fired a bullet into his dog.

What was that noise? Cobra jacked his body up from the sagging mattress and listened. Goddang, all that noise sounded like a real live gunshot. Between the Hueys and gunfire, his sniper days in 'Nam were flashing like white lightning in his weary brain. His heart pumped. His head pounded. He pulled on faded jeans and grabbed his battered Glock 17, the one he'd found in a dumpster. His hands shook so badly, he could hardly hold the gun.

Who was *that*? When Cobra cracked the bedroom door, he could hear the voices, speaking in the same Elvin drawl. *Must be friends from Memphis.* Something in the hostile tone of their voices…

Cobra crept along the darkened hallway, his gun close to his side. The gunfire on the television persisted, loud and clear, the blades of the Huey whirred. He felt the chills and sweats and every little hair on his neck. His chapped hands trembled. Cobra knew he wasn't in a jungle or on a battlefield, and yet, the god-dang panic attack persisted. He just needed a single cigarette—fiendin' like a crackhead on Saturday night.

He inched his way behind the glass beads and listened. The voices escalated. Cobra felt dizzy. He wanted to lie down and never get up again, but somehow his finger landed firmly on the trigger of the Glock 17. It insisted on remaining there.

The lyrics of CCR blared the words that Cobra knew so well. Something about ain't being no fortunate son. No, he thought, I'm not. But, I'm lucky Suggs found me when he did, or right now, I'd be dead. There, in the dim hallway, he waited and listened, just like he had in 'Nam. It was Cobra, the lucky, dizzy sniper, with one finger on a trigger.

He could see them now. Fatso and Whitey had guns on Elvin. God, what he would do for a scope. He guessed with a target like Fatso, he didn't need one. The Glock poked between the rows of glass beads. He aimed straight between Arnold's demonic eyes.

Mark. Fire.

The Glock's muzzle fell. *Okay, Whitey.* The sights steadied.

Mark. Fire.

Two down. Fortunate son, indeed.

Walter's knees collapsed. His gun dropped. Blood sputtered from his mouth. His lips curled in an ugly sneer. "I'll get you back, Suggs, I swear to God, I'll get you, you, you, you..." His white-haired head drooped like a day old daisy.

Arnold hadn't made a sound.

Neither had Don. And, this wasn't the jungle. Why, then, did it feel like a war?

Elvin sobbed and cursed. Still, he gathered the dog in his arms to carry her to the backseat of his old Cadillac. "Cobra! Help me, buddy! Help me!" was all he could manage to say.

Cobra jammed the Glock into the waistband of his worn

jeans. "What do you think I've been doing, Suggs?"

"Are you all right, buddy?" He reached for the door. "We've got to get this bullet out of Vanna's leg. If you hadn't just killed those maggots, I would have done it myself. I just hope you're alright."

"The truth of it is, I never felt better than right now." Cobra crinkled his nose and sniffed the air. "Do you smell what I smell?" Elvin cracked the door and knew.

"Fire! We've got to get everyone out."

In the hall, sizzling smoke seeped from the front door of Belle's apartment. "Buddy, you knock on these doors and run like the devil. I've got to get Vanna outside." Elvin dashed for the landing. Vanna's breaths were shallow and short. "Hang on, baby, I got you. Now, let's get Di." Heading for the door, Elvin yelled through the smoke and fumes, "Get Di for me, buddy. She was going back to G 'cause she thought something funny was going on." He ran for the landing with the panting terrier in his arms.

Belle's Apartment

A scream penetrated the smoke, Cobra knew the voice. He couldn't leave yet. Di was in here somewhere. He dashed among the rooms, searching. "Di, answer me!"

"Di!" He darted among the rooms. When there was no answer, he proceeded to the rear of the apartment, where he found Di and Rose, struggling over a large kitchen knife. Its steel blade gleamed like a sword in the shadows. The nurse barely turned her platinum head as he entered the room, the scuffle was so intense. Belle Torrez lay motionless on the bed, an oxygen tank beside her.

"Get out, the place is on fire!" yelled Cobra. "Get the old lady!"

"She's already gone, Cobra," screamed Di. "So am I. This woman's a killer. Go on, save yourself!"

"Damn you!" Rose hissed. She grappled the knife from Di,

who had hit the floor. Rose aimed for her back. Di twisted, and Rose stabbed her in the thigh. Di clutched her leg wailing in agony.

"Drop it!" Cobra raised his pistol and gauged his opening between the two women.

"Gotcha!" yelled the nurse as she yanked the blade from the wound, yet still, Di struggled to crawl.

"Sit real still, now." Rose cackled. Clearly, she planned to plunge the knife into Di's back. Cobra's bullet penetrated her left temple and she fell to the floor, the point of the blade stuck through her own throat.

"Hold on, gal!" shouted Cobra, as he lifted Di's lacerated body. Smoke seared his eyes, but he reached the door. His weakened knees buckled beneath the dead weight. His strength sapped, determination spent, he had nothing left to give. His knees collapsed. The shame of failure drained his spirit. Sooty smoke swirled in the shadows.

He heard it before he saw him. "Hey! Buddy! I said, hey buddy, you in there? Di! Di! Can you hear me?"

It was a hand—Elvin's hand—reaching through the grimy smoke. "Grab on, buddy. Oh man, look at you, Di—got an ambulance downstairs, hon. C'mon."

"Move it!" Cobra said hoarsely, choking on the sooty smoke. "There's an oxygen tank in there!"

Twenty-Eight

Reggie pulled up to The Jewel Arms just before noon. It was a poignant moment, yet he felt an odd sense of relief. Whatever had happened within those walls, he decided, was now history. Firefighters struggled to save the neighborhood landmark, but the brittle wood and dry walls burned like old newspaper.

Wearing his initialed bathrobe, Dent lingered on the sidewalk beside Reggie. Together, they watched the voracious flames devour the secrets of anonymous lifetimes.

Elvin's Cadillac sped to the best Emergency Room in the city, the "Hot Box" at People's Clinic on 14th and Lafayette Streets. According to Parry, there was none finer in a 500 mile radius—and he should know.

Di was seriously wounded. After weeks in the VA Hospital, and too many visits from Elvin and Cobra, she returned to Elvin's meticulous home care. Elvin proved to be quite proficient, especially since he had nursed Vanna himself. Of course, they had to stay in Valentino's apartment, because the Jewel Arms had exploded. For once, Rick Valentino was grateful for a place of his own called "REHAB". Di kept saying she couldn't believe she survived. The hard truth became more and more evident when she recounted those final moments of their struggle, and the shocking truths that Rose revealed.

It was another week before Reggie could speak to her in his downtown office. He tapped the tape recorder and nodded. "Let her rip, Mrs. Redding."

"It was pretty simple, really," said Di. "Rose Honeycutt was running from the law. She had a past to hide. She was a mercy killer with a cause. Anybody who knew her identity was in danger of losing their life—particularly if Rose believed someone was suffering."

Reggie clicked his ballpoint pen and set it down, leaning back in his chair. "I don't get it. Take Torrez, for example. What could possibly be ailing a guy like him? He was a good-looking guy-fine clothes, nice cars, plenty of money. So, where's the problem?"

"Edith Mars told me Belle ran his life for him. His father, Tony, abandoned them when Matt was just a baby. She'd convinced him all women were dangerous and something to be avoided—all except for her, that is. Whenever he got involved with someone, she warned him to break it off; and he would. But, Matt yearned to start a life of his own. He couldn't trust women, couldn't get as far as a relationship, even though it was the thing he wanted most. Where even simple friendships with women were concerned, he needed confidence. He was a nice enough guy."

"I'm sorry," said Reggie, sitting up in his chair. "That just doesn't seem like a reason for a murder."

"Well, there was something else. When Rose confessed to me that she had killed him, she told me he was dying anyway, so she didn't see it as a murder."

"Why?"

"She claims he thought he had AIDS."

"AIDS? Why did he think that? You know, now I'll have to check into that possibility. This is one screwy case, man."

"Well, it seems his taste in women ran to those readily available, if you get my drift. He favored 'dates' with prostitutes, because he knew they would accept him, even if it was only for a certain amount of time, even if it meant he had to pay a price for their services. He understood that part only too well. He was, first and foremost, a businessman.

"When he told Rose he thought he had AIDS and was going

to propose to Valerie, so he could have some kind of life before he died, he asked for his mother's diamond ring. Rose gave him a fake."

"Why did she have one? Why did she care what he did with Rose's ring?"

"Elvin did a lot of checking into her background. Turns out Rose Honeycutt is an alias. Her name is Florence Sills. Sills was wanted for murder in at least two other states. Her victims were terminally ill patients. She told me that she kept something from each victim to remember them by—'mercy killings' is what she called them. The imitation ring was one of them."

"So, Belle never knew about any of this?"

"No, Belle never knew about the ladies, especially Valerie Gains. In Rose's opinion, it would be better for both Matt and his mother if he was dead, rather than married to a woman like Valerie." She laughed. "She said it would just kill Belle."

"So, do you know what happened to Belle's diamond ring?"

"I'm getting to that. Turns out Edith Mars knew Rose for years before either of them came to The Jewel Arms. Edith was Sills' baby sister. Torrez was desperate for a nurse to care for his mother; so desperate he neglected to do a background check. Edith knew about the murder charges, but didn't believe them."

"What does this have to do with Edward Mars' death?"

"Sills told me she had to kill him. Edward Mars knew about Mattie's murder and his illness. At first, she paid him, to keep him quiet. She had to pawn part of her jewelry, but Edward wanted more. With Mattie gone, she wanted to quit taking care of Belle. With Edward around, she couldn't make a clean break."

"Where is Edith now?"

"She died in the fire, I presume."

"Okay, about Belle's diamond ring—"

"I'm getting to that. Sills knew about the Silvers' marriage. Everybody who lived at The Jewel did. It was a violent relationship, to say the least. The night Annie died, she went over to Belle's, as she sometimes did, to 'borrow' some beers. Sills had actually started keeping it in for her, as well as vodka and wine. She felt sorry for her."

"I still don't see…"

"Hold it. Florence told me one night, Annie was sitting with her, talking about how their wedding anniversary was coming up, and she held up her hand to show Florence her plain gold wedding band. 'Someday before I die, I'm going to have a big diamond ring to go with it, Florence,' she said. 'Ben promised.'"

"Sills had already decided to kill her out of 'mercy'. In fact, she planned to kill her in Belle's apartment, and drag her over to her own, but Belle was too sick that night. She waited until Annie went home, and later, brought Belle's ring over to her. She rang the bell, and presented it to her, but Annie insisted she couldn't accept it, even though Sills said Annie tried the ring on her finger before she placed it back in the box—before Florence stabbed her."

"So," said Reggie, "the ring we found in the Silvers' apartment is the real diamond?"

"I believe so."

"The ring in Mattie's pocket was an imitation?"

"That's an imitation ring that Sills stole from a former patient."

"Man. I'm worn out just listening to all of this." Reggie laughed. "You know, the scary thing is, if she looked hard enough, she could have found a reason to kill us all. Living means suffering, at least part of the time. Makes you happier when things go right, you know?"

🐕

Elvin and Cobra lounged in a booth at the Night and Day Lounge and gobbled the famous cheeseburger platters. Di sat across from them, picking at a taco salad.

"Hey Brenda, babe!" Cobra slapped her on her derriere as she passed.

Elvin chuckled and shoved a French fry into his mouth. "Ain't no one but you she let do somethin' like that, Cobra."

While they ate, the city traffic whizzed past, people faceless behind the wheels of their cars.

"It's a shame about The Jewel." Cobra dipped a fry into a puddle of ketchup. "Good news about Vanna, though. She's a tough gal."

Di glanced up and then down at her salad, pushing the lettuce around with her fork.

"What?" asked Elvin, aware of her silence.

Di sighed, and looked up. "It's a shame about Matthew Torrez, Mr. Mars, Tasha, Annie, and…" She stopped short of mentioning Cherie. The omission was not lost on Elvin. "I guess I better think about looking for another place to live."

"You could come to Memphis," said Elvin.

"You going back there?" asked Cobra.

"Don't know, buddy. To tell you the truth, things are a lot tougher in St. Louis than I expected them to be. 'Course I could keep pretty busy in a place like this." He stopped and stared at Cobra. "You could, too." They both stared at Di, her head in her hands.

"You gonna have to get over all of this, girl," he said to Di. "You know, it might be better that The Jewel burned down. Make a fresh start, and all that."

Di shook her head. "I never thought Rose, or whatever her name really was, could do such a thing. I mean, she bragged to me she killed three people. I guess she would have eventually killed Belle if she hadn't died on her own."

"All that talk about pain. Is pain always a bad thing? Bad enough to kill someone over? Why did she think she should be the one to end the pain, anyway?"

Cobra wiped his mouth with a white paper napkin. "Hell, yes, pain's a bad thing. I've seen guys hurting. You have, too. I've hurt myself bad enough I wished I was dead."

"You didn't answer my question," said Di. "When you saw guys hurting, why didn't you shoot them then? Why didn't I? I'm a nurse just like Rose was. Why didn't I? I'm saying, is it really wrong to end someone else's pain?"

Elvin shrugged. "What if they ask you to? Is it right to turn them down? What kind of person wants to see someone suffer, especially when the pain is never going away?"

Brenda shoved the check between the salt and peppershakers. "If you ask me, life is pain. Try to quit smoking if you don't believe me. Better yet, go on a diet, or get a divorce. If you ask me, we start hurting the day we're born."

Di reached across the table to hold Elvin's hand. "I just never thought I'd be alone at this point in my life. Everything I had just went up in smoke." She snapped her long fingers. "Just like that. All I've got now is a beat-up Suburban—and my friends."

Elvin smiled. "You want me to stay here?"

"Yeah El, I guess I do."

Elvin glanced at Cobra. "What do you say we go into the detective business together—you and me? Like you said, you've got the kind of skills nobody advertises for, and I'm free as a bird."

"We hardly know anyone here," said Di.

"We know each other, and, I'll bet Parry Leach could use a job about now." Elvin winked. "I'm sure he's got a few connections around town. Word about us gets out, it won't be long before some kind of trouble finds us." He took a final sip of his soda and leaned back in his chair. "This town is tougher than it looks. I was reading this paper at a gas station over on Vandeventer—think it's called The Whirl. Sakes alive! I couldn't believe what goes on here. 'Course you can't believe everything you read, now."

"Hey, say we look for a house, maybe set up an office in the living room or something," said Cobra.

"Paint it yellow, maybe, with a backyard for Vanna."

"I'm in." Cobra crumbled his napkin. "I'm starting to feel real good about all of this."

Di grinned at both of them. "Cobra's right. Together, we're unbeatable. Maybe we could finally have some good times again." She laughed and raised her empty glass. "Here's a toast to our new life." Elvin and Cobra raised their glasses.

"To us!" said Cobra.

"Shore 'nuf," said Elvin. "Just don't forget the best part."

"What's that, El?" said Di. "Okay, my mistake. How could I forget Vanna?"

"Looks like you can't, Di. Cobra flipped on the television. "It's time for Valerie's dog food commercial. And you know who the dog star is."

"How'd you find out about this show, buddy?"

Cobra grinned. "I'll bet your dog never thought she'd be doing commercials with the likes of Valerie. Hey, do dogs think?"

"Oughtta be coming on any minute now." He leaned back into a creaky wooden chair. "Yep, there we are."

There, clad in the regal robes of King Barksalot, was an awkward Cobra, accompanied by none other than Queen Barksalot, a.k.a. Valerie Gains. Between them, sat a very large Airedale Terrier, sporting a sparkling tiara.

"When did you make Vanna a celebrity?"

Cobra winked at him. "You jealous or something, Suggs?"

"Everybody be quiet," said Reggie.

"I searched for months for the right food for my loyal subject," said the King. "But, I never dreamed I would find the perfect combination of taste and nutrition."

"It was out there all the time," said the Queen. "You were looking too hard to see it."

The King nodded. "I finally found all I need in Barksalot chunks. Now, I can sleep at night, knowing the ones I love are happy. Isn't that right, loyal subject?" The camera focused on the Airedale, smiling as only a happy dog can, her fuzzy neck encircled by the Queen's fond embrace. "So, look for Barksalot in your kingdom," she said. "May all your dreams come true!"

Cobra punched the remote. The television screen faded to black. The weary group sat, deep in thought. Finally, Cobra spoke, and his words seemed to spring from the well of an aching soul. "I just want to say thank you."

"Aw, that's all right buddy."

"No, I want to tell you Suggs, but I just want to say it out loud to whoever else might be listening. Because, see, I don't know why we're still here."

"I don't read you," said Elvin.

"Okay, why did you find me that night? Why are we still here? You lost Cherie, right?" Elvin looked away, and stroked Vanna's head.

"Sorry. I mean, I'm thinking about that and what the Queenie there just said about being happy and making dreams come true. She's right, Suggs, and by the way, she's my type, I think. Where do I find that lady?"

"There are a number of places. Right now, I think you ought to thank your lucky stars for your life. And focus on those dreams. Your Miss Gains will be around, at precisely the wrong time and place. Trust me on that one."

"What about Parry?" said Elvin. "He's free to go, sure enough? Because I need him more than a jail does. You can trust me on that one."

Reggie headed for the door. Ready to lecture the group, he turned to face them, and suddenly his voice dissolved into laughter. "Have a good day, folks. And Cobra there, you're right. We should be saying 'thank you' to whoever's in charge. I don't know why we're still here, but it's probably got something to do with those dreams on Queenie's commercial. Didn't you guys say something about a detective agency? What are you waiting for? We've got plenty of stuff to keep y'all busy. Here's my card again—keep in touch, hear?"

"Sure enough, Reg. We'll let you know where we end up. Hey, what's that sound?"

"It's my phone. Hold on just a second, willya?" Reggie put the receiver to his ear, and his smile was transformed into the frown of a frazzled detective. "Okay, what does she look like? Yeah, that's her, all right. It's spelled G A I-N-S." Reggie hung up the phone and chuckled. "What did I tell you? Queen Barksalot, I mean our own little Miss Valerie Gains, always gets what—or who—she wants. I guess I'd better get back to the station before she appoints herself Chief of Police. Watch yourself, Suggs." Reggie ventured into the misty twilight, alone.

Elvin wrapped his coat tighter around his taut body. He strode to his car in the blustery wind. "I always do, Reg. I always do."

Claire Applewhite is a graduate of St. Louis University, where she earned an AB in Communications and an MBA, Finance. A past participant in the Summer Writers Institute at Washington University, she is a contributing writer for the St. Louis Post-Dispatch Book Blog, Stltoday.com, Entertainment. Her novel, Night and Day was a 2007 Finalist in the William Faulkner Creative Writing Contest, and two additional mystery novels were named Semi-Finalists in 2005 and 2006. Her short story, Moonlight Becomes You So, will be published in a mystery anthology, also by LL Dreamspell. Visit www.Claireapplewhite.com for details.

Claire is a current Board member of the Midwest Mystery Writers of America. Since 1999, she has been a charter member of the St. Louis Chapter of Sisters in Crime. In addition, Claire is an active member of the Missouri Writers Guild, St. Louis Writers Guild, Heartland Writers Guild and Mystery Writers of America.

A mother of three grown children, Claire lives in St. Louis, Missouri with her husband and two Airedale Terriers, Jack and Sydney.

♥

AFTERWORD

My first Airedale Terrier was a rescue dog named Gracie. At 13 months old, she weighed 59 pounds, had hypothyroidism, and was somewhat combative. Hey, it's okay. Nobody's perfect. When she died of cancer, I went to a nationally known breeder to get an Airedale from a cancer-free line. I purchased a puppy, and named her Savannah, Love Me Tender. Like Gracie, Savannah also died young. In my imagination and my writing, however, they both live on, and they always will.

Vanna, the Airedale featured in this book, is a composite of Airedales I have known and loved, especially Gracie and Savannah. Historically, terriers are tenacious dogs that are not supposed to surrender to pain or threat of attack. Faithful and courageous, protective, fun-loving and high-spirited, Airedales can occasionally become rowdy and stubborn. Any disobedience is usually intended and willful. Still, Gracie and Savannah wanted nothing more than to be a great companion—on their own terms.

The characters in this book react predictably to Vanna's behavior. I've observed those same reactions on the faces of my own family and friends as they grapple with toddlers, teenagers, and even grown adults—adults like me. Like Elvin, I sometimes feel that Vanna and I have a whole lot in common, particularly when we chase what seems to be impossibly out of reach. You know, like a dream I once had about publishing a book. Shore 'nuf.

♥